CAN'T MISS HER

Emily Slate Mystery Thriller
Book 5

ALEX SIGMORE

Dark Woods Press

CAN'T MISS HER: EMILY SLATE MYSTERY THRILLER BOOK 5

1st Edition

ebook ISBN 978-1-957536-20-0

Print ISBN 978-1-957536-21-7

Prologue

SUMMER SANFORD SAT ACROSS THE TABLE FROM HER HUSBAND, watching him avert his gaze. Whatever this was, it wasn't going to be good.

In an uncharacteristic move, her husband, Brady, had suggested they go out for dinner and to leave the kids with her parents for the evening. They hadn't had a "date night" in who knew how long. At least six months. Their schedules had just been too packed. If it wasn't him working overtime, it was her covering an extra shift at the library. Or one of them needed to take Elliott to soccer practice or Judo. Or pick Ashleigh up from horse riding. Their lives were a constant treadmill of trying to get from one thing to another without tripping over each other all the time.

Summer hadn't expected married life to be like this. They'd fallen in love and married young, and Elliott had come along only a few months later. What little time they'd had for each other melted away. When Ashleigh was added into the mix it only made things more complicated. Had her parents not lived close, Summer wasn't sure how they could have coped. As it was, they were barely getting five hours of sleep per night, and they were fighting all the time. In fact, she'd argued against this meal because their finances were a mess right now and they really couldn't afford it. But Brady had insisted.

"Here we are," the waiter said, approaching with their plates. "Shank steak for the gentleman, medium rare, and a chicken cobb salad for the lady, dressing on the side." The waiter clasped his hands together and glanced at both of them. "Is there anything else I can bring you at the moment?"

"Another glass of wine," Brady said, tapping his nearly-empty glass.

"Ma'am?" the waiter asked.

Summer shook her head. Her glass of Pinot was still full. But Brady had sucked his down like it was pure sugar.

"Very good, I'll be back in a moment," the waiter said, heading off at a brisk pace.

Brady had brought her to one of the nicest restaurants in town, The City Grill. It was upscale enough that their prices were listed in whole numbers and the bar was four shelves tall and backlit, stocked with everything imaginable, so it was a centerpiece of the restaurant. The kitchen was open, with seats around the U-shape so patrons could watch their dinners being prepared. Summer supposed that was nice for them, but it had to be nerve-wracking for the cooks. She used to wait tables back in college and couldn't imagine someone watching her try to do her job all night long.

The rest of the restaurant was lit with ambient mood lighting, to accentuate the romantic aspects of the place. It was just enough light to see the other members of your table, but not to be distracted by anyone else around you. A single real candle burned in the middle of each table and its light reflected off their wine glasses as Brady began cutting into his steak.

"Brady—" Summer began.

He waved her off. "I know. But we have the food now,

there's no going back. Let's just try to enjoy the evening, huh?"

Summer pushed a long breath through her nose. Her husband's ability to blind himself to the reality of their situation was astonishing. How could he just pretend like they weren't drowning in debt? Or that Elliott hadn't been suspended this morning for getting into a fight with another student. He'd protested, but she hadn't had the patience to hear it. Ever since he'd started hanging out with that friend of his he hadn't been the same little boy she'd once known. It was bad enough Elliott had to take summer school to catch up with his grades, but to be suspended? There was no way he would move into the tenth grade this year.

"How am I supposed to just pretend like nothing is wrong?" Summer asked. "You can't just wish your problems away, as much as you'd like to."

Brady sighed and set his knife and fork down, looking at her under hooded eyes. He was about to speak when the waiter returned with the wine bottle and refilled his glass without a word. As soon as he left, Brady decided the wine was more important than actually talking to her and greedily drank from his glass.

She didn't like when he did that; it meant he had some bad news, and she wasn't sure she could take anything else right now. "What are we doing here, Brady?"

"Do you remember when we first got married?" he asked, stretching his hand across the table for hers. She took it, reluctantly.

"Of course."

"Remember how it was just going to be the two of us, against everyone else out there? That we'd be there for each other, no matter what?"

She withdrew her hand. "What did you do?"

"Whaddaya mean?" he asked, too quickly, pulling back as well.

"You only get sentimental like this when something is wrong. Just come out with it already. I've had a long day and we have another early morning tomorrow. I don't have the energy to get you to open up. Either tell me or don't say another word."

Brady took a long look at her, then took another generous gulp from his glass. Great, she supposed she'd be driving them back tonight. *After* they hiked back to the car, which had to be parked half a block away due to construction around the restaurant.

"I…uh…" He let out another breath before continuing, which only produced a pit in Summer's stomach. What the hell could be so wrong that he couldn't even start the conversation? What was he buttering her up for?

She took a drink from her glass too, trying to mentally prepare herself for whatever was coming.

"First off you have to know it's over. I cut it off. But I thought…I mean…we're not supposed to have secrets from each other, right? So it's important that you know—"

"Just say it already," Summer demanded, her heart pounding. She wasn't so naïve as not to expect the next words out of his mouth to tear her in two, but she held on to a sliver of hope that wasn't the case.

"I…I had an affair. But I ended it."

His words hit her like a bag of crushed glass. They left little cuts all over her, seeping deep into her skin, into her soul, confirming her worst fears about him. She had always known Brady to be a flirt, but he'd never taken it anywhere beyond that. But to actually go and get involved with another woman behind her back, to break the trust they had built up over fourteen years of marriage, all for what? A couple of good orgasms? She couldn't believe her ears.

"Summer, honey?" Brady said.

Tears formed in the corners of her eyes, threatening to break through. How dare he do this here! Where he knew she couldn't make a scene. Where he'd be "safe" from any kind of emotional outburst on her part. He knew her that well, at least. He'd engineered this whole thing to lessen the impact on him, the selfish bastard.

Summer wasn't one of those women who made a spectacle of herself; in fact it was her goal to move through the world with as few people noticing her as possible. She never liked being the center of attention, even when it was warranted; it only made her feel like she had to be "on" for everyone, and that was not something she enjoyed. Whenever they had an argument in the past, they would always wait until getting home before she would even show a hint of emotion. But this was something else entirely. This threatened to overwhelm her.

She looked away from him, unable to stare at his stupid face for one second longer, trying to remember to breathe. The arrogance. The absolute entitlement. He wouldn't get away with it. What, did he think they would just never go home again? That he could keep her out here forever and never have to face the true consequences of his actions?

"I need to use the restroom," Summer said, and got up, making her way to the back of the restaurant. She wanted to scream at the top of her lungs, but instead kept a calm demeanor as she moved past the other patrons and found her way into the bathroom.

She locked herself in one of the stalls and allowed the first wave of tears to overtake her. Her breath hitched and she knew if she wasn't careful, she could end up hyperventilating, which would only make things worse. She gave herself five full minutes to cry before she left the stall and composed herself again.

When she emerged, another woman stood at one of the sinks, applying her makeup. The woman was a knock-out, and Summer couldn't help but think had Brady had sex with *her*, or someone like her, as implausible as that was. She'd forever be looking now, wondering if any of the women she passed on the street had been her husband's secret lover. She wasn't sure she could take that. But she wasn't powerless here; the first thing she would find out would be who the woman was. While it might not make any difference, at least she'd know.

Beyond that, what was she supposed to do? They had built a life together. And with their financial situation, a divorce was going to be expensive and time-consuming. How was she supposed to deal with this on top of everything else?

"Rough night?" the other woman asked, glancing at Summer in the mirror.

"My husband just confessed his infidelity to me," Summer said. Normally she wouldn't have opened up to a stranger like that, but she had just been gutted. She didn't really care about consequences right now.

"Oh, honey," the woman with the silky red hair said. "You go back in there and throw his drink in his face. I can call you an Uber if you need."

A small smile tugged at Summer's lips. "No, thank you, though. I just need…" What did she need to do?

The other woman put a reassuring hand on her shoulder. "Take as much time as you need. Make the bastard wait."

"Thanks," she replied.

"I'd go do it for you, but I don't want to deny you the plea-sure," the woman said as she made her way for the door. "Good luck with it. And don't be afraid to take him down a few pegs."

Summer gave the woman a nod, thankful that she didn't judge her. Normally she would have expected a woman like that to think Summer had not been able to satisfy her husband, and that's why he'd wandered. But her reassurance only formed a resolve in Summer. She was going to take care of this *her* way.

She took one good look in the mirror, setting her features and stormed back out of the bathroom and to their table, noticing Brady had already finished half his steak. Had he been *eating* while she'd been in there crying her eyes out? If she wasn't resolute in her decision before, she was now. "Get up," she said.

"What?" he asked, looking at her.

"We're leaving."

"But what about——"

"Find the waiter, pay him, and get your ass outside that door," she fumed.

Brady looked at her like he didn't know who she was. She had never been this forceful with him before, always kowtowing to his decisions, his wants. Well, no longer.

As Brady headed off to find the waiter, Summer noticed some of the other patrons staring at her. She grabbed her wine glass and downed it all in once gulp, not even tasting it as it went down. She then headed outside the main doors, waiting in the evening warmth. Part of her thought she should just go to the car and leave his ass here on the sidewalk, but she wasn't about to let him get away with it that easily. No, he was going to tell her everything, and then she was going to make him pay for this.

A few minutes later, Brady appeared beside her, his hands in his pockets. "So, should we——"

"Shut up," Summer said. "I don't want to hear your voice again unless I ask you a question, got it?"

He nodded.

She headed in the direction of the car, clutching her small purse. Inside was little more than a few tissues, her ID, and some credit cards that were close to their max limit. She was already thinking about how much she could spend on getting away from him before her credit was completely down the drain. Mom had always told her to keep a reserve fund Brady didn't know about and for the first time in her life, Summer wished she'd listened.

"I want to know who she is," Summer said, walking a few

paces in front of Brady as they made their way along the street back to their car.

"What does that matter?" he asked, having the hubris not to answer right away.

She spun on him, only to see a pair of headlights coming down the street dangerously close to the sidewalk. Brady looked at her with expectant eyes, as if to ask her if they really needed to go through all this. But before he opened his mouth again, Summer saw the muzzle of a gun poking out the window of the car barreling toward them.

She screamed.

Chapter One

I'M USUALLY NOT THIS NERVOUS.

But as I wait outside the small café, my heart pounds inside my chest. It's funny, as an FBI agent I've faced down killers, kidnappers, psychopaths, and everything in between. And yet, here I am, nervous about nothing more than a little lunch.

I spot her turning the corner and I force a nervous swallow down. My sister-in-law stands out in a crowd, as much as she doesn't try. With her dark, raven hair contrasted with her fair complexion, she's hard *not* to notice, something that's punctuated by a man passing by who takes a second look. But Danielle doesn't so much as acknowledge him. She's looking in my direction, her face lighting up when she sees me. Even though we're not related by blood, we aren't too dissimilar in how we look, though Dani usually wears something much more stylish than me. I'm so used to wearing suits for work I don't really have any other clothes that fit right, which is why I'm here in my normal blazer and matching slacks. Early August in D.C. is always murder and this year is no exception. Fortunately, the overhang of the row of buildings blocks out the direct sun, but the ambient heat is still enough to make me feel like I'm cooking inside.

But Dani looks like she's in a protective bubble of some kind, her makeup expertly applied and no hint of sweat along her brow. She carries a nice handbag as she strides toward me with purpose, her smile clear and her green eyes bright. "Hi, Em, so glad you could make it."

I reach in for a half-hug, catching a whiff of her perfume. It's subtle and smells of something expensive. Dani's a marketing coordinator for a local company who represents some high-dollar clients. Because I haven't seen much of her in the past six months, I didn't realize how well business must be going. "Thanks for the invite." I pull back. "I was surprised to hear from you so soon."

"We have a lot of catching up to do," she says.

It was only a few days ago that she and her husband, the brother of my dead husband, welcomed me back into their lives after six contentious months. They had partially blamed me for Matt's death, whether that was conscious or not I don't know, but there was a lot unspoken between the three of us. And yet they had been willing to take care of my dog while I was away on cases. After someone broke into my apartment to spy on me, I decided it was best to let them keep Timber until the danger was gone for good.

"Let's grab a seat," Dani says.

I'm still uneasy about all of this. Up until a week ago, my relationship with both of them was strained, to say the least. We hadn't even really spoken beyond a few shouting matches since the funeral. But after finally laying everything out, it seems they've had a change of heart and are willing to welcome me back into their lives again. Part of me is grateful because I don't have any blood relatives left. Both my parents are deceased, and I never had any siblings. The rest of my family I rarely speak with, except for the odd text message around holidays sometimes. We just never got along.

That's why I leaned so hard on Dani and Chris when I first got married. For the first time in my life, it felt like I had a family I could count on. When Matt died, all of that was ripped away again. So I'm understandably cautious about this turn of events. It isn't that I don't trust them; but I've felt that sting before and I need to prepare myself for it to happen again should they change their minds.

We stroll in and take a couple of seats along the wall. The café isn't very busy yet, seeing as it's just past eleven on Monday morning. But this was the only time I could meet. I'm due in for a briefing right after lunch.

"It's so good seeing you again," Dani says, hanging her purse on the back of her chair.

"It's only been a few days. I'm still nursing the hangover from that night."

Dani laughs. It's a bubbly sound. "I really think Chris thought he could take you. I tried to warn him."

"I hope he wasn't too bad the next morning. I didn't see him before I left."

She shakes her head. "He was fine. He had me to play nursemaid all day." There's a twinkle in her eye as she says it, and a flood of feelings come back to me. Feelings I haven't felt since before Matt passed…feelings of belonging to something again. Feelings of acceptance. "Are you still staying at the apartment?"

I nod as a waitress brings us glasses of water. She seems to notice we haven't looked at the menus yet and gives us a few minutes without a word. "I don't have much choice. I'm not going to move."

"Em, are you sure it's a good idea to stay there? I told you the other day, you can take our guest room. We don't mind."

I give her a pinched smile. As much as I appreciate this heel turn, I need to take it slow, for my own mental well-being if nothing else. I can't rush headfirst back into their lives like nothing ever happened. "Thank you, but I'm not going to let this person run me out of my own home. I'm a trained federal agent. If she wants to come for me, she's welcome to try."

Dani sits back, her eyes wide. "Wow. I don't think I could ever do that. I jump whenever Chris opens the garage door. How can you be so calm about it? I mean, this *is* the person who killed Matt, right?"

"Exactly," I say. "And I'm not going to miss a chance to interrogate her. If she comes to me, all the better." Normally I don't reveal information about ongoing cases to people outside the Bureau, but in this case, I felt it was warranted. Chris and Dani deserved to know the truth about what happened to Matt. There isn't an official case open on it yet. My boss, Janice Simmons, is still working with her superiors to figure out how to approach this. When I found recording devices in my apartment a few weeks ago Janice tried to set up a sting to catch the person responsible, but unfortunately she was one step ahead of us again and never showed. Ever since then Janice has been unofficially spearheading the search for the woman who I believe not only killed my husband, but is my primary suspect in a serial killer case. We're still trying to figure out how they're connected.

"I don't see how you do it, Em. Day in and day out. It must be mentally exhausting," Dani says.

"There's a reason there's a mandatory limit on how long you can be in the Bureau," I reply. "The mental stresses can be extreme. But it's a rewarding job, especially when we know we've made the world a better place. The Bureau has had its fair share of problems in the past, but that's why Zara and I, and people like us, keep going. To make it better than it was, to change things for the better."

"It's a lot more noble than marketing research," she says, grinning and taking a sip from her glass. "So you think this person is just out there, waiting for you?"

"I think she's waiting to see what I'm going to do." I never told Chris and Dani about the warning message I received while I was working my last case up in New York. But the assassin called me, trying to warn me off. She also emailed me some disturbing information about Matt, indicating he wasn't who he said he was. I haven't told them that part either. And I don't plan to, not until I get to the bottom of it.

"I just don't understand why she did it," Dani says. "Matt never hurt anyone."

"That's what I plan on finding out. Part of me hopes she does come after me, because then I'll finally get a chance to ask her all these questions." I also don't tell her that the assassin warned me if I didn't stop looking into Matt's death, that I'd be next. But that just makes me want to look harder. If she's willing to threaten the life of an FBI agent to get me off her case, then I know there has to be something solid there. I just need to find out what it is.

"So what's the next move?" Dani asks.

"Wouldn't you rather talk about something more…I dunno, normal?" I ask. This is the first real conversation I've had with her alone in over seven months.

She laughs again. "I'm being morbid, I know. It's just all so fascinating! I mean, I could tell you about this new marketing push that's supposed to get people to drink more soda water, or we could talk about how the dogs got into a mud hole yesterday and we had to spray them off and give all three of them baths before letting them back in the house. But it all seems so mundane in comparison. You lead such an interesting life, Emily. I can't believe I've missed so much of it."

"I can't argue with that." I smirk. "But I'm just taking it one day at a time, working what little evidence we have. As soon as I have a development, I'll be sure to let you know."

"Good," she says, picking up her menu. "I'm famished. Chris was up early for work this morning and I can't sleep when he's getting ready, so I've been up since five. My stomach is about to tear itself in two."

I admit I'm hungry as well. Eating in my apartment is more nerve-wracking these days, I'm always on edge that something might happen, so I can never really relax. Which means I often don't even finish what I fix. But this, this feels much better. I'll probably down two entrees while I'm here.

"Oh and this is on me," Dani says. I move to protest but she cuts me off before I can. "And don't even think about arguing. We have a lot of missed lunches to make up for and until we do, the family hero gets to eat for free."

"Dani…I can't—"

"Yes, you can," she says earnestly. "Chris put you through hell and I didn't help. Let me try and start to make that up to you."

I pinch my features together but finally give in. She was never as bad as Chris toward me, but she never stopped him either. And that hurt for a long time. If she wants to try and atone in what few ways she can, I won't stop her. I'm just glad things are getting back to normal.

"Okay," I say. "You win."

Chapter Two

AFTER LUNCH, I MAKE MY WAY BACK TO MY CAR PARKED across the street. However, I don't get in the driver's seat and instead slide into the passenger side, frustration seeping from my pores.

"Good lunch?" my driver asks, and I have to bite my tongue to keep from saying what's really on my mind, which is that I don't need a babysitter to watch me all hours of the day.

I turn to my driver, Agent Liam Coll, a recent graduate from Quantico. He looks the same way he did back in Virginia three months ago, perhaps with a steelier look in his eye. But he's the same handsome, clean-cut man I met investigating the Veronica Wright case. Afterward, Liam had become so fed up with his own corrupt police department, he'd left Stillwater and applied to become a federal agent. Now, three months later, here we are again. Up until three days ago, I hadn't seen him since that last day in Virginia, before I found out that someone had murdered my husband. I'll admit I was nervous to see him again; we'd developed a rapport, and he'd been easy to get along with. Maybe in another life we could have had something more, but he'd had his path, and I had mine.

I'd hoped the reunion would be as easy as things were the first time, but right from the beginning it hasn't been the same. What warmth was there is now gone, and Liam acts more like a robot. His primary job is to watch my back and keep me safe. Janice says it's for my own protection, but I know if the FBI loses another agent to an assassin so soon after the last one, it's going to cause big trouble for the Bureau. They can't afford the bad press if the woman hunting me decides to go through with it. So I get a chaperone.

"Fine. Ready?" I ask.

He starts the car and pulls away from the curb. He'd parked right where he could keep an eye on me the entire time I was eating with Dani. But I've already thought more than once about ditching him, despite how bad that might look to my boss. Maybe the problem isn't Liam, instead it's me. I don't like someone standing over my shoulder, checking my work all the time. And I certainly don't need protection.

"How's the leg?" he asks, not taking his eyes off the road.

"What?"

"The leg. I haven't seen you limping on it."

I think back before I realize what he's talking about. He means from when I was stabbed at the scene where we captured Wright. "Oh. It's fine. Why?"

"Just curious. I figured an injury like that would leave some lasting effect."

"Just gets sore sometimes," I say. I'd needed stitches, but they'd repaired the artery and it had healed beautifully. But you can still see the wound, even now. It was a deep one. "Is this your attempt at conversation?"

He doesn't say anything, doesn't look at me with those hazel eyes of his that I found myself becoming lost in last time we were together. I'm frustrated he seems so closed off, not because I want to start any kind of romantic relationship with him, but because I could do with a few more friends these days. Especially with what I'm facing. But it seems Liam's time at the academy has changed him in some fundamental way.

The drive back to headquarters is silent, the two of us sitting there, not saying anything all while I'm only becoming more and more agitated by the situation. As soon as the briefing is over, I'm going to suggest to Janice that she reassign Liam. It's a waste of an agent to have him following me around all the time. If the assassin comes after me, I'll be ready. I *want* her to. It's the only way I'll get the answers I need.

We get out of the car and Liam escorts me to the door, opening it for me. The first few times I tried to fight him on it, but he insisted, saying that he was there to take care of the little things so I could focus on the big things. I think I can open a freaking door on my own, though.

Once we're in the building, he relaxes a hair as we make our way up to my floor. I manage to beat him to the double doors that lead into my department. The last thing I need is Zara seeing him opening doors for me before I'm hit with an onslaught of wisecracks at my expense.

As soon as I see her, her eyes brighten, and she smiles. Her platinum blonde hair is beginning to grow out, though she's done little to maintain the color. I think she's hoping Janice will let her go back to pink or electric blue, though as long as she's a field agent, that's unlikely.

"So," she says, grinning at me as I take my seat. "How was girl's lunch?"

I roll my eyes. "Fine. Pleasant."

Zara watches as Liam passes our desks and takes a seat a couple of desks down. "What did she want to talk about?"

"Mostly my job," I say. "She said she was trying to make up for lost time."

"You must have really put the fear of God in them," she says, turning back to her work.

"I think *you* put the fear of God in them. My brother-in-law specifically."

She grins. "What are friends for?"

"Slate!"

I glance over to see Janice standing in her doorway. Right. The briefing. I stand and head over to her office.

"Coll, you get in here too," she calls.

"I thought this was just a personal briefing," I say.

Zara looks up, watching Liam as he passes back by and joins us in Janice's office. She closes the door without addressing my comment. "Take a seat, both of you," she says.

I don't like this. Janice is as straight as they come, but she's being more standoffish than usual. What can be going on?

I take a tentative seat while Liam takes the other, shooting me a look. It's the first unspoken communication we've shared. But I don't have any idea what's going on here.

"I've just spoken to the Deputy Director," Janice says, perching on the edge of her chair. "He's concerned this experience with your stalker could damage the Bureau's reputation. He wants you on leave until it's taken care of."

I have to physically restrain myself from shooting out of my chair. "*What?*"

Janice shakes her head. "I don't like it either. But he feels like you are too much of a liability to the Bureau right now. And with this money-laundering operation we're working on, we can't afford any black eyes right now. This involves some very powerful people in high places. The Bureau has to be airtight."

"That's not *my* fault," I say, realizing how I'm sounding as I say it. "What I mean to say is, I can still be an asset to the Bureau. You don't have to bench me."

"I agree," Janice says. "But I want to impress on you how serious the Deputy Director is taking this. You're in someone's crosshairs, and we have no idea who this person is or what they want with you." She turns to Liam. "Report."

He shakes his head. "Nothing out there. If someone is watching Agent Slate, they're being damn careful. I haven't caught so much as a whiff of anyone poking about."

Janice stands and exhales. "Here's what we're going to do. Things seemed to have calmed down when you were out of state. I'm assigning you to a case over on the Peninsula. Looks like it could be a domestic case."

"A domestic case?" I ask. "Why don't the locals just handle it?"

She turns her back to us, looking out her window on the bullpen. "Because the victim was from Delaware, but was killed across state lines in Maryland. And there's apparently some sort of tiff between the local sheriff and the police chief of the closest town, both on either side of the border." She turns back to us. "I'm giving you a softball, Slate. I want you to go, investigate, and do what you do best, which is see what no one else sees. And for your own sake, take your time. I don't need you back here in three days telling me you're ready for another one."

"So you *are* benching me," I say, standing.

"I'm doing the only thing I can to keep you active until this situation is resolved because I know if I send you home you'll either go stir crazy or go rogue, neither of which is ideal." She turns to Liam. "You're to stick by her, keep an eye out for anyone on your tail. Seeing as it's close to the city, maybe this will help draw the assassin out."

Wait, Liam's coming with me? "But Zara—" I begin.

"—is going to continue to work on your case here," Janice says. "Look, Agent Foley has skills I can use on this. And you'll forgive me, Agent Coll, but you're still fresh. Which means you get guard duty. I can't send *three* agents to Mardel without due cause. Plus, this will be a good chance for you to get some hands-on experience with a case."

I have to admit, I'm getting a little sick of being sent away just because I'm inconvenient. At least this time I won't have to confront my in-laws about taking care of my dog, they already have him. But this is not what I wanted. I had hoped when I got back from New York I'd be working on finding this mystery woman who seems so intent on stopping me from investigating Matt's murder. Unfortunately, it seems like I'm too much of a burden to keep around.

"Any other protests?" she asks, but she barely gives me time to speak up. "Very good, I'm emailing you the case files now. The murder happened last night. Get out there as soon as you can and get set up. You will be taking your time with this one, but I don't want it to look like we're dragging ass, got it?"

"So take my time, but do it quickly," I say.

She points a finger at me. "And try not to be such a smartass. Good luck, I know you'll come away successful." Janice turns to Liam. "And you, listen to her. She knows what she's talking about."

"I've seen that for myself, ma'am," he says, though he doesn't look at me. But I appreciate his vote of confidence from the last case we worked together.

Janice takes her seat again. "I know this isn't what you want, Slate. But this is the best I can do, given the circumstances."

I give her an appreciative nod. "I know. I won't disappoint you."

As we leave her office my phone buzzes with an email. Probably all the case information. "Give me a few minutes," Liam says. "I just need to button up some things then I'll be ready to go."

I pull my phone out and open the files, giving them a quick once-over. "Yeah, okay." He heads off for his desk and I take my seat at my own again, shoving my phone back in my pocket.

"Now there's a grumpy face if I've ever seen one," Zara says.

"She's sending me back out. Delaware/Maryland state line."

"Great." She smiles. "When do we leave?"

I shake my head. "We don't. She told me to take Liam so he can watch my back and I can show him some first-hand experience."

Her face falls a little. "Oh. That makes sense, I guess."

"I'll be honest, I'm getting a little sick of being sent away every time I feel like I'm getting close to this woman."

Zara leans forward. "I know it can be frustrating. But don't worry. I won't let you down. I've already got a couple of ideas on how to proceed. When you get back, I'm going to have something concrete for you, trust me."

"Is this another one of your bets?" I ask, laughing.

"I could do with a little wager. How about if I find some big piece of evidence, something that really moves the case forward...you have to go with me to the *Rich Boy Poor Boy* concert. Floor seats."

"That's the one where the come out into the audience, isn't it? You are like an introvert's worst nightmare." I stand back up as Liam approaches. "No way, cause you'll do it just to spite me. Not taking the bet."

"C'mon, whatsa matter? Chicken?" she teases.

"Yes, absolutely," I say, nodding. "You won't be happy until you me get into a mosh pit. Not doing it."

Liam comes back over, nodding at me that he's ready.

Zara gives him a pointed look. "Liam, will you please tell your new partner she needs to loosen up a little? Mosh pits can be fun, exciting new experiences. You feel like one of those cinnamon buns smashes up against all the others."

"Um..." he says, looking at her then at me.

"C'mon, I need to go home and pack," I tell him.

"I'm taking that as a maybe!" Zara calls after me. She's already hooked me into karaoke and roller coasters. This is where I draw the line. I give her a final wave as we head out.

Chapter Three

THE CITY OF MARDEL IS ABOUT TWO AND A HALF HOURS AWAY. Situated on the Delaware side of the border, it's not much to look at from the satellite photos I pull up on my phone. A significant downtown, though it looks like the town hasn't grown in seventy years. I do notice a few large houses farther out from the city. It's possible some D.C. bigwigs live there if they only have to commute in once a week or so. Nanticoke county isn't much better. It's the county that sits on the Maryland side of the border, where the murder took place. The seat is a little town called Fairview, about half the size of Mardel.

I had a few things to wrap up before leaving, so we didn't end up getting on the road until first thing this morning, after yesterday's briefing. I'm sure Janice would have preferred we leave right away, but the truth is I didn't like the idea of being shooed off so soon after coming back.

We've already been in the car a good hour getting out of D.C. and Liam has barely said a word, other than to comment on the traffic. I've been trying to go over the case notes while he drives, but I feel like I can't take it anymore.

"Okay, this isn't going to work," I finally say.

He glances over at me before returning his attention to the road.

"What the hell is going on? The first time I see you in four months and you act like we've never met before. Then you spend the next three days being all standoffish, despite the fact we're around each other all the time."

"Just...trying to keep things professional," he says.

"Look, if we're going to work this case together, we've gotta be able to communicate. I can't have you giving me the silent treatment when I need to know what you think about the case. I mean, did I do something to put you off? To make you act this way? Stillwater did happen, right? I didn't imagine it." I'm just so mentally exhausted by this game that I don't want to play. Yet he seems determined to push my buttons on it. If Zara were here, we'd already have ten different theories about what could be happening in Mardel but with this guy I've got nothing. It's like he's a stranger.

"No, it's not...you didn't do anything," he says, sounding frustrated for the first time since he's been back. "I just..." Liam takes a deep breath and sighs. "Back in Stillwater I was closing in on senior detective, despite only being on the force a couple of years. Still, it felt like I knew what I needed to get ahead. And then everything happened with Burke and I realized I didn't want that small-town life anymore. But when I got accepted to the program and started the FBI training..." he trails off.

"What?" I ask.

"I felt like I was a tiny fish in a big ocean. Like I knew next to nothing. And looking back on it now, I can't imagine how you must have seen me then. Like a yokel who didn't know his head from his ass. And you would have been right." He gives me a mirthless laugh. "I didn't know a thing, despite all my bravado." He turns and looks at me. "I didn't want you to think I was that same person. FBI agents are serious business.

I need you to know I'm serious about this job. I'm not going to screw this up."

I let out a long breath. "Is that what all this has been about?" I ask. "You're afraid of looking stupid?"

He turns back to the road. "Despite the fact that Stillwater is only a few hours outside D.C., my accent is pretty strong. That was made clear to me at Quantico. And despite what everyone says, when you sound like a country bumpkin, people treat you like one."

"I don't," I say. "And you're not stupid. I never would have trusted you back in Stillwater if I thought you were."

"Thanks," he says. "My classmates weren't so generous."

I give him a knowing nod. "Yeah. It can be a little brutal. Despite all the inroads we've made, I swear some of the worst people qualify for this job. Or at least, it seems like it sometimes. It's like being an FBI agent requires some special kind of asshole attitude, like it's ingrained in the fabric of the job."

"You're not an asshole," he says.

"Oh, I am," I reply. "But only to people I don't like. I know that much about myself. Thankfully people like Zara and a few others are willing to put up with me." I turn to him. "And you think that people in this job can't have a sense of humor? You have *met* Zara, right?"

He laughs and his shoulders relax for the first time in four days. "Yeah, I guess that's true. Both of you have treated me with nothing but respect."

"Then get out of this headspace," I tell him. "You wouldn't be here if you weren't qualified. I knew when we worked together in Stillwater, you'd make a good agent. You have that determination about you, that unwillingness to take no for an answer. And we need more agents like you, rather than some of the more…traditional agents."

"You mean the loudmouths?" he asks.

"I wouldn't be so polite about it, but yes." I grin. This feels better. More like old times. "What did your dad say when you passed the academy?"

"He was over the moon," Liam says. "Said he'd have preferred I go work for MI5, but he guessed the FBI was okay too."

I laugh. "Maybe not as glamorous. Did you tell him we don't issue our agents Aston Martins?"

"I think that might break his old cop heart." Liam chuckles. "Sorry I've been...weird the past few days. I just wasn't sure how to act. This is the big leagues."

"It is, but as you'll soon find out, we have our smaller cases too. Doesn't mean they don't deserve our full attention."

A silence stretches between us, and I start to feel that wall going up again. But before I can say something, Liam pipes up. "I read your report on the person who bugged your apartment," he finally says. "I never got to tell you I was sorry about Gerald Wright. That never should have happened."

And just like that, the wall is gone again. I didn't realize he'd been looking in on my reports. That shows the same initiative I knew he was always capable of. "No," I say. "But we didn't know what we were up against. This woman is a cold-blooded killer. A true professional. If someone had been in her way, I don't doubt she would have killed them too, in order to carry out her mission."

"It's just crazy," he says. "Maybe I *should* have gone into MI5, help you figure out who this mystery woman really is."

"I don't think she's the kind of person you find. She's the kind that finds you, when she's ready."

He glances over. "You think she's coming for you?"

"Seems that way. A couple days ago, when I was still in New York, she sent me an email, telling me my husband wasn't who I thought he was. When I didn't stop my investigation, she called and threatened me. I can only imagine her final recourse will be to confront me. Because I'm not going to stop looking, no matter what." The phone call and the email aren't in the official report yet. Janice decided it was best to keep that off the desk of the Deputy Director, unless I wanted to be placed under house arrest. He's already nervous enough, if he knew I'd been directly threatened, he'd blow a gasket.

"I had no idea it was that serious," Liam says.

"We'll keep a sharp eye out while we're on this case," I say. "She might be following us here from D.C. Somehow, she manages to keep a close eye on me no matter where I go. I want to find out just how committed she is."

"I'll be watching carefully," he says. "If she shows, I won't let her get away."

"Good, I'm glad we're in agreement on that point." I glance at the clock. We've still got an hour and a half before we reach our destination. "Now, let's go over the particulars of the case. I want to see if we can't figure a few things out before we get there."

"Didn't Janice say to take your time?"

"That's just her trying to tell me to stay away for a few days. She knows once I have a case in my hands I don't stop digging until I've hit something solid."

"Okay," he says, taking one hand off the wheel and stretching out his back. "I didn't get a chance to read anything before we left. Hit me with it."

I smile. Maybe this will work out after all. If Liam and I can stay on the same wavelength, then we should have no trouble working together. It's still a little strange, given how close we are in age and yet I'm technically four years his senior. But I'm not about to let that get in the way of us doing our job. I know what he's capable of, and for the first time I feel lucky that Janice assigned him to this case with me. If all goes well, we'll have it wrapped up in no time. Then maybe I can get back to finding my assassin.

"Case number LV425," I say, reading from my phone. "We have a white male, DOA, shot in the back of the head…"

Chapter Four

THE NANTICOKE COUNTY SHERIFF'S OFFICE LOOKS LIKE IT WAS built sometime in the 1960s and then forgotten. It's an old, one-story building consisting of concrete walls with slim windows on the outside and nothing but wood paneling on the inside. The lobby has the smell of old books that have been left in the basement too long, like it's permanently baked into the building. At the desk in the front sits an older woman, probably in her sixties with gray hair that's come straight from a salon and a gaze that could cut through glass. She eyes us as Liam and I make our way up to her, our badges already on display.

"Agents Slate and Coll, here to see Sheriff John Black," I say. Normally we would have headed out to the crime scene first, but Janice impressed on me that this case needs some kid gloves. So we decided it was best to try and introduce ourselves to Sheriff Black first, then head across the border and speak with the police chief over there before we dove in. As I understand it, both departments are claiming jurisdiction and it's going to be our job to sort all of this out *and* uncover our killer.

Given the vibe I'm receiving from Mrs. Marple here, I'm starting to think that might not be so easy after all.

The woman doesn't say a word, only smacks her lips once and then again, eyeing us the entire time, as if she doesn't trust we really are who we say we are. It isn't hard for me to imagine she's got one hand on a weapon hidden under the desk, just in case she doesn't like the cut of someone's jib who happens to enter.

"We were sent by SAC Janice Simmons, from Washington." I attempt to add more authority to my voice because we really don't have time to be standing here while she decides if we're worth the sheriff's attention or not.

The woman narrows her eyes, then makes a quarter turn to the left. "*John!*"

"What is it, Irma?" a booming voice yells from down the hall.

"Coupla *feds* here to see you. From *Washington*." Somehow she manages to keep an eye on us and yet direct her attention back behind her. The disdain in her voice is palpable. I can already tell this isn't going to go well.

"Christ. Send 'em back," the voice says.

Irma makes a motion with her head that we should go around the desk, past the swinging half door and down the hall to the voice. I lock eyes with her and make my way down there, not looking in front of me but instead giving back as good as I got from her. I finally have to break eye contact when we reach the doorway.

Inside the room sits a heavyset man with a salt and pepper beard that's as thick as wool. He seems to have a hard edge to him, like he's one of those men who has seen too much to talk about, so he just keeps it all bottled up inside. I'd peg him in his late fifties, though, given the size of his belly I hope he's watching what he eats. From the ashtray full of spent cigars, I'm guessing health isn't on the top of Sheriff John Black's agenda.

He glances up as we walk in, pushing himself up with a grunt and extending a hand. Although I'm in front, he manages to find a way to take Liam's hand first, then gives mine a bare squeeze.

"Sheriff John Black," he says. "But most people just call me Big John."

"I'm Agent Emily Slate, this is Agent Liam Coll. We understand you have a jurisdiction issue."

He glances at me, like he's surprised I'm taking the lead on this. "We do. That bitch over in Mardel stole my corpse, and I'll be damned if she's gonna get away with it. Crime happened here, in my county. So I don't give a rat's ass who or what says different, I'm taking the investigation."

I'm taken aback by his abruptness, but it's nothing I haven't heard before. "I assume you mean Chief Quaker?"

"Who the hell else would I mean, sweetheart?" he asks, more than condescending before turning back to Liam. "The woman has been gunning for me ever since she was appointed. Don't matter what it is, she sees a chance to get under my skin, she'll take it. And now she's gone too far. Her kind just don't seem to know when to quit, do they?" There's a smile on his face as he says it, but then he seems to remember I'm there and it disappears.

"That how you feel about all women, Sheriff?" I ask.

"Now don't go readin' into somethin' that's not there," he says, a drawl coming out of his defensive posture. "It was just a figure of speech."

"Uh-huh," I say, nonplussed. "Exactly how did she remove the body from your care?"

"She and that damn medical examiner of hers. He's behind it. Took possession of the body before my deputies could stop him, now they've got it back across the border. I want you to go over there and get it back so I can get on with this investigation and find my killer."

"Sheriff, this is *our* investigation now," I say, more than happy to lay a bit of condescending tone into him. "Since you and your neighbors can't play nice, we're taking over and will find Mr. Sanford's killer."

"Wait a second now, you can't do that," he says, then looks to Liam for backup. "She can't do that."

"She can, and she is," Liam says, and I can tell he's attempting to suppress a smile himself.

"Then you need to reason with her," Sheriff Black says, his beady eyes going wide, talking about me like I'm not even here.

"*She* doesn't need to be reasoned with," I say. "*She* has already made her decision."

"Look here now," he says. "I've already got one pair of tits breathing down my neck, I don't need another."

"*Excuse me?*" I say.

"You heard me," he replies, pointing a chubby finger at me. "You can't come in here and take a case away from me, I'm the lawfully elected representative of this here county. And I'll be damned if some smartass *fed* is going to come into my station and tell me how things work. I was protectin' the people of this county before you were born, little miss."

Out of pure instinct I grab his finger and twist counter-clockwise. His arm and then the rest of his body follows in an attempt to keep it from breaking and he yells out as he hits the desk. "You listen to me," I growl. "I'm not going to stand here and be berated by some arrogant asshole who thinks he can just push people around because they're in his way. We're taking over this investigation. And unless you want a dozen federal officers in your station in the next hour, leading you out in handcuffs, then I suggest you start to cooperate. Don't think because I happen to look young that I'm stupid as well."

He grunts, then nods in agreement. I let go of his finger and he pulls it close to him massaging it. "You're right, okay," he says. "I...apologize. That wasn't very...welcomin' of me.

Would you be willin' to start over? I've had a rough day. This business with the body and Quaker is getting' under my skin."

I suspect that's not all there is too it. In addition to the cigar smoke, there's the slight hint of whiskey in the air. Since it's not out, I imagine he's got the bottle stashed in his desk somewhere.

"Listen, Sheriff," Liam says, leaning closer over the desk. "You're not doing yourself any favors here. You should be grateful to have Agent Slate on the case; she's got a stellar record at the Bureau and can be a big asset here. While calling us names isn't an offense per se, it doesn't really help your case very much if you want to remain part of this investigation."

"I understand," he says, still holding his finger. Technically I could get into a lot of trouble for that finger. Assaulting an officer of the law by a federal agent could bring a whole heap of shit down on me that I'm not willing to deal with. But in the moment, I just snapped. Hopefully he'll be too scared of what could happen to him if he actually makes a report, seeing as he instigated the entire event. "Like I said, could we maybe…start over?"

I take a deep breath, willing myself to calm down. It won't be helpful to the case if I'm so wound up over this man that I can't think straight. "Fine. Anything you can tell us about the victim or the scene before we head out there?"

He flexes his hand a few times, then grabs a nearby file, opening it on his desk. "Brady Sanford, age thirty-nine. White, college-educated, married with two kids." He closes the file again. "Looked to me like a domestic issue. As far as I can tell, the couple set their kids up with the grandparents for a date night, had dinner at a restaurant over here, then as they were on the way back to the car, the wife popped him and ran."

I exchanged glances with Liam. None of this is in the file. "You have evidence that the wife did it?"

He shrugs. "She's missin', ain't she? We didn't recover any shell casings from the site, which means she either picked 'em up or they got lost, but it looked to me like a close-up job. But since I can't have my own man confirm that, I'm just speculatin'." I've noticed he's begun addressing Liam again, though I'm not sure he even realizes it. It's like he can't seem to believe I can add any value to this case.

"We got patrols out lookin' for the wife now," he adds, grabbing the file again. "Summer Sanford. Age thirty-seven."

"What about the rest of the family?" I ask.

"No contact yet, not to her kids or parents. The grandparents are keepin' the kids for now, obviously." He hands the file to Liam. "Guess you'll be needin' this more than me. Will you keep me updated on the progress? We don't get a lot of murders out here and people are gonna be up in arms. If I don't deliver somethin' quick, I'm gonna start gettin' more phone calls than I'm ready to handle."

"We'll keep you apprised," I say, taking the file from Liam. I hand over my card. "And let us know if your deputies find Mrs. Sanford or anyone else of interest." I make sure to emphasize this last point to him as he takes the card. "Don't go behind our backs on this, sheriff. Understand?"

He flits a look to Liam then back to me. "'course not."

I narrow my eyes at him, then turn and leave, pushing past the swinging half door again out into the lobby. I don't even bother looking at Irma or seeing if Liam is close behind me. I just have to get out of this building before I explode. When I finally feel the sunlight on my skin again, I take a few deep breaths before heading back to the car.

Liam catches up with me a few minutes later. "Hey, you okay?" he asks.

"I shouldn't have done that back there," I say, leaning up against the car.

"No, probably not. But I don't think he's about to tell anyone he just got his ass handed to him by someone half his size," Liam says with a smile. "Trust me, he wouldn't want the embarrassment."

"Still, it was unprofessional. And it could get the Bureau in deep trouble," I say.

"It was a slip. And given the way the guy was acting; I don't blame you. If someone shoved their finger in my face, I'd want to rip it off too."

I let out a long breath. "Thanks." I usually don't slip like that. Maybe this business with the assassin has me more on edge than I thought. I have felt extra tense ever since coming back from New York, like someone was out there lying in wait for me, and could pounce at any second. I need to just focus on the case in front of me and try not to think about it right now. Zara will take care of things back home while we work on finding Mr. Sanford's killer.

"C'mon," Liam says. "We've still got to meet the other side of this feud."

"Yeah," I say. "And figure out how to smooth things over so we can actually find the killer. I've never heard of an M.E. moving a body out of the jurisdiction, have you?" Honestly, Sheriff Black has good reason to be pissed. Maybe if he wasn't so overtly sexist, I'd actually have some sympathy for him.

"Not unless there was something irregular about it," Liam says, climbing in the car. "Let's go see what we can learn."

Chapter Five

"I DON'T KNOW ABOUT YOU, BUT THAT GUY GAVE ME CHIEF Burke vibes," Liam says as we head down Route Eleven toward the Mardel town limits.

His words pull me from my thoughts. I can't quit thinking about how I nearly twisted Sheriff Black's finger off and didn't even consider it. But now that Liam mentions it, I have to agree. "Yeah, fortunately guys like him are few and far in between. At least on the surface."

"So far I'm batting a thousand," Liam says. I furrow my brow. "I'm trying non-soccer-related metaphors. Apparently when you say something like 'coupla sweet strikes,' no one in this country knows what you're talking about."

I turn back to the road. "I'm not much of a sports person either way."

"I remember," he says, and there's an undercurrent of mischievousness about him that's come out of nowhere.

"What, are you going to show me the error of my ways?" I ask.

He shrugs. "Maybe. Can't hurt to give it a try now and again. We could start together; learn why they call it America's pastime."

A surge of nervousness runs through my stomach. I think I might actually be nauseous, only to realize it's something else, something psychosomatic. Liam has an undeniable attraction about him, and now that the wall between us is down it's on full display. I'd almost forgotten about it in my frustration with him, but it isn't like I could ever do anything about it. As far as I'm concerned, I'm off the market, even though my husband is dead. Dating someone else now, so soon after his death would feel too much like cheating, and I'm just not ready to go there. I don't know if I'll ever be. It's not something I've given a lot of thought to, nor do I plan to. I need to stay focused and keep my head in the game.

"I appreciate the offer," I say. "But it's really not my kind of thing."

His eyes drop for only a second before he's all business again. Rejection is never easy, but it's better than leading him on when I know it will never go anywhere. I just hope it doesn't affect our working relationship.

"So, how are we going to handle this? It sounds like Chief Quaker actually did remove the body illegally. Do we go and arrest her?" he asks, his tone back to normal.

I shake my head. "I want to get her side of the story first. We really don't have time for this bickering, not with a killer out there on the loose. Though I'm not sure I buy Big John's explanation of what happened."

"That guy's ex-wives probably have their own support group," Liam says, which causes me to chuckle.

"I wouldn't be surprised," I say. "But let's get the facts first, then we can decide on a course of action. It's too early to make any kind of decision."

Liam nods as the town of Mardel comes into view. It sits right on the other side of the Maryland/Delaware border, and looks smaller than the satellite photos suggested. A sign right at the state line confirms as much, placing the population at only twenty-five thousand.

It's a typical American town; a bunch of gas stations and chain restaurants line the main highway, which ends up making it look like most any other high-traffic place in America. But once Liam gets off the main street and the town itself comes into view, it's like we've stepped back in time. Small brick buildings line the streets of the miniscule downtown, looking like they're at least eighty or ninety years old. The town only has a few stoplights, though I'm surprised to see a few businesses still in operation, and it seems Mardel has had something of a resurgence. Boutiques and café's take up spaces once held by what look like law offices or old warehouses. The town is in the middle of a transformation.

A couple of old houses sit between the commercial buildings and at the corners of some of the streets; more than likely historic homes belonging to people who were once important in the town. A rail line runs through the middle of town as well, though its tracks are old and rusted. It's not hard to tell that it was the industry that built this town back when it was booming. It seems like whoever is in charge of city planning is doing their jobs as far as bringing people back. Even on a Monday there is some foot traffic out and about. I hesitate to make the assumption, but I think they're tourists.

"Cozy place," Liam says as he pulls up to the police station on the far side of the main square.

"It's okay," I reply.

We get out and head through the doors of the police station. Strangely, unlike the Nanticoke county office, Mardel has a police station that looks new and renovated on the inside. It's clean with polished floors and glass partitions at the small information desk. A young man who sits behind the desk wearing a town uniform looks up as we enter. "Welcome, can I help you folks?"

"Agents Slate and Coll to see Chief Quaker," I tell him.

"Right away," he says and grabs a headset, slipping it over his head. "Chief, the FBI agents are here. Yes ma'am." He removes the headset with a smile. "I'll buzz you through. She's all the way back on the left." He indicates the glass door off to the left of the desk.

"Thanks," I say. A soft buzz indicates the door is open and I push through. Despite how fragile it looks, the door is heavy, telling me it's probably reinforced glass and could probably stop bullets if need be. Not only does the place look more welcoming, but it seems they've done a good job with security too.

We head back down the open hallway until we reach the very last door, which is open. Before I can knock to announce ourselves, a woman appears in the doorway. She's small, no taller than five-four, though the lines on her face tell me she's probably close to the same age as Black. But she's in much better shape. Her face is taut and sharp, while her uniform is open around the collar enough for me to spot a defined clavicle underneath. People don't get those unless they really work out, and Chief Quaker comes across as one of those people who works out obsessively.

"Agents," she says, extending her hand, taking mine first. "Glad to have you here. I'm Mary Quaker, been the Chief of Mardel for about five years."

"Pleasure," I say, then introduce us. While this is a much more enjoyable experience so far than the one we had with Sheriff Black, this woman potentially authorized an illegal seizure of human remains. That's not something we can just let slide no matter how polite she is.

"Come in, come in, can I get you a water or something?" she asks, rounding the desk and taking a seat on the other side. Her laptop is open and she begins tapping away.

"No, thank you," I say as Liam and I take our seats across from her. "You know why we're here."

She quits tapping and pushes the laptop aside. "I can surmise the reason. We don't get too many murders out this way. And when we do, they're usually homeless or gang-related. Not a lot of white, college-educated people being gunned down in the streets. Sadly, it's often the people of less means, the minorities."

"Before we get into the particulars of the case, we need to address the body," I say.

Her mouth turns into a frown. "The body?"

"Sheriff Black says you removed it from his jurisdiction without permission," Liam says.

Quaker sits back and rolls her eyes. "So you've met Big John. I'd ask if the encounter was pleasant, but I already know the answer."

"Still, this is a serious accusation," I say. "Regardless of the jurisdiction, removing a body without due cause—"

"Agent Slate, let me stop you there," Quaker says. "I didn't remove anything without permission. The closest medical examiner on the Maryland side of the border was over an hour away. My guy was fifteen minutes. Due to the extreme nature of the crime, I thought it was better to have *someone* on site as soon as possible rather than wait and possibly lose evidence. He met Black's men out at the scene of the crime and tried to get them to let him bring the body back to their morgue, but Black refused him access. Said he wasn't turning over his facilities to someone he didn't hire." She gives us a heavy sigh. "It's probably because he knew Robert was my guy. So I told Robert to bring the body back here so he could begin the autopsy. Considering the victim is from Mardel, and we didn't have anywhere else to start working the case, I thought it was the best option at the time. I didn't realize Black would throw up such a stink about it, though I should have."

"Why is that?" Liam asks.

She shakes her head. "He's always had it out for me; hasn't liked me since I became chief. I'm not sure what it was initially, but now the blood has been bad for so long there's just no way we can work together. As soon as I get anywhere near him, I'm the recipient of an onslaught of insults and I've just had enough."

I nod. I guess I can't blame her, I wouldn't want to work with Sheriff Black either if I didn't have to. "He neglected to mention his own examiner couldn't get to the body in time."

"That sounds like John. I'll be happy to return the body to him, but at this point the autopsy is almost done, there's nothing left to do. I'm still trying to contact the family to figure out what to do with his remains when the time comes, but I can't reach Mr. Sanford's parents or brother, all of which live out of state."

"What about the wife's family?" I ask. "I understand her parents are here and are keeping the kids."

"Considering we don't know much about the case yet, I was hesitant to contact them other than to ask them if they'd seen their daughter, which they said they haven't," Quaker says.

"Sheriff Black seems to think the wife was the one who committed the murder." I can't help but wonder if Quaker shares the same theory or not.

Something flashes in her eyes, but it's gone too soon for me to recognize it as anything more than a passing reaction. "I'd heard that, but so far we don't have any evidence to substantiate that theory."

"You said the autopsy is almost done; can we take a look as soon as your man is finished?" I ask.

"Of course, give me your information and I'd be happy to loop you in." I hand her my card and notice she begins typing the information into her computer as soon as I do.

"I don't want to step on any toes here, Chief," I say. "But Sheriff Black wasn't very happy when we informed him, we'd be taking over this investigation. Do you have a problem with us being here?"

She passes my card back to me. "Here, no need to waste one on me, I keep everything electronic now. But to answer your question, no. I understand we have something of a unique situation here and given we can't seem to sort it out ourselves, it only makes sense that you would come in and take over. At least this way we can be assured the investigation will be done properly and won't have to worry about any tampering."

"Is that a common problem here?" Liam asks.

"Just once, but never again," she replies without elaborating. That's something I may press on later. Not that I care at the moment, but something has wedged itself between these two and it might help to know what that was. But in the meantime, I have a body and no killer or weapon. We need to get moving.

"Thanks for this, Chief," I tell her. "We'll be back in touch after we take a look at the crime scene and speak to the family. Hopefully by then your man will have the autopsy done." We stand and she does the same.

"Looking forward to it," she says, taking each of our hands again before showing us out.

Once we're back on our way to the car, I look over at Liam. "Well?"

"Definitely a lot friendlier," he says. "But she's hiding something."

A smile stretches across my face. I was afraid he might have missed it. "Why do you say that?"

"She's too eager to help us. I see what you mean now, about not all local LEOs being the same. But she's like the flip side of Black. Just because she was nice to us doesn't mean she wants us here anymore than Black does."

"Bingo," I say, shooting him a finger gun and winking. "She's repressing something there. And there has to be some cause to this rift between them. Whatever it is, it's not good for the people of this community, or the next one over. I think solving this case and apprehending the killer will go a long way to showing both of them they need to find common ground."

"Sounds good to me," Liam says. "Where to first?"

I slip into the passenger seat. "We'll start at the beginning. The crime scene."

Chapter Six

"THIS LOOKS PROMISING," I SAY, BENDING TO LOOK AT THE blood stain on the concrete sidewalk that's about halfway down the block from The City Grill, a family-style restaurant that has managed to re-invent itself over the past few years as an upscale place, given the décor Liam and I just witnessed. The staff there couldn't tell us much about the couple, other than the fact they were arguing on the night in question and the woman went to the restroom before leading them out in a hurry. Unfortunately, the restaurant doesn't have any security cameras. In a small town like this, I can't imagine security is a huge priority. The entire town's losses from theft are probably less than a grand per year. The sad fact is most people here are all in the same boat, and I'd be willing to bet if someone decided to steal then everyone else would know who did it by the end of the week.

It's that kind of community gossip that I'm hoping will help us find Mrs. Sanford and our killer, if they're not one and the same person.

"I'm assuming you're being facetious," Liam says, standing over the spot on the other side. The entire sidewalk has been roped off with police tape and one of Sheriff Black's patrol cars sits nearby with two of his deputies leaning up against the vehicle with their wide-brim hats and sunglasses. One of them is even chewing on a toothpick.

"I am," I say, standing. "There's literally nothing here but a bloodstain from where the poor man's brains bled out onto the sidewalk."

"Black did say they didn't recover a shell casing," Liam reminds me.

"Mm-hm," I say, taking a broader look around, hoping I'll spot something the deputies missed. But there seems to be nothing. It's an average sidewalk, cracked from age and lack of upkeep. The road beside it isn't much better. I glance back down to the restaurant. It only took us about three minutes to walk this far, but it was enough of a distance that we're not in view of the building any longer. Though I can still see the top of one of the construction vehicles in the parking lot over the brush that borders the far side of the sidewalk.

"How long did they say they've been working on that parking lot?" I ask.

"Um." Liam pulls out his notebook. "A month. It's going slow because of the funding."

"So the couple parks down there." I point to the end of the block where a gravel lot serves as the restaurant's temporary parking. "They walk the five minutes down to the restaurant, eat, have an altercation, and begin walking back. But halfway something happens, and the husband gets shot in the back of the head, and the wife is nowhere to be found." I turn back to the makeshift parking lot. "So why didn't she just leave in her own car?"

Liam turns and looks at the parking lot himself. A blue Toyota Highlander sits in the lot along with half a dozen other vehicles.

I place my hands on my hips. "If I recall, isn't that the vehicle that's registered to the Sanfords?"

"No way they missed that," he says as we both make our way over to the vehicle. "They *can't* be that incompetent."

"It wasn't in Black's report," I say as we head that way. I motion to the deputies to follow us and catch them exchange a glance before complying. When we reach the vehicle, it doesn't look as though it's been disturbed or vandalized in any way. "Check the license," I say.

Liam goes around the back then pulls out his cell. "Hey Pruitt, can you run a plate for me? Delaware. Zero-Three-Nine-Three-Eight-Four." He taps the side of his leg as he's waiting on the information, giving the deputies time to catch up with us. "Yep. Okay, thanks." As soon as he hangs up, I already know it's their car before he can confirm it.

"We need to get this dusted for prints," I tell the deputies. "It's the Sanfords' car."

"Dammit," one of them says under his breath and goes off to make the call into tech services.

"How'd you boys miss this?" Liam asks, walking over.

The other deputy shrugs. "Black told us to focus our investigation on the scene of the death and the restaurant." He's going for nonchalance, but even I can tell he's frustrated by the way he's holding himself. Local LEOs don't like it when the feds come around but they *really* don't like it when we show them up. He knows this is a crucial part of the investigation and given the fact it was just missed, makes it hard for me to have any sympathy for them. Someone should have caught it.

"This screams chief William Burke all over again," Liam says, exasperated as soon as the other deputy is out of earshot. "I can't believe they'd be this negligent."

"I don't think it's negligence," I tell him. "I think Black is so blinded by his little feud with Quaker that he's allowing it to affect his performance." I glance over at the deputy who is inspecting the vehicle. "And it's bleeding into his troops." Black is a pompous, arrogant ass, that much is for certain. I think it'll be better if we just keep him at arm's length through this entire investigation. Otherwise, he could end up derailing us and compromising our results.

"The question remains then," Liam says. "If Mrs. Sanford didn't leave in her car, where did she go? Did she make a run for it on foot?"

I consider the question. "If you'd just killed your husband, would you take your easily-recognizable car out and around the city where everyone could see you?" I ask. "Or would you have planned for this and had a backup ready?"

"You think Black's theory might have some weight to it?" Liam asks.

I take a long, hard look at the car, then back at where Brady Sanford was killed. "I'm not sure. We need some more information. Let's go talk to the grandparents, maybe they can shed some light on this situation."

"What about the car?" Liam asks.

"Leave it to Black's men. They already screwed this up once, they're going to be on their best behavior not to do it again."

On the way to the grandparent's house, we swing by the victim's residence, just on a hunch. But after a couple of knocks and no answer, we leave empty-handed. I didn't actually expect Mrs. Sanford to be there, or even if she was, to actually answer. But something told me it would be a bad idea if we didn't head over there just to check anyway. My main concern is finding this woman and then figuring out what she knows. Unfortunately, there isn't much we can do for Mr. Sanford anymore, but his wife is still out there somewhere, probably very scared. Either that or looking over her shoulder every five seconds. Depending on how this goes, we may need a warrant for the home anyway.

When we pull up to the house of Summer Sanford's

parents, it strikes me as quaint. It's a one-story brick building that looks like it was probably built sometime in the 1940's. The driveway is little more than two concrete runners that lead from the street to a covered pad. Copious amounts of grass grows between the runners, almost to the point where it's taken over. But the house seems like it's in good shape otherwise, and while small, is well-taken care of. None of the shutters are missing and the roof is clean, which is more than I can say for most of the rest of the houses in this neighborhood.

Liam and I make our way up the walkway to the front door and give it a good knock. A moment later the door opens to reveal a young girl, probably no older than ten, with bright, blonde hair in pigtails staring up at us. I instinctively take a step back.

"Hi there," Liam says. "Are your grandparents home?"

The little girl nods and runs off, leaving the door wide open.

"Still dealing with the kid thing, huh?" he asks.

I wince. I shouldn't have let that happen; it's been more than six months since my incident back in D.C. I shouldn't still be so jumpy around kids. "Old habits, I guess."

"You want me to take the lead? Like back in Stillwater?"

I shake my head. "No, I got this. Thanks, though." Had Liam not been there to help when we were interviewing Gerald Wright before we suspected him of murder, I'm not sure I would have ever listed him as a suspect. His young children had been playing close to us and had been a major distraction for me. Fortunately, Liam had managed to take control of the questioning; it was that afternoon that eventually led us to suspecting Wright as our killer. But I'm not about to let that happen again. This time I am present, and I can handle being around kids. I have to be, it isn't like they're going anywhere.

A few moments later an older woman appears at the door.

She's probably in her late seventies or early eighties, and is dressed modestly. She has long, silver hair that's tied back. I can almost see the young woman she was once; she's one of those women who has a timeless beauty about them. "Can I help you?" she asks, with a gentle, yet firm voice.

"Good afternoon. Are you Adelaide Thompson?"

"I am," she replies.

"I'm Agent Emily Slate with the FBI. This is Agent Liam Coll. I understand you've been informed about the events of Sunday evening."

"I have, yes." No reaction. Apparently no love lost for her daughter's husband.

"We've taken over the case from the local authorities," I say, hoping this will reassure her that we're serious about finding out what happened. "Have you had any contact with your daughter since that evening?"

The woman smiles, then looks down at the little girl who is hanging close behind her. "Go find your brother. I need to speak with these nice people for a few moments."

"But he never wants to play, gramma," she whines.

"For a few minutes, Ashleigh. Go on."

The girl rolls her eyes then heads off while Mrs. Thompson joins us out on her front porch, closing the door behind her. "I haven't had any contact with Summer since Sunday when they dropped off the kids," she says. "If I had, I would have informed Chief Quaker."

"Do you have any idea of where she might be?" I ask. "We found her vehicle was still parked in the lot by the restaurant."

Mrs. Thompson shakes her head. "It isn't like my Summer to disappear like this. She loves these kids dearly and wouldn't leave them for anything. It was insinuated to me that she might have killed Brady herself, but that would be impossible."

"Why's that?" Liam asks.

"It wasn't in her nature. They had problems just like any family, but she wasn't the kind of girl who solved those problems with a gun. She doesn't even own a gun as far as I know."

"How often did you speak with your daughter?" I ask. "Was it on a regular basis?"

"Semi-regular. She'd call a few times a week, or I would call her. Charles and I were always happy to take the kids whenever they needed us to. But their schedules were always so busy that it was hard to find time. This date night of theirs was the first one they'd had in months."

"You mentioned they had problems," I say. "Do you know what kind?" I see some hesitation from Mrs. Thompson, as if she thinks she'll be betraying her daughter's confidence if she tells us. "I know it's not easy," I say. "But at this point we need all the information we can get if we're to find your daughter."

The woman averts her gaze and lets out a long exhale. "They were having money issues," she finally says. "But I don't know the extent of it. I just know they were barely making ends meet. Summer wouldn't tell me any more about it."

"How long had this been going on?" I ask.

"At least six months or more. But then, I found out Elliott had been suspended from summer school. He was there to make up a class he failed last year, but now he'll have to do all his work from here. I just found out this morning when I tried to take him and drop him off." She looks at us again. "They had a lot on their plates."

I exchange another look with Liam. We'll need to start diving into Summer Sanford's financials if we want to corroborate any of this. But it does give us the potential for a motive. I hate to say it, but Black's theory is looking better and better by the minute.

"Can you tell us anything else? Did Summer ever mention

to you where she might go if she was in trouble, or who she might contact?" Liam asks.

The woman shakes her head. "She never said anything about that. She's not that kind of person. Summer, God love her, but that girl can't plan worth a damn. It took her a year to unpack her closet from when they moved into their new house. And she's called me twice because she's run out of gas on the side of the road and is too embarrassed to call her husband for help. She's just...she's so locked in her own head sometimes she forgets to look up."

I give the woman a knowing smile. "Okay, thank you for your help. Please, if you think of anything else that might be useful, feel free to give me a call, day or night. There are no hours on here for a reason." I hand her one of my cards.

"You don't think she really did this, do you?" Mrs. Thompson asks.

"I don't know what to think yet," I tell her. "I just know we need more information if we're going to find your daughter."

She nods. "I'll be sure to call. In the meantime, the kids will be safe here with us. Might do them some good to live under some rules for once." She gives me a small wink then heads back into the house.

"C'mon," I tell Liam. "Let's find a place where we can set up and see if we can't corroborate some of this. It might just be what we need to find Summer and button this entire thing up."

"Lead the way," he says.

I smile as we head back to the car. It was as I thought, a simple case. And once it's all over then I can finally get back to the real issue at hand. Though part of me isn't sure if I'm ready to handle it yet or not.

Chapter Seven

ON CHIEF QUAKER'S SUGGESTION, WE HEAD OUT ALONG Route Eleven until we come to a diner marked *Traveler's Barrel*. I'm not sure what a barrel has to do with anything, but it seems like a nice-enough place. There's no one else in the parking lot, which means we won't have to worry about being disturbed. I'd initially thought about heading back to the Mardel station, but I don't want to look like I'm playing favorites here, even though I definitely am.

I want to take a minute from the warring factions to go over what we have so far, see if we can't figure out where Mrs. Sanford is before she manages to get too far.

As we push through the door, a small bell above us rings, announcing our presence. A woman sticks her head out from behind a partition near the back. "Hey there. Ya'll just sit wherever you like. I'll be with you in a minute."

We make our way to one of the back booths, away from the restrooms or any potential traffic, in the unlikely event we're here long enough for the place to get crowded.

As soon as we're sitting, I've already pulled up my laptop with the secure server Zara set up for me when we got back to D.C. "I'm going to dig into their financials, see if the grandmother was telling the truth," I say. "Start checking with coworkers, known associates. See if you can't find anyone who might know something useful."

"Got it," Liam says, and begins working between his phone and the case file for friends and coworkers of Brady Sanford. The waitress brings over a couple of cups of coffee for us and leaves two menus on the table. I don't plan on eating anything, we're here purely for a quiet place to work for a few minutes.

Meanwhile I take a few minutes to log into the secure FBI servers before starting the deep dive on the Sanford's' financials. I'm not great at this kind of thing; normally Zara is the one who takes care of all the computer work. While it's nice to have Liam here, I miss the way Zara and I can work effortlessly off each other, anticipating each other's moves before we've made them. It makes the casework go a lot faster and it keeps my head free of distractions while I'm working, because I know she'll come through for me.

And while I don't doubt Liam's skill as an investigator, I can't help but think back to what he told me in the car, about not wanting to disappoint me or come across as stupid. Are those things influencing how he's approaching this case, and could they potentially be compromising him? I'm sure I'm worrying for nothing, but until we become more comfortable around each other, I'm going to have these lingering thoughts in the back of my head.

As I go through the various programs to look at the litany of transactions over the past year, I have half a mind to call Zara and ask her how things are going on her end. Maybe that's just because I miss her, not because I want an update on the search. Part of me does, but another part of me thinks maybe it's better if it remains a mystery, at least until I get back. The last thing I'd want is for Zara to find the assassin and bring her in while I'm stuck out here working what seems like a simple murder case.

I shake my head, turning my thoughts to the case at hand. We still have a missing woman out there, and it's beginning to look more and more like she's on the run. Finding Summer Sanford will be the key to her husband's murder, though I'm still not convinced she was the one who did this. Her mother seemed adamant that Summer just wasn't this kind of person; that she wouldn't have the wherewithal to pre-plan her husband's murder. While I'm waiting on the financials to go through, I check the gun registry for Delaware to see if she has any weapons registered in her name.

"Hey." Liam looks up. "I just pulled the registry on Summer Sanford. No weapons in her name, but her husband has a .22 and a .38, both handguns. Both registered in his name. Do we have any info back from the medical examiner about the caliber of bullet used?" He checks what notes he has. "Nothing yet. I assume it will be in the autopsy."

I check the time on my phone. "What is taking Quaker's M.E. so long? He's had the body for over a day now. You'd think he would have had this finished yesterday."

"Maybe he was backed up," Liam says.

"Except that Chief Quaker's entire reason for using him was he was closer than Black's own examiner. So what, they take the body then just sit on it for a day? Why, to piss off Black?"

He chuckles. "I wouldn't put it past her."

"Ya'll have a chance to look at the menu?"

I look over to see the waitress has returned, pen and pad in hand.

"Nothing for me, thanks," I say.

"I'll take a plate of fries," Liam says. "Extra salt."

"Salt's on the table, honey," the waitress says with a smile. "Looks like you're working hard."

"This? No, this is just a normal day for us," he replies and I arch my eyebrow at him. He returns the gesture, adding a little smirk.

"One plate of fries, coming up," she says and heads off.

"What was that?" I ask.

He gives me those puppy-dog eyes of his. "What? Just being friendly. Can't hurt, right?"

"Uh-huh." Finally, the financial information populates on my screen. "Here we go." Liam looks up and I motion for him to come to my side of the booth so we can both take a look. He slides in the booth and I catch a whiff of his aftershave. That familiar sensation of butterflies in my gut is back, but I push it back down. Not happening, not even in the cards. At least he doesn't seem to notice.

"Okay," he says, scanning their bank accounts as I click through them. "Adelaide was right, they're just barely hanging on. What are all these withdrawals?"

The Sanfords have three accounts, two checking and a savings. But someone has been withdrawing a thousand dollars every two weeks from the savings account, causing it to dwindle to so low they're getting hit with low balance fees every month.

"Who's withdrawing the cash? The husband or the wife?" Liam asks.

"I guess there's only one way to find out," I say. "We'll need to head over to First State Credit Union."

The waitress returns with the plate of hot fries. "Here you go, enjoy."

I fold up my laptop and put it away. "We're going to need those to go."

"There are only a few reasons I can think of to withdraw large amounts of cash every few weeks, on a schedule," I say as Liam drives to the only credit union location in town. I'm praying they have security cameras, though given what I've seen of Mardel so far, nothing is guaranteed.

"Stowing money away for a getaway," Liam says.

I nod. "Or they were using it to pay someone off. Either way, it doesn't look good. And without more information, we'll never know where that cash went. I'm just hoping if we can find out who was withdrawing it, it might give us a direction to head in."

"Sounds like a long shot." He pulls into the parking lot of the credit union.

"Half the time it feels like that's what this job is all about," I reply. "Stay here and keep working on friends and cowork-ers. Someone has to know *something*."

"Good luck," he says, grabbing a few fries from the Styro-foam container on the dashboard.

I smile. "Save me a couple."

The credit union is a standard bank building, probably repurposed from a local branch that was merged long ago. But as soon as I get inside, I spot security cameras in the corners of the large lobby, and I breathe a sigh of relief. I take a minute to inform the closest teller who I am and why I'm here before she heads off to grab the manager. A few seconds later an older man in a blue suit appears, his hand extended. "I'm Arthur Montgomery," he says, "Branch Manager. I understand you're looking for information on one of our customers."

"Agent Emily Slate." I shake his hand. "I'm hoping you can tell me who has been withdrawing cash from this account over the past few months." I hand him the written account number.

"Follow me, please," he says and leads me into his office. It's sparse, with a cheap wooden desk and a few shelves, but few items that would tell me anything about the man himself. As I understand it, banks tend to move their managers around a lot, so it isn't a surprise that he hasn't taken to decorating.

"Let's see, oh yes, the Sanfords, I know them well," he

says, pulling up the account. "Nice family. In a town this small you tend to learn a little bit about everyone."

"When was the last time you spoke to either Mr. or Mrs. Sanford?" I ask.

He scrunches up his face. "Maybe a week ago? I'm sorry, I can't remember the exact date. But Mr. Sanford was in here for something." He looks at his computer a moment. "Ah, it seems he was probably making this withdraw you're inquiring about. The thousand on the twenty-second, is that right?"

"Correct. Can you tell if he was the one who made all the other withdrawals as well?"

He types a few more times. "Looks like it. All were made with his debit card, not the one registered to his wife's name. I'd have to check the security feeds for each of these to be a hundred percent sure, but I can say with a good degree of confidence that Mr. Sanford was the one making all of these withdrawals."

"Would you mind reviewing the security footage and copying it for me?" I ask, handing him my card. "You can either email it to me or I can come back to pick it up."

"Can you tell me what this is about?" he asks. Apparently, the news of Brady Sanford's death hasn't reached everyone yet, which is good news for me. I figured in a town this small the news would have spread faster. But then again, considering he died across the border, maybe there is some unspoken barrier there that prevents the two communities from inter-mingling. It wouldn't be the strangest thing I've ever seen.

"I'm afraid I can't discuss an ongoing case," I tell him. "But it would be very helpful to us to have that confirmation."

He gives me a serious nod. "Very well. But it will take me some time. I have other duties to attend to."

"That's fine," I say. "Thank you for your help."

"Always happy to help the FBI," he replies. "Good luck with your investigation."

I head back out to the car to find Liam deep in his phone.

When I open the door, I'm hit with the smell of fried potatoes. I crack open the container to find he's left at least half of them and a little pile of ketchup squeezed from packets.

"Any luck?" he asks.

"Looks like Brady was the one making the withdrawals," I tell him. "Did you find anything?"

He nods. "A couple of college friends, one who is local. He seems like our best option."

I check the time; we're closing in on five p.m. It's already been a long day, but I'm anxious to button this up as quickly as possible. "Where can we find him?"

"He's an insurance adjuster with Delfarm. Which means he works a nine to five."

"Got an address?"

Liam smiles. "I knew you were going to ask that. Seatbelt."

I find I'm hungrier than I thought and manage to finish the remaining fries before he can even get back out on the main road. But the whole time I can't quit wondering why Mr. Sanford was withdrawing that money.

It seems this case isn't going to be as open and shut as I had first thought.

Chapter Eight

"GLAD I ORDERED THE LARGE," LIAM SAYS, LOOKING AT THE empty container that used to contain the fries.

"Sorry," I say. "I have a problem about not eating while I'm on a case. Zara gets on my back about it all the time."

"Maybe once we talk to Mr. Vogel we should go get a proper meal," he says. He pulls the car up to Delfarm Insurance just as a middle-aged man is closing up and locking the front door. He doesn't turn and look as we get out of the car, more concerned with making sure his office is secure for the evening.

"Daniel Vogel?" I finally cause him to turn.

"Yes?" he asks. He's a stout man, with a thin beard and moustache, certainly nothing that could rival Sheriff Black's. He also wears a pair of eyeglasses that have shaded in the afternoon sun. I didn't know they even made those anymore.

"I'm Agent Emily Slate with the FBI. This is Agent Coll. We'd like to ask you a few questions."

"FBI?" he asks with a frown. "What's this about?"

"Do you know Brady Sanford?" I ask.

"Of course, why?"

"When was the last time you spoke with Mr. Sanford?"

Liam asks, coming around the other side of the car. Vogel remains in front of his door, holding a briefcase in one hand.

"Maybe last weekend. But we text a few times a week. I haven't heard from him in a few days, though."

I exchange a look with Liam. In my haste to find out about this case, I've neglected to realize that we'll have to inform Mr. Vogel of Brady's untimely demise. It's the worst part of the job, and sometimes you have no idea how it's going to go. Some people just go numb, while others break down into hysterics. I hate to say it, but we often watch how people respond to the news in the event they are or could become potential suspects. It's a difficult job, sometimes.

"Mr. Vogel, I'm sorry to tell you this, but Brady was murdered on Sunday evening."

His eyes go wide. "What?" The word comes out as barely more than a whisper. "No, that can't be. Are you sure it's him?"

"He's been positively identified, yes," I say. Vogel drops his briefcase, which clunks on the ground and then falls over. He leans back against the building, his hand up at his temple as he takes deep breaths. "Do you need to take a seat?"

"I…I think so, yes." He turns to the door automatically and fumbles with his keys a moment before finally finding the correct one and turning the tumbler. He pushes through and takes the first seat inside the door. We follow him in, and I flip the lights back on. Liam and I stand off to the side to give him a few minutes to collect himself.

"I just can't…*murdered*." Vogel shakes his head. He's bent over, almost to the point where his head is between his knees. "Do you know who did it?" he finally asks, looking up.

"We're working on that right now," I tell him. "Had Brady been acting strange at all for the past few months?"

He cocks his head at me. "Strange?"

"Different than normal. Like he had something on his mind."

"Oh," he says, and his shoulders fall. "You're wondering about Isobella."

"Isobella?" I ask.

He looks between us. "Yeah, I figured you already knew. The woman he was seeing on the side. They'd been meeting at his office while everyone else was out for lunch for a few months now." He sits back, tilting his head up at the ceiling. "I tried to tell him not to get involved, but he claimed it was love and that they weren't just fooling around."

Liam gives me a pointed look. Another mark against Summer. If she found out about the affair, the motive writes itself.

"Do you know Isobella's last name?" I ask.

He shakes his head. "Never met her. Brady only told me about her a couple of times. Said they had something he just didn't have with Summer. He still loved her, but this was something else and he didn't know how to explain it. The way he talked it sounded like he was really head over heels for this girl."

"Did he ever say anything about paying her?" Liam asks. "Or that she ever needed money?"

Vogel squeezes his eyes shut for a minute like he's in physical pain before opening them again. "I told him, and he just wouldn't listen. I said, 'She's taking you for a ride, man.' But he was adamant they were in love." He turns to Liam. "I think he was giving her a couple grand a month. Maybe more."

"Is there anything else you can tell us about Isobella? Where she lives, where she works?" I ask. This is starting to look very bad for Mrs. Sanford. Her husband was taking money from their savings account to give to a woman he was sleeping with behind her back. Maybe this is what they were discussing that night at dinner and why they left so suddenly.

"I never met her," Vogel says. "I'm not even sure Isobella is her real name. Brady used his real name, but for all I know she could be someone completely different."

"You said they met at his office sometimes?" I ask.

He nods. "That's where they always met. He was too cheap to get a hotel and said she liked the thrill of it."

I look over at Liam. "Maybe his coworkers saw something. We need to find this Isobella, right now."

"Do you think she was the one who killed him?" Vogel asks. "Why? He was paying her. She kills him and the payments stop."

"Thank you, Mr. Vogel, we appreciate your time and help," I say. "And I'm very sorry for your loss." He brings up a good point, though. I don't think this "Isobella" is our killer, but who's to say she didn't have another guy on the side who found out about Brady and decided he wanted Isobella all for himself? There could be a million different explanations. All I know is the deeper we get into this case, the more complex it becomes.

We leave Vogel in his office and head back out to the car just as my phone buzzes in my pocket. "Slate."

Chief Quaker clears her throat before she continues, "Agent, I'm glad I reached you. I wanted to let you know Robert has finished the autopsy. He said he'll be in his office first thing in the morning to go over the results with you."

"In the morning?" I ask. "Can't we do it now?"

"I'm afraid he's already left for the day," Quaker says.

"Chief," I say, trying to remain diplomatic. "I don't mean to be intrusive here, but we have a killer on the loose and a missing woman. Possibly the killer herself. Waiting until tomorrow morning costs us precious time in finding her."

"I'm sorry, Agent Slate, I don't know what to tell you," she replies, though it doesn't sound like she's sorry at all. "Robert is strict about the hours he keeps."

I can't believe this. Is the medical examiner really going to put this entire investigation on hold because he's "done for the night"? "Can you call him back in, for special circumstances?"

"Frankly, Agent Slate, I don't know how many times you

can ask the same question. The answer remains the same. He'll be in at seven-thirty in the morning and will go over the details with you then. I'm calling you as a courtesy." She sounds offended that I'd even suggest her examiner work past five p.m.

"He's putting this investigation at risk," I finally say. "And so are you by allowing him to just leave like this. Agent Coll and I don't quit until we've found our killer."

I can hear a huff of indignation on the other end of the line. "Then I guess you'll just have to put up with our uncivilized ways," Quaker says. "Goodnight, Emily."

"Chief," I say, but she's disconnected the call. "Son of a—"

"What was that all about?" Liam asks.

I feel a rush of adrenaline that urges me to throw my phone across the parking lot, but I manage to refrain. "Quaker. She sidelined us. And here I was worried about Black."

"The autopsy?"

I nod. "She says her examiner will speak with us in the morning. And not a moment before."

Liam shakes his head. "Unfortunately, I'm familiar. That's something else I noticed about the FBI. You guys are like tanks, you just keep going until you've reached your destination. Things back in the precinct were slower, more manageable. If you needed to take the afternoon off for something, you just did it and came back to the investigation later."

"Some agents may work like that," I say. "But not me. Not when people's lives are on the line. I have half a mind to find out where the examiner lives and go knock on his door."

"I'm sure that would ingratiate him toward us. He'll definitely want to share what he knows then."

I give Liam the side-eye but eventually relent. He's right. No amount of foot-stomping is going to change the fact that we're at this man's mercy. If he decides to wait until tomorrow, there's little we can do about it. It isn't like he works for us. It's just I've never encountered a medical examiner or coroner who wasn't willing to stay up half the night to get us the information we needed for the case. I guess I've been taking that for granted.

"C'mon," Liam says. "We can still speak with Brady's coworkers. We can even work straight through dinner if it will make you happy."

I give him a light shove. "Ass."

He grins. "Eh, comes with the territory."

"Who's first?" I ask.

"Charlotte Dunlevy," he says. "She's the office manager for Alltown Realty, where Brady worked."

"Okay, I tell him. Switch."

"What?"

"I'm driving."

Liam hesitates. "I've seen the way you drive. I just about threw up on that trip back to Stillwater down the mountain."

"Then lucky for you there are no mountains around," I say and get out of the car. I'm sick of being driven around like I'm someone's charge. I need to get behind the wheel and burn off some of this frustration.

Liam gets out of the driver's side. "I'm supposed to keep you safe. Which means I'm the one driving and keeping a lookout for any dangerous vehicles or anyone who might try and make you a target."

"It's Delaware," I say. "And if she is out there, she's just watching, like always." Though I hate the idea of someone keeping an eye on my every move, I've had to come to accept it as a normal part of my life, at least for now. Otherwise, I'll go crazy trying to find her and I can't get distracted, not while this case is tying me up in knots. Finding Summer Sanford is my number one concern. I'll deal with the assassin later.

Liam presses his lips in a line and finally tosses me the keys as we exchange seats. "That's more like it," I say, turning the car over. I'm full of pent-up rage at both Quaker and Black. Some time out on the open road will do me good.

I back out of the space, doing a hairpin three-point turn before we're headed back out to the main road. Before we reach there Liam has the "oh-shit" handle in a death grip. "Funny enough, Zara never complains about my driving."

"That's because she's as nuts as you are," Liam says. "You two are cut from the same cloth."

I laugh; she'll get a kick out of that. I back it off a little; I'm not so arrogant to think I'm the only driver on the road. But being in control of the car for the first time during this investigation feels good. "All right. Let's see what Mrs. Dunlevy has to say."

Chapter Nine

"THANK YOU FOR YOUR TIME," I SAY AS MRS. DUNLEVY closes her door and returns to finish preparing dinner for her family. While she hadn't been too happy to interrupt her evening schedule, she did give us some important information.

"So we know Brady Sanford was not only taking money from the account he shares with his wife, he was more than likely giving that money to a woman known only as Isobella, that he happened to be sleeping with," Liam says. "And even though we have a description, we have no positive ID. Is that about the long and short of it?"

"You got it," I say. Mrs. Dunlevy had spotted a young woman coming and going from Brady's office in their building a few times over the past few months but had never met her personally. She managed to tell us the woman was olive-skinned, with dark hair and was trim, dressed professionally. As descriptions go it's pretty vague, but it's better than nothing. She also indicated she wasn't surprised he was sleeping around on his wife; he was known to flirt in the office. Though considering she was ten years his senior, she hadn't been willing to put up with it herself. She just hadn't been able to say anything because Brady had been her boss.

"So now we have a host of other suspects," I say. "Pretty much any woman in his office could have a motive, depending on how far Brady pushed things."

"I take it to mean our workload just got a lot bigger."

I shake my head and attempt to stifle a yawn. We've been going ever since we pulled into this town first thing this morning. I feel like we've been working on this case for a week already. "Unfortunately, yes. We'll have to interview and alibi all of them, if for no other reason than to eliminate them from the suspect pool. Which only slows us down and doesn't get us any closer to finding Summer."

"Okay, I'm calling it," Liam says as I begin to pull out of Mrs. Dunlevy's driveway.

"What?"

"You're tired, I'm tired. We need food, considering all we've had to eat today is a container of salty fries. We can start fresh tomorrow."

I put the car in park and gape at him. "Did you not just hear me tell Quaker that we don't stop until the case is solved? What was that, half an hour ago?"

"Em, you're exhausted," Liam says. "I can see it on your face. Maybe Zara will let you get away with pulling all-nighters, but I need rest, and so do you. You're getting frustrated and you need to recharge otherwise you're not going to be good to anyone, much less Summer. I say we go check into the motel, find a place that has something not bathed in beer batter and then hit the sheets so we can be up early to talk to the medical examiner. All of these people we need to interview can wait until tomorrow."

I take a deep breath and glare at him, hating that he's right. We've been going full steam ever since we got here and all I've really done is managed to alienate the two warring factions I'm here to try and build a bridge between. This clearly isn't going to be the open and shut case I was hoping for when we drove up this morning. I can feel my mind beginning to cloud as all my thoughts jumble together. And somewhere in the distance my stomach is rumbling as well. He's right, we can't make it on a day of coffee and French fries alone.

"Fine, you win," I say. "Where are we staying?"

He looks at his phone. "Best location I found was the *Delta River Inn*. It's the least infested hotel in town according to Yelp."

"Please tell me you're kidding," I say.

He chuckles. "No, it's actually pretty nice." Liam turns his phone where I can see it. The pictures of the rooms look updated and clean. It actually has interior hallways, which is always a plus. In this line of work we tend to work with what we get.

"Yeah, okay," I say. It only takes us another ten minutes to reach the *Delta River Inn*, which sits right on the outside of Mardel, close to the Maryland border. As Liam is checking us in, I wonder if Summer herself is holed up in one of these rooms, waiting for things to calm down. Somewhere deep there's an urge to go knocking on every door, except I realize I don't have to.

"Hey," Liam says as I come through the lobby door. He's leaning over the counter as the man behind it processes his credit card.

"Sir," I say, getting the attention of the man behind the counter. "Has a woman checked in here since Sunday night? She could have been alone or with someone else. Late-thirties, dark blonde hair, wearing jeans and a red blouse?"

"Are you two cops or something?" he asks.

"FBI," I say, showing him my badge.

"No, no one like that since Sunday," the man replies, handing Liam his card back. "We've only had two check-ins since then. You and another, older man with his grandson who were passing through on their way to Virginia Beach. Made a big deal about going over the Bay-Bridge Tunnel."

I sigh, deflated again.

"C'mon, Em. Let's drop our stuff off and find a place to eat," Liam says.

For some reason I can't seem to let this go, even for a few hours. Maybe it's because we don't know if Summer killed her husband or not. Or maybe it's because I don't like the fact she hasn't shown up anywhere since his death. None of her credit cards have been used, her car is still where they parked it, and there is no sign of her anywhere in town or otherwise. She either planned this out with precision—unlikely according to her mother—or we're looking for the wrong person.

Liam was right, the hotel room is nice. It's classy, but not in an old-fashioned, out-of-date or dingy way. The windows have nice curtains, a solid oak table sits in the corner and the bed has a headboard that looks to be made out of the same wood. Surprisingly, there's no carpet. Instead, a laminate faux-hardwood covers the floor, while the bathroom has a nice tile. It's not as nice as some of the chain hotels, but for an independent business relying on Mardel's "booming" tourist population, I have to give them some credit. They've done a good job.

After dropping our stuff off in our respective rooms, Liam takes us to a nearby restaurant which boasts a vegetarian menu. I find I'm hungrier than I thought and manage to demolish a chicken Caesar salad and half a dozen breadsticks. We manage to talk about anything but the case or my situation back in D.C., which is a welcome relief. I hadn't realized how much I needed that. And by the time we're on our way back to the hotel, I'm beginning to feel sleep paw at the edges of my consciousness. Liam was right, this was exactly what I needed. But I don't want to admit to him that he was right, that'll just encourage behavior like that in the future.

Still, I'm grateful.

"Bright and early?" he asks, once I have my door open. His is the next room down.

"Up at five-thirty," I tell him. "Maybe we can grab breakfast at that diner before we go talk to the medical examiner."

"You're the boss," he says and gives me a small salute before heading into his room and closing the door. Some deep, dark part of me is inclined to follow him, but I smash it down as soon as the thought pops in my head.

I head into my own room and settle in for the night, grateful that I have someone I can trust watching my back. It's a far cry from where we were this morning when we set out for Mardel.

What a difference a day can make.

Chapter Ten

HE'S GOT TWO MORE MINUTES BEFORE I GO KNOCK ON HIS door.

After a great night's sleep, I was up early this morning strategizing on the case. When I work a case like this, I'll sometimes get inspiration while I sleep. Something came to me last night. Which was why I was up and showered and ready by five-twenty. I've been checking my phone every thirty seconds for the past fifteen minutes now, waiting on Liam to make an appearance, but I've been out of luck. Somehow, I manage to stop myself from pacing in front of his door, but I'm not above giving the door what Zara calls one of my "police knocks". As in, it sounds like the entire door is going to cave in as I'm pounding on it.

Just as I've decided I'm going in, the door swings open to reveal Liam, fresh and ready. He jumps slightly as soon as he sees me, but even as he does, there's a smile on his face. He checks his watch. "I thought you said be up by five-thirty."

"I didn't think it would take you half an hour to get ready," I reply. "We're burning daylight here."

He frowns, looking out in the distance. "The sun isn't even up yet."

"You know what I mean. C'mon. Let's get moving. I'm hungry."

"You're one of those early birds, aren't you?" He stifles a yawn as he makes his way over to the driver's side of the car. "AKA, the most annoying people in the world."

"And you're one of those late sleepers, I bet. Always showing up right before the buzzer. How late would you have slept in if I hadn't said five-thirty?"

"I plead the fifth, your honor," he says and pulls away from the hotel. "My secrets die with me."

"You know, getting up early is conducive to a sharp mind. Getting the blood flowing early helps generate new ideas and jumpstart the cerebellum to perform better."

"You would say something like that," he replies. "I'm not even sure I believe it."

"That's the beautiful thing about science, whether you believe it or not, it's still true." I grin at him.

"You sure are chipper for this early in the morning," he replies.

He's right. I am in a good mood. Enough that I don't even mind telling him so. "That's because you were right. I was burning out yesterday. Usually, I would have worked for a few more hours, then gone back and had a drink at some bar to calm down before going to bed late before getting up earlier than my body would have liked. But thanks to you, I got plenty of rest, so I'm ready to get this started."

"I'm glad I could help." He sits up a little straighter, pushing his shoulders back. "So what's this great revelation that your wonderful night of sleep gave you?"

"Who said anything about a revelation?" He catches me off guard. Am I so easy to read?

"You're the one talking about getting the blood flowing, about churning out a productive day. I have to assume that means you had some sort of breakthrough. Otherwise, I don't think you'd be this animated, especially after everything we learned yesterday."

"It's more complex than I gave it credit for, I admit. But I didn't solve it overnight, if that's what you're asking. I had a thought, though. We should start checking Summer Sanford's passport to see if she's used it in the past forty-eight hours. In addition, we should get her face all over the surrounding towns and counties. Someone has to have seen her if she's on the run."

"You definitely think she's running?" he asks.

"It's looking more and more likely. It doesn't all add up yet, but I'm hoping we can find her to ask her ourselves. She's our best chance at solving this thing."

"I guess that means we'll need to coordinate with both departments to begin the manhunt. I'm not looking forward to that."

"Me either," I admit. "Black already doesn't seem to even acknowledge I'm there and Quaker turned cold last night when I began grilling her about her medical examiner. We're missing a piece of the puzzle there somewhere, but regardless, we don't have a choice. We were sent here to solve this, and I don't think we can do it without either of them."

The sound of Liam's stomach grumbling erupts in the car. "How about we wait until after breakfast?"

When Liam pulls up to the *Traveler's Barrel* at six a.m., there's already a small line at the door. Mostly hard-looking men who probably have early shifts somewhere in town. The doors to the diner are open before we get to the line, so by the time we're in, the place is already bustling.

"Just take a seat, we'll be right with you," one of the waitresses announces and we head down the same way we did yesterday. Part of me hopes the same booth is open; I liked that spot. But when we reach the booth, I almost do a double-take. Sheriff Black is sitting right where I was seated not more than fourteen hours ago, sipping on a hot cup of coffee.

"Sheriff?" I ask.

He glances up as he's taking a long sip before putting his cup back down. "Agents," he says. "You're up early."

"What are you doing on this side of the border?" I ask.

He chuckles. "It ain't East and West Germany, sweetheart, we come and go as we please. And the *Barrel* has the best pancakes around. I'm here ev'ry Wednesday."

I inwardly wince at his condescension, but I don't let him see it. Instead, I slide into the booth across from him. "Actually, this is good timing. We need your help with something."

He takes another sip from the mug. I notice he pulls his other hand away from me, the one I wrenched yesterday. "Anythin' I can do for the FBI."

"We need to start building a net for Summer Sanford. That has to start here, where she was last seen. I want you to coordinate with the other local counties in Maryland to get her face out there. Start with the media, someone has to have seen her. We'll have Chief Quaker do the same on this side of the border."

"So then you think I'm right, she offed her husband," he says.

"That seems to be where the evidence is pointing us. Get any prints off that car of hers?"

He tenses for a second before taking another sip of coffee. "Still in processin'. But I don't expect to find much. Both of their prints will be all over that vehicle."

I press him. "Hard to believe you just missed it."

Black looks up at Liam for support, but Liam doesn't give him an inch. "It was a chaotic scene," he finally says. "We had a body with a hole in its head bleedin' on the sidewalk, and it was dark. That temporary lot of theirs don't have any lights around it."

"Where did you think they were walking? Back home?" I ask, more snark in my voice than is probably called for.

"Agent," Black says. "I'm tryin' to be civil here, especially after our little misunderstandin' yesterday. But I won't have you questionin' my competence. Tell me you've never made a mistake on a crime scene before."

I could push back. I could berate the man for missing such a huge piece of evidence, and I might even get him to admit he was too upset about the body being moved to keep working the scene. But none of that will help me find Summer Sanford. In fact, it would probably do the opposite, and just piss Sheriff Black off, which means he'd be much less likely to cooperate. "None of us is perfect," I say.

He gives me an appreciative nod and goes back to his coffee. "I'll get in contact with our local news as soon as I'm done with breakfast. It won't make the seven, but it'll be there for lunch and the evenin' news."

"That works, thanks, Sheriff."

"Ya'll stayin' for breakfast?"

I look around at how busy the place is and only two waitresses covering the whole diner. We could sit a couple booths down from Black and make this awkward, and right now I don't feel like putting myself through it. We've had a small win here, last thing I want to do is stick around and risk saying something I shouldn't to screw it up.

"Actually, we have an early meeting. I was hoping they wouldn't be this busy. We'll just grab something to go from somewhere."

He lifts his mug to us as I slide back out of the booth. "Have a good day." It's definitely not the friendliest goodbye I've ever received.

"You too," I reply and follow Liam back out to the car.

"I thought for a second you might actually make us sit and eat with him," Liam says, a heft of relief in his voice.

"Not a chance," I reply. "I wouldn't want to give him the satisfaction, even though it would probably be as uncomfortable for him as it was for us."

We both get back into the car. "Fast food?" he asks.

I nod. "I know our options are limited, but the less greasy, the better."

"Em, I think you're asking for a miracle there," he chuckles as we pull away from the *Traveler's Barrel*.

Chapter Eleven

LIAM WAS RIGHT, FINDING SOMETHING THAT WASN'T FRIED OR bathed in gravy in a town like this seemed impossible, so we opted for some hash browns and coffees from a chain restaurant. I don't usually eat a lot for breakfast, but I need something in my stomach to start the day. I can't operate on just caffeine alone.

We make sure to be back at the Mardel Police Station promptly at seven-fifteen and are there to greet Chief Quaker when she walks in ten minutes later.

"Good morning," she says with a smile. "How was your first night in town?" The angst from yesterday is gone, like it never existed in the first place.

"Surprisingly well," I say. "Though it helps we went to bed at a reasonable hour."

"Glad to hear it. I know we're all anxious to receive the report, if you'll follow me, I'll take you over to see Robert." She leads us back outside.

"The morgue isn't connected to the station?" I ask.

She shakes her head. "Nope. It's part of the city's new medlab, a couple of miles out. Don't worry, it's a short drive."

We follow in my car as she leads us to another building

about twenty minutes away. We have to head back out to Mardel's main drag and down quite a few blocks to reach it, and when we do, I can tell it's new construction. It has that recent "office park" look to it, all made out of gray brick with a sloped roof, so it doesn't stick out so much. It's the only building with its own parking lot though, so it isn't hard to recognize.

Quaker leads us inside the lobby, which is bright, clean, and tastefully decorated, like the rest of the building. In front of us is an antechamber which has doors leading in three different directions.

"This really is a nice morgue," I say.

"Thank you, we're quite proud of it," Chief Quaker, says. "The city keeps approving our budget year after year, so now we have this. I've always been of the belief that the police can't do their jobs if they're stuck in old, outdated locations. Not only has each individual officer's performance improved since we renovated our station and moved all our med-tech services here, but community sentiment about our department is at an all-time high."

I shoot Liam a glance and he smirks. *Really?* I think. *She believes people are happier with the police because of their building?* I can tell by the look on his face he's thinking something similar, but Quaker keeps prattling on about community wellness and approval ratings. Clearly, this is one of her main concerns. Considering she can be replaced by the city's mayor at any point, she's probably doing everything she can to keep the department's reputation as shiny as possible.

She leads us down the leftmost corridor, and I recognize the familiar smell of formaldehyde and a few other chemicals that always seem to penetrate the halls of every morgue I visit. We enter a large room where the body lays on a table, still uncovered. Usually, the medical examiner will at least cover half the body for their modesty, but there is no sheet to be found covering the naked body of Brady Sanford. This is the first time I've seen him in-person, and all the color is gone from him, as is to be expected after an autopsy. A y-shaped incision begins at his collarbones and meets at his sternum before proceeding all the way down past his abdomen. There's also a small tag on his toe, indicating his identifying information.

"Agents Slate and Coll, this is Dr. Robert Metcaffe, our resident examiner," Quaker says with a smile. A tall man with a shock of white hair and a thin moustache turns around from typing on the computer set up in the cabinets along the wall. He's thin and gangly, with dark eyes and zero humor or friendliness about him.

"Doctor," I say, extending my hand.

He doesn't take it. Instead, he turns to the body. "After an extensive process, I have completed my findings. He died via a gunshot to the back of the head, causing massive tissue damage and hemorrhaging. The death was near-instant, and when he fell, he fractured his frontal lobe. I found no other injuries on the body."

"Can you tell what size round was used on the body?" I ask.

"Of course, it was still embedded in the brain," he replies, turning and picking up a tray with a small, red-stained bullet on it. "Judging from its size, it's from a .22 caliber weapon."

I bend down and inspect the cartridge carefully. There's some damage on the nose where it impacted Brady's skull, but otherwise the round is intact. "We need to find out what kind of gun that came from," I tell Liam.

"I'll bag it up for you," Metcaffe says. He deposits the bullet into an evidence bag for us using a pair of tweezers.

"Can you tell us anything else?" I ask.

"Mr. Sanford had steak in his stomach when he died," the man replies. "His last meal, obviously. And his blood-alcohol level was point-zero-eight. He was above the legal limit to drive."

"And possibly be aware of his surroundings," I say. All that tracks with what we know from his dinner with his wife on Sunday.

"There was also no residue on the back of the head from the gunshot," Metcaffe adds. "Which means the killer was standing at least four or five feet away. Far enough so there wouldn't be any powder transfer from the weapon. Also, given the bullet didn't completely penetrate the skull, I estimate the killer was more than likely ten to twenty feet away. The momentum from a closer shot would have drilled the bullet all the way through the other side."

I take the bag from Dr. Metcaffe. "Chief, do you have a forensics team here? We need to analyze this bullet and find out what kind of gun it came from."

"Sure," Quaker says. "Jerry back at the station is a wiz with this kind of thing. I'll ask him to take a look."

"If we're done here," Metcaffe says. "I'll put the body back in storage. I have some paperwork I need to catch up on."

I push down the sense of frustration that's bubbling up inside me. Not only did this guy make us wait twelve hours for what he could have told us in five minutes, but now he's trying to push us out of his hair. Metcaffe strikes me as the kind of man used to getting his way most of the time. Someone who hasn't had to change their routine in a couple of decades.

"No, I think we're finished," I say.

Without a word, he wheels the table out the open door and down the hallway to where I'm assuming the cold storage is located.

"Here, let me take that," Quaker says, and I hand her the bag. "I'll get Jerry to take a look. Maybe we'll get lucky."

"There's something else," I say, then outline the same plan I presented to Sheriff Black. We need to get her face out there so if anyone sees her, they can contact us. Given this most recent evidence, I have to assume she's on the run. And I'll admit, it doesn't look very good for Summer Sanford.

"Sure, I can do that," she says. "I'll get the word out this morning and contact the surrounding counties, especially around the bridge and tunnel towns. But I have to point out, if she left town Sunday night, she could be in Colorado or Canada by now."

"I know. But we need to do it anyway. Just in case. After speaking with her mother, I'm not so sure she'd just up and leave her kids, no matter how bad things became. We're going to need a warrant for her house to make sure she's not hiding out in there."

"I'll have it within the hour," Quaker says. "Anything else I can help with?"

I have to admit I'm surprised by this turn in her demeanor. I'd expected her to begin to stonewall us after the little tiff last night. In my experience, once you've upset the local LEOs, they don't let you forget it. But it's almost as if it never happened in her mind. "No, but thank you. Let me know as soon as you have the warrant, and we'll perform the search."

She nods and heads back down the hall while I hold Liam back. "We may have a very serious problem."

"You mean about the .22?" he asks.

I nod. "You said Brady had a .22 and a .38 registered to him. We need to find those weapons because I'm guessing one of them is our murder weapon."

"Wouldn't Summer have thrown it away, especially if she was on the run?" he asks.

"Probably. But that's another reason why I want to search the house. And we need to find out as much as we can about their marital problems. I know we were going to look at Brady's other coworkers, but it might be better to focus on Summer's coworkers instead. If she knew something was going on, maybe she said something."

Liam steps back and grins.

"What?"

"You. Is this how you are on every case? You won't leave any avenue unexplored, will you?"

"Just because you spent your time slacking off in Stillwater doesn't mean I don't expect you to pull your full weight around here," I say, doing my best to keep the smile off my lips. It's easy bantering with him. I need to be careful. The last thing I want to do is make this seem like something it's not.

"Yes, ma'am." He gives me a salute. "Where to next?"

"The library where Summer worked. Then we can go back to Brady's office if we don't find anything. Hopefully by then we'll have a warrant for the house."

As we make our way back out of the medlab to the car, Liam pauses before getting in. I pinch my brows at him.

"Can I ask you a personal question?"

Whenever someone asks that, it always means you're about to be insulted or things are about to get a lot more complicated. Still, I trust Liam as much as I do Zara. We're working closely on this case together, so maybe we should get to know each other a little better. "Okay," I say, hesitant.

He screws up his face. "You know what? Never mind. It's not a big deal."

I shake my head. "No, really, it's fine."

"I just…I don't know how to put this delicately." He takes a deep breath and my heart picks up the pace. What is he about to ask me?

"Was it…was your work ethic like this before your husband died? Or did that…did it…" he trails off, not sure how to finish the sentence.

"Oh." I wasn't expecting that question. And I'm not sure how I feel about it. It doesn't feel like he's asking because he's jealous or upset. It feels like genuine curiosity. But I've never really thought about it. After Matt died everything just… changed. I can barely remember what things were like before, despite having a wonderful life with him. I recall the broad strokes, the big events, but I feel like I've lost the day to day. Isn't it supposed to be the other way around? Aren't you supposed to remember everything with such clarity that you take it to your grave? If I can't remember, what does that mean?

"I'm sorry, I shouldn't have asked," Liam says. "It was too personal."

"No, it's okay," I say. "I just…I'm not sure how to answer because I really can't remember. Is that bad?"

"I don't think I'm the right person to ask that question," he replies. "I worked for a corrupt boss for years, knowing full well something wasn't right, and yet I kept on doing it anyway. If you're looking for a moral compass, I'm not it."

"You're too hard on yourself," I say.

"Something we have in common," he replies.

Deep down, I know he's right. But it still doesn't answer the question. I give him a small smile, an understanding coming between us that no further discussion is needed. Our heads need to be in the right place for this case. We're close to finding Summer, I can feel it. We just need these few pieces of evidence to come through and we'll finally have our answers.

Chapter Twelve

"JAY, WAIT UP!" ELLIOTT CALLS, TRAILING BEHIND HIS FRIEND. It seems like they've been walking for hours now, trudging through the thick brush. Elliott has scraped his legs twice already, one of them deep enough that it even bled a little. But he can't show Jay it hurts, he'll think he's nothing but a wimp. Elliott already knows he's on thin ice, after not taking a swing at Troy a few days ago when Jay told him to. But Troy hadn't even done anything, just worn a Minecraft shirt to school. Despite that, Troy went to the principal anyway and *said* Elliott had hit him. So it hadn't even mattered. He'd done the right thing and was still punished for it.

And now he might not even start tenth grade next year. He tried to explain to his parents, but they wouldn't listen, no matter how hard he tried. They'd just automatically assumed he was guilty just because he'd started growing his hair longer and hanging out with Jay last year. He knew what they thought; they assumed Jay was a bad influence on him, that Elliott couldn't even make his own decisions for himself anymore. They assumed he'd fallen in with the "bad" crowd.

"What's wrong Sanford, hill too steep for ya?" Jay teases from about twenty feet ahead. He has at least six inches on

Elliott. It hadn't been that way last year when they'd started hanging out. But in the past six months Elliott has noticed how much bigger his friend seems every time they hang out. He wishes he would finally start the growth spurts his parents keep telling him are coming. It just seems like everyone else is getting older and he's just staying the same.

"Nah, I got it," Elliott replies, grabbing the branch of a tree and hoisting himself up. The truth is he's exhausted already; they've been exploring out here for what seems like an hour, but according to his phone it's only been about thirty minutes. Jay says they're headed to this place he'd found, he heard that the juniors and seniors hang out here sometimes. Elliott knows what that means. Sophie Blackburn. Jay hadn't been able to take his eyes off her during the regular school year, despite her never even acknowledging he existed. He said she just didn't know what she was missing yet, he just needed to get a few minutes alone with her outside of school was all. And since everyone else who hadn't failed English is out on summer break, now's the perfect time to find her.

"Hurry the hell up, I ain't got all day here," Jay calls.

"Yeah, yeah," Elliott replies, hiding how hard he's breathing. "You really think she'll be there?"

Jay shoots him a sly smile as Elliott catches up with him. "I dunno, man. They all come out here to screw and smoke pot. Seems like the perfect time to find her."

Elliott has to suppress a laugh. "You really think she's going to even talk to you?"

Jay smiles, making a smoking motion with one hand. "You never know. People are different when they're high. You still ain't tried it yet. Tellin' you, man, it opens you up, makes you experience the world as it really is. All the bullshit is gone, and you just feel like your authentic self."

"I already feel like my authentic self," Elliott says.

"You *think* you do, but until you try it, you'll never know."

Elliott rolls his eyes and follows along behind his friend. It isn't like there's going to be anything out here for him; and what if Sophie Blackburn really is here? If, by some miracle, she ends up talking to Jay, that'll leave Elliott by himself again. Part of him wants to just go back. If his grandmother knew he was out of the house she'd throw a fit, as she likes to say. But he'd been able to bribe his sister with some time on his phone later if she kept her mouth shut about him being gone.

He doesn't see why they have to stay with their grandmother anyway. He's old enough to stay at the house by himself and watch Ashleigh. What's even more frustrating is that no one will tell them anything. They'd had to go back over to their house on Monday to get some clothes as grandma said they'd be staying with her for a while. When he'd asked where their parents were, she said they had taken a short vacation.

But that didn't make sense. They hadn't been talking anything about a vacation. In fact, he'd overheard them complaining there wasn't enough money to do anything. Unless someone had won the lottery. Plus, they hadn't called.

The other possibility is they're getting a divorce and want to keep him and his sister out of it. Though that doesn't make much sense to him. But honestly, most things adults do don't make sense to him. Like all those times his dad is always on his phone late at night, after Mom has gone to bed. Does he really think they're all so stupid they don't know what he's doing? He sees the same look on some of the kids in his school's faces when they think they're alone. He's wanted to tell his mother, but she's so stressed out about everything else he wasn't about to add more to her plate. But the fact is his dad is talking to someone he shouldn't be, and he doesn't want anyone to know about it.

He can only imagine that's what all of this is really about. Mom must have finally found out, and whatever it was, it was bad enough she filed for divorce.

"Man, would you hurry up?" Jay calls. "I swear to God, you're the slowest person I know."

Elliott trudges on. How deep into the woods were they going? It probably helped to have longer legs so you didn't run into so many branches. "How much further?"

"We're almost there," he calls back. "What's going on with you today?"

"Whaddaya mean?" Elliott asks.

"You're so mopey," Jay calls back. "Get your head out of your ass and come on. Bridget Templeton might be there."

"Why would she be there?" He knows Jay's just saying that to get him to hurry up. Bridget is in their grade; she wouldn't be hanging out with juniors and seniors. Not to mention he doesn't really care about Bridget Templeton. She's nice enough, but he's not interested in her. When Jay put him on the spot last year, he'd said the first name that came to his mind, which had been Bridget because she had been standing in his eyeline a few feet away. Now Jay thinks she's the only person Elliott is interested in and never misses a chance to remind him of it.

But Elliott can't tell him the truth. That would be social suicide. Especially in a place like Mardel.

"Here, finally," Jay says as the underbrush begins to clear.

Elliott pushes through to a small clearing with a few large rocks. It doesn't look like anything special to him, just a bunch of stones in the middle of the woods. And other than a couple of fast food wrappers and discarded liquor bottles, there's no sign of life here.

"Juniors and seniors hang out here, huh?" he asks, glaring at Jay. "Good call."

"Shut up," Jay says, heading closer to the rocks. "I didn't say she'd definitely be here. At least we found it."

"Yeah, cause if she was, she'd be making out with Braden McCoy. And now we have to go all the way back. I'm glad I risked getting grounded for this."

Jay gives him a disingenuous smile and begins walking around the largest rock, looking at the ground.

"What are you doing?" Elliott asks.

"Seeing if anyone left anything in one of these bottles. My pop finally got wise to me stealing from his stores. Stopping bringing it home."

Elliott has tried Jay's dad's vodka a few times. The first time he nearly threw up, but he's gotten a little more used to it since. It's never been enough for him to really feel anything. Unlike Jay who never seems to know when to stop. That is part of his charm, he supposed. Jay wasn't afraid to do anything, no matter what anyone said.

Elliott sighs and follows Jay around the rock, kicking at a few of the empty bottles. Part of him hopes no one will be here; he doesn't feel like sitting around while a bunch of older kids do all the stupid shit teenagers typically do. But this also means he has a unique opportunity.

Suddenly Elliott's heart is hammering. Can he really do this now? He hadn't planned on it, but the more he thinks about it, the more it feels like the right time. When else is he going to get Jay away from his drunk-ass father or their other friends? When else will he have a chance to talk to him one-on-one?

But then there is the other side. What if it all backfires on him? Elliott isn't a popular kid and can't just start hanging out with the football players or the theater kids. If this goes wrong and he burns this bridge, it's possible he'll be a pariah forever. He'll have to endure another three years of ridicule, at least. And that might as well be an eternity.

But still, the thought of doing it at all is tempting. He's never really thought he'd be brave enough, that a time would come when he'd be willing to put himself out there like that. And what if things go right? Hasn't Mom always told him to look on the bright side? Instead of planning for what can go wrong, he should plan for things going right instead? He has no idea if Jay feels that way, but maybe he's just like Elliott. Maybe he hides it all deep under a façade because of where they live.

After all, Jay had been the one to approach him and strike up a friendship. Not the other way around.

He's going to do it. That's what life is all about, right? Taking chances? And maybe his mom is right too. Maybe things will go just like he wants them to.

"Holy shit!"

Jay's voice brings Elliott out of his thoughts. He's out of sight, around the other side of the rock. But his voice has the edge of panic to it. Elliott races around the rock, to find Jay standing about ten feet away, frozen in place. "What?" Elliott yells. "What's going on?"

Jay doesn't respond. It is like he's been immobilized by some kind of mind control, like Professor X has a hold of him.

A chill runs down Elliott's back and he approaches Jay slowly, unsure what was going on. But then he sees the body and he stops cold. For a minute he can't comprehend what he's seeing. It doesn't make sense. And in that instant all thoughts of Jay, failing school, or even the fact they have to walk all the way back through the woods leaves Elliott's mind. None of it matters anymore.

He screams at the top of his lungs.

Chapter Thirteen

I STARE DOWN AT THE BODY OF SUMMER SANFORD, RACKING my brain for answers. Liam stands beside me, both of us drenched from the hike up here in the heat. Around us Chief Quaker's people are securing the scene, while a different examiner from Metcaffe's office crouches off to the side, her medical case open as she's examining the body.

"Robert's not much of a hiker," Chief Quaker says, coming up beside us. "But Sandra has his full confidence."

The medical examiner, Sandra, looks up at the mention of her name then goes back to her work.

Summer Sanford is naked from the waist up. She's missing all of her clothes except for her underwear, including her shoes. If I hadn't been staring at pictures of her for the past two days, I might not recognize her. Her lips are blue, and her eyes are frozen open in a panic. Around her neck are purple marks that scream strangulation, but I'm not about to make that assumption until we get the official word from the medical examiner. I only hope Sandra is quicker than Metcaffe.

Chief Quaker puts her hands on her hips, shaking her head. "I just can't believe it. What do you think happened?"

I've been asking myself that question ever since we got the call. We'd been on the way to Mrs. Sanford's place of employment, the library, when we received a call from the Mardel dispatch. Some kid named Jay had shown up, claiming he and his friend had found a body out in the woods and that his friend wouldn't leave it alone. That had been enough to pique my interest, but when I learned the kid was Elliott Sanford and the body was that of his mother, you could have dropped a nuclear bomb beside me, and I wouldn't have noticed.

The fire department had followed the kid up through the woods and were the first ones to come upon the young boy, screaming at the top of his lungs beside the body of his dead mother. They had to literally pick him up and carry him out of here to the ambulance waiting at the nearest road. I can't even imagine what kind of psychological damage that kid will have to endure.

"How long has she been out here?" I ask.

Sandra takes another look at the body after having performed her initial examination as soon as we all got here. "I won't know for sure until I do a full autopsy but based on my experience and given the weather we've had the past couple of days I'd say at least thirty-six to forty-eight hours."

"Since Monday, then," Liam says.

"I'll call the surrounding counties," Quaker says. "Tell them to call off the search."

"No," I say, turning to her. "Someone still may have seen something. Keep her face out there, at least for the adjacent counties. I want to know if she was seen with anyone around town. She obviously didn't get far."

"So much for our working theory," Liam says.

I shake my head, dumbfounded by all of it. The evidence had suggested Mrs. Sanford had been the one to kill her husband and then took off running. But not everything had lined up. For one thing, her mother had insisted Summer wasn't a killer, but more than that, she wasn't someone who could meticulously plan anything. It seems she was right.

"Couldn't she still have killed her husband?" Quaker asks.

"What was her plan? Kill him, then run off with someone who decides to double-cross her?" I ask, sarcasm tinting my words. "The profile doesn't fit. More than likely the same person who killed Brady Sanford killed his wife too. But it's strange they both weren't murdered in the same location." I turn to Liam. "We need to rethink this, find out if the Sanfords had any enemies, anyone who would be looking to do this."

"We still need to talk to her coworkers at the library," he says. "But I feel like Vogel would have mentioned it when we told him Brady was dead."

I run my hand down my face in frustration. Now we're looking at a double homicide. And given how the body of Summer Sanford was found, most likely a sexual crime as well. "Did the kid touch the body?"

Quaker furrows her brow, then goes to speak with a few of the firefighters who are still on the scene.

"What are you thinking?" Liam asks.

"That we missed something. Something big." I should have seen this before we spent so much time going after Summer Sanford. Were she and her husband targets for something else they were into? We need to start a deep dive into the Sanfords' lives, leaving no stone unturned. Now that we know Summer is dead, it should be a lot easier to get access to all their records, especially since we could be dealing with a potential serial killer. Based on how professionally these two were killed, I'm willing to bet this isn't the killer's first victim.

"I want you to see if you can find anything out about Brady. Figure out where all that cash was going and to whom. Meanwhile, I'll head over to the library and speak with Summer's coworkers."

"What about the family?" Liam asks. "Don't they need to be notified?"

I think back to Adelaide. The news is going to be a terrible blow to her, whether it comes from us or her near-catatonic grandson. But I believe she will be able to handle it in time. It's the kids I worry about. Having lost my own mother when I was still a pre-teen, and the way in which she died...

I shake my head violently, trying not to relive the memories. It's an involuntary tic I started not long after she died. It doesn't happen much anymore, but if I allow myself to go back down that road, to relive those memories, it will put me out of commission for days. Maybe even a week. And we have a killer to catch; I can't let my past impact my job anymore.

"What was that?" Liam asks.

"What was what?" I repeat, playing dumb.

He narrows his eyes. "Nothing. We need to head in different directions. You take your car. I'll grab a ride with one of the officers back to the station. Maybe they can help me figure out how to find an untraceable cash transaction." Liam produces a sly smile and I know he's teasing me. I've given him a potentially impossible assignment.

"I just want to make sure they're not slacking off down at Quantico since I was there," I shoot back. "They practically raised us on impossible cases."

"Uh-huh," he says with a grin, then heads off for one of the officer's cars.

I glance back at Sharon, who is taking her time processing the body. "When will you begin the autopsy?"

"Right away. Metcaffe left right after his meeting with you this morning," she replies. "He probably didn't expect another body so soon. The man is nothing if not a slave to his schedule."

"So I've seen." I place my hands on my hips and look around. "I appreciate all the speed you can give me. It's looking more and more like time is of the essence here."

She nods. "You got it. I'll get your number from Quaker."

"Thank you," I reply, then head back to my car.

"Agent Slate!" I look up to see Quaker herself heading over, her hands on her belt as she jogs back to me. "Wanted to let you know they don't think the boy touched anything, so we shouldn't be seeing any kind of contamination. Also, I spoke with the D.A. That warrant for the Sanford's house just went through."

"Does he know about the body?" I ask.

"He does now. He was with Judge Cooper in his chambers when I called. The judge signed it on the spot."

"Great," I say. "I'm headed over to the library to interview Summer's coworkers, then Liam and I will head to the Sanford house."

"If you don't mind, I'd like to be there when you examine the house. Another pair of ears and eyes can't hurt, right?" She's practically bouncing on the balls of her feet, though I can't tell what her angle is. It's not unprecedented for local LEOs to head out on site with us, but Quaker is acting like a little kid at Christmas.

"Sure," I say, though I'm somewhat cautious. I'm still not convinced I can trust Quaker any more than I can trust Sheriff Black.

"Great. We're going to nail the bastard, aren't we?"

"That's the plan," I tell her. She flashes me one last smile, then heads back to the site. If I didn't know better, I would say Chief Quaker was excited about the possibility of a serial murderer in her town. Usually that's not a good thing, but maybe for a police chief who hasn't delivered on a lot of her promises it offers an opportunity to make good with the town council and mayor.

I shake my head. Everyone has their own priorities, I suppose.

"How's my favorite sleuth doing?" Zara asks.

I sigh, glancing down at the phone mounted to my dash as Zara's voice comes through my speakers. "It looks like I'll be longer getting back than I originally thought." I'm headed back into Mardel to the library. It's a long shot, but maybe Summer Sanford let something slip to her coworkers.

"That sounds ominous," she replies. I can tell she's wedged her phone between her ear and shoulder, and from the ambient noise, it sounds like she might be driving as well.

"Where are you headed in the middle of a weekday?" I ask.

"I have cases of my own, you know," she teases. "Some of us actually work around here rather than going off on field trips."

She always knows how to make me smile. "You're just mad because you didn't get to accompany me to the most boring town in the most boring state in the country."

"Ouch," she says. "Shots fired at Delaware. Careful, they'll sic their gray foxes on you."

"Gray foxes?" I ask.

"Yeah, it's the state animal," she replies. "Everyone knows that."

"Literally *no one* knows that except you," I reply. "How do you have so much useless information?"

"You think that's useless, try this one on. Their state fish is the weakfish."

"Weak as in strength or duration of time?"

"The first one."

I suppress a laugh. "I don't believe you."

She doesn't even acknowledge the fact. Instead she changes subjects. "So what's going on? You didn't call to talk about fish."

"You're the one who brought it up!" I say. "It's just this case. What looked like a simple domestic situation gone wrong has turned into a possible double homicide."

"Whoa." I can tell by the timbre of her voice she wasn't expecting that. "Why is it you tend to gravitate to all the really messed up ones?" she asks.

"Trust me, I'm wondering the same thing myself," I reply. "It's like I'm a magnet for the sickest, most twisted minds out there."

"You know, now that I think about it, that actually explains a lot," she quips.

"You're hilarious, you know," I reply.

"Yeah? And how is Agent Coll? Is he still dreamy as ever?"

I rub one of my temples with my free hand, keeping the other on the wheel. "Zara…"

"Okay, okay. So you have a difficult case. It's nothing you haven't faced before."

"That's not the point. It's just…I was supposed to be back so I could help you hunt down our mystery woman and here I am, stuck again on something that's outside the city, away from where all the action is. This is the second time Janice has sidelined me and I'm starting to take it personally."

"Let me ask you," she says, her voice suddenly serious. "Is this an important case?"

"They're all important," I reply, already knowing what she's doing.

"And are people's lives at stake?"

"Yes," I say, grumbling more than saying the words.

"Then you already know what I'm going to tell you."

"I need to put the public good above my own," I say.

I can already hear the victory in her voice. "Right. We can't pick and choose which cases are important and which ones aren't. We have to treat them all the same, and we can't put our personal needs above those of the general public. Lucky for you, you have a friend in the FBI who just happens to be working on your case at the same time."

I scoff. "Yeah, I guess I am pretty lucky."

"Work the problem down there and leave this mess up to me. I might be getting somewhere."

I perk up. "Really?"

"No spoilers until I'm sure," she replies. "But you'll be the first to know, trust me."

"I hate that you're right all the time," I say.

"You already knew it, you just needed someone else to tell you," she says. "Who do you think instilled that in me?"

"Thanks," I tell her. "Though the way this is looking, I might be in Mardel for a while. It seems each layer we uncover about this mystery opens another level we didn't even know was there."

"That's how the best ones go," she says. "Listen, I gotta run, but I'll be back in touch as soon as I have something. Be careful out there."

"You too," I say. "And thanks, Z."

I can practically see the smile on her lips. "What are friends for?"

Chapter Fourteen

THE MARDEL TOWN LIBRARY ISN'T A HISTORIC BUILDING BY any means. It looks more like a converted preschool than what most people probably imagine when they think of a library in a town that was founded in the 1880s. But instead of a stone exterior with some prophetic saying above a row of Doric columns, it's a one-story brick building with a flat roof and thin windows which allow me to see little of the rows and rows of books inside. It reminds me of my own elementary school, though when you're a little kid you never notice those things. You just think buildings are buildings. It isn't until much later you realize they're all their own characters.

Inside it smells of air fresheners and soap, and there's a small circular desk near the door where a woman sits, reading a book. She doesn't even look up as I enter, though I take a moment to get the lay of the building. A large children's section sits near the rear, with brighter colors and animal mascots either painted on the walls or on the endcaps of some of the shelves. There are also some kid-height tables back there, where they can sit and read. The rest of the library is tame by comparison, nothing really notable about it. It also seems that I've come at the slow time of day as there are only two other people here.

"Excuse me," I say, walking up to the desk. The woman glances up at me through cat-eye glasses. She's probably no older than forty-five or fifty, and she has her dark hair tied back loose so it stays out of her eyes.

"What can I do for you?" she asks.

I show her my badge. "I'm Agent Slate with the FBI. Do you know Summer Sanford?"

The woman's pleasant smile disappears as soon as she learns who I am. Upon mentioning Summer's name, she blanches. "Oh, my goodness. What's this about? Is Summer okay?"

"I'll take that to mean you know her," I say. "Are you two close?"

She doesn't hesitate. "We often work the evening shifts together during the school year. But in the summer, there aren't as many people around, so the library just keeps one person on staff in the evenings. What is this about?"

Because we technically haven't informed the family yet, I don't want to say anything revealing about Summer's demise. Which means I'll have to be a bit more stealthy if I want to find any useful information. "Unfortunately, it looks like she's missing," I say. "Her husband, Brady, was found, shot in the head across the state border."

I wouldn't have thought the woman could go any whiter, but somehow she manages it, putting her hand to her mouth. "Oh my God," she says.

"Did Summer ever mention anything to you about her relationship with her husband? Any problems the family was having with anyone?" I ask.

"No, nothing like that," she replies. "Although...she did mention her parents had cut her and her husband off a few months ago."

"Cut them off?" I ask.

She leans forward conspiratorially. "I don't know all the details," she says in a hushed voice, "but I think they were still relying on her parents for income. The library doesn't pay a lot and apparently they had some finance issues. I think her husband might have been gambling all their money away."

She's not far off. "How long had her parents been supporting them?"

"That I'm not sure of," she replies. "I just know it had been going on for some time. She came in all upset and I practically had to pull her ear to get her to spill what was going on. I think she was embarrassed about needing money from her mother and father."

Funny. Adelaide never mentioned any of this when we spoke with her earlier. I'll need to interview her again. Maybe now that Summer is dead, she'll be willing to provide more details. Then again, she could be so distraught that she won't say a word to me. I think maybe I have a fifty-fifty chance of getting something tangible out of her.

"Anything else?" I ask. "Anyone threatening them? Maybe someone looking to collect on more debts?"

The librarian shakes her head. "Not that I know of. Summer is a rather private person. Oh, I do hope she's okay. Is there anything I can do to help? Organize a search committee?"

I hold up a hand. "Thank you, but that's not necessary. We have the search well under control."

"Is there anyone else you can think of that I should speak to about her?" I ask. "I'm looking to talk to anyone who saw her regularly."

"I'll talk to the rest of the staff here," she tells me. "If any of them know something, I'd be happy to send them your way."

I pass her my card. "I would appreciate that."

"Good luck," she says, though she doesn't return to her

book. Instead, she watches me as I leave, all the way out to my car.

———————

"Please tell me you have something," I say, walking back into the main bullpen at the Mardel police headquarters.

Liam looks up from the station he's been using, a few of Mardel's beat cops standing behind him. "Maybe," he says.

"Maybe?" I mimic, with a little too much enthusiasm in my voice. I hadn't expected him to actually find something, though I have to admit the trip to the library had been little more illuminating than I'd expected.

"We're not sure yet," he says. "We pulled surveillance data for half the city and have been pouring over it on the days when Mr. Sanford withdrew the money. I think we might have spotted him, but I can't make a positive ID."

"Let me see," I say, circling around his station. The beat cops all take a step back out of my way.

Liam taps a key, and a video fills the screen. It's green and pixelated, showing the outside of an establishment, though I can't tell what kind. The angle isn't great and the resolution is only barely legible.

At the upper-left side of the screen, a man with his hands in his pockets makes his way down the sidewalk. He's wearing a baseball cap and t-shirt with cargo shorts. I can't get a good look at his face because of the hat and the low resolution of the video.

The man stops outside the main doors to the establishment, and speaks with another man—a bouncer of some kind —for a moment. They shake hands, and the bouncer lets him inside, his hand going to his pocket quickly. No doubt to pocket the bribe the man just paid him. A second later, he opens the door for the man, who disappears inside.

"Okay," I say, once the video is over. "Is that it?"

Liam nods. "No cameras inside the club, that's how it works."

"What club?"

"Sandriders," one of the beat cops says.

I glare at him. "Sandriders?"

"It's the name of the local biker club," Liam says. "Apparently, it's like its own society in there. They have a hierarchy. There's the king, then his subordinates, then their subordinates, and on and on."

"So it's a pyramid scheme, got it," I say. "What does this have to do with Brady Sanford?"

"We think that's Brady," Liam says. "It's on Thursday the sixteenth, the same day he made a large withdrawal from his shared account with his wife, all in cash. And the timing lines up." I check the timecode on the video he's showing me. It's three-oh-five in the afternoon.

"When did he withdraw the cash?" I ask.

"Two thirty-nine, according to the bank records," Liam says. "And Sandriders is roughly twenty minutes from the bank location. So, it's not unreasonable to assume he drove straight here from making the withdrawal."

"*If* that's him," I say. "When does he come out?"

Liam shakes his head. "Never does. There must be another exit somewhere that doesn't have a camera. This was the only thing I got."

I take a deep breath. "Okay, well, it's worth a shot at least." I'm not sure what a white-collar guy like Brady Sanford would be doing at a biker bar, but then again apparently there's a lot about the man I don't know. Maybe this will help put some of the pieces together.

"Should we search their house first or head here?" he asks.

Honestly, at this point I'm feeling like their house won't give us very much. Obviously, Brady didn't keep any records of what he was doing with their money and since Summer more than likely didn't kill him, we're unlikely to find evidence that can help us. We still need to do our due diligence, of course, but I feel like the more urgent priority should be investigating the biker bar. We're much more likely to make some progress.

"Definitely the bar," I tell him. "Let's get a couple of printouts of his face. See if anyone recognizes him and is willing to talk."

One of the beat cops scoffs.

I turn to him. "Problem?"

He shakes his head like I'm the dumbest person he's ever met. "Those guys do things by their own rules down there. They're not going to give two shits about a couple of FBI agents who've wandered into their midst."

"You sure about that?" I ask, squaring my shoulders. "Willing to bet the outcome of the case on it?"

He swallows, his eyes shifting to his two cohorts. He obviously didn't expect me to stand up for myself. But I've been doing that since day one. I'm not about to stop now. "I just mean they don't have any reason to talk to you. You can't force them to say anything."

"No," I say. "But I can be persuasive when I need to be."

Liam stands. "Want to head over there now?"

I check the time on my phone. It's close to five already. And I expect a place like Sandriders will be more active during the evening. There's a better chance we'll find something there tonight. "Let's grab a bite first. I'm always better at interrogating people on a full stomach."

The cop scoffs and he and his cronies head off. I just have to let it roll of my back. If I tried to engage every ass out there who thought I didn't belong in this job, I'd wouldn't have time for my real work.

"Good job," I tell Liam as we head out. "I didn't actually think you'd find anything."

"Glad to know I can surprise you," he says with a grin. "But I have to thank those guys. They helped me get through all the video data quickly. I think they softened a little when I told them I used to be a detective over in Virginia."

I eye him as we make our way out into the parking lot. "You know, you might just be what we need to make nice with the locals. You're like the missing link."

He laughs and I can't help but feel that slight pull again. It's too easy to be comfortable around him. Liam is the first guy I've felt anything toward since my husband died. And I admit I like messing with him. Am I crossing a line? I feel that familiar stab of guilt run me through like a lance and I shut it down again. We're colleagues, nothing more. I can't pretend the situation isn't what it is, and I'm not willing to turn it into anything different. Not when my husband's killer is still out there.

That silence falls between us again and I curse my awkwardness as we get to the car. This is why I like focusing on the job, it keeps me distracted from all this other…stuff.

But as we're getting in, I catch Liam shoot me a glance. He turns away like he was looking at something else as soon as I catch him, but there was something unsaid in that glance.

I just have to pretend like I didn't see it.

Chapter Fifteen

"So, what's the play here?" Liam asks. "I'm leaving this one up to the professional."

We're both standing outside Sandriders, looking up at a gray brick façade with no signage whatsoever. The only indication there's something here are two metal doors that look like they lead to a loading dock instead of a bar. A man sits outside on a stool, scrolling on his phone. But I can tell his attention is laser-focused on us, even though we're still a good twenty feet away. He's subtle about it, but based on how he's holding his head and how he's positioned himself, I can tell his posture is designed so he can keep as wide of a lookout as possible. I don't see a weapon anywhere on him, but he's a big man, and there's a good chance he has a concealed gun under his shirt or tucked into the waistband of his pants. He'll be the club's first line of defense if something goes wrong. The canary in the coal mine, if you will.

"Did you find out anything about any other rival gangs in the area?" I ask.

"Didn't have time to do a lot of digging," Liam says, "But I heard one of the other cops mention the eighty-eights. I think they're a white supremacist group that operates off a farm around here somewhere."

"Great, just what we need," I say. "More domestic terrorists. Remind me to put in a call to counterterrorism after we're done here. I want to make sure they have eyes on this place."

"Got it," he replies.

"As for the play, we'll focus on Summer. No one knows she's been found yet, so who knows, maybe whoever knows Brady in here would like to point the finger at him and out themselves in the process."

"Will that actually work?" Liam asks.

I shrug. "It's either that or start accusing people. And I get the impression if we do that, they're bound to form ranks around each other. We don't need to do anything that's going to make us their enemy."

We make our way up to the man on the stool. As we reach the ten-foot mark, he's off the stool, his phone gone from his hand and he's glaring at us, attempting to use his imposing stature to get us to turn the other way. "You folks need to head the other direction," he finally says when we get close enough.

I pull out my badge. "How about you let us in, instead? We've got a missing person and word was her husband liked to visit this place."

He glares at me under hooded eyes. "Not sure I can do that."

"Okay," I say, nonchalantly. "We can always come back with a warrant and the SWAT team for an official search. We just thought this would be less intrusive to your bosses and their operation." I'm completely bluffing. I'm pretty sure we couldn't get a warrant based on what little video evidence we've found, but K2 here doesn't know that.

"Not supposed to let you in if you're armed," he says. He's looking for any excuse to turn us away that's not going to make it look bad on his bosses or interrupt their operation, and he's quickly running out of options.

"I'll go ahead and assume most of your club members are carrying," I say. "And I'd be willing to bet more than a few of those don't have accompanying paperwork, am I right?"

He shakes his head. "This is a legitimate business. We do things by the book here."

I give him a solid glare. "Are you a hundred percent sure? If I call my bosses and get them to raid this place, are you telling me that every single person in there has all their licensing up to date and no one is carrying an illegal firearm?"

His eyes slip to the side and I catch the reflection of a small camera aperture built into the wall. Given that we're losing light quickly, and his body was blocking part of it, I'm not surprised I missed it. But now I see the bouncer really doesn't make any of the decisions.

He hesitates a moment longer, then nods. The handle of one of the doors has a small black pad built in and I notice the bouncer place his thumb directly on the pad before I hear a small click. Then he turns the handle and opens it for us.

Zara would have loved that, I think as we walk into the dark space. It takes my eyes a second to adjust and I see we're at the beginning of a long hallway, with lights along the floor illuminating the walls on both sides in purples and blues.

"This is not what I was expecting," Liam says as we begin walking down the hallway.

"Me either," I say. "Are you sure we're at the right place? This looks more like the entrance to a strip club."

"It's the same place that was on the video," he says.

When we reach the end of the hall we're met by another man, though this one is dressed considerably nicer. He's wearing a dark gray vest and matching pants with a white shirt and purple tie. He can't be more than twenty-five. His hair is immaculate, and his beard is trimmed close, and cut along his jawline to perfection. He wears a small earpiece and the sleeves of his shirt are rolled up to reveal the corded muscles of his arms. "Welcome," he says. "I understand you're with the Federal Bureau of Investigation."

"That's right," I say, unsure what's going on here. "We'd like to make some inquiries with your members."

He gives me a half-smile. "We know why you're here. But if this becomes anything more than an inquiry then the boss will ask you to leave. First, politely. Then, not so politely. Understand?"

"Are you threatening two FBI agents?" I ask him. *The balls on this guy.*

"Just telling you how it is. Our members pay for the privilege of not being hassled. Because there's been a murder, we're willing to assist, but our generosity only goes so far."

I don't like how this is shaping up. This isn't foreign soil; they can't just choose not to listen to law enforcement. But at the same time, we're likely to be outnumbered in there. We need to keep a low profile and not make any waves, especially if we want their help. These people might be the only ones in town who can tell us about Brady Sanford. But there's also the possibility someone in here had a hand in his and his wife's deaths. The last thing I want to do is spook them.

"I understand," I say.

The door behind him has a similar biometric lock as the one outside and it requires his thumbprint to open, which it does, to a raucous and flashy interior. The door had blocked out all sound—some of the best soundproofing I've ever seen.

We enter the main room, and while it's loud, it's not deafening. A couple of people glance at us as we walk in and I'm suddenly starting to feel like the cowboy from out of town who pushes his way through the swinging bar doors.

This is probably the nicest biker bar I've ever seen in my life. A large island sits in the middle of the room, which is at least twenty feet tall. They've managed to convert an old warehouse into the bar, so it's huge. But the island bar in the middle is at least twenty feet square, and has shelves that reach high up to the second floor. Tables and chairs surround the main bar, while a stage sits along the far wall, complete with curtains and instruments, which, at the moment, are not being used. It looks as though a band has just finished a set or is about to begin. Rock music plays from unseen speakers, and the air is thick with smoke and marijuana. Two bartenders, dressed exactly like the man we just saw, are running the bar, efficiently from what I can tell.

I don't know why, but I expected this place to be full of a bunch of old men with long, gray beards and leather jackets, with women in their fifties hanging off them, wearing their tight leather pants. But everyone in here is dressed...*nice*. Most of the men are wearing suits, or some variation thereof, and the women are almost all in long dresses. A few are wearing suits themselves. The place has an air of sophistication about it and feels more like a private club than a biker bar.

I turn to Liam. "Have any of Quaker's people actually been in here before?"

He takes another look around. "I doubt it. Doesn't look like the kind of place where cops are welcome."

"We better get on it," I say. He nods and we split up, heading in different directions. I approach the first table, which is surrounded by high-back chairs, allowing the people around it to lounge back. The seats are pointed at the stage, so I must assume the show will be starting soon.

"Good evening," I announce myself to the two men and the woman who are at the table. "I'm looking for anyone who knows this man." I pull out my phone and show them a picture of Brady Sanford. I catch the women exchange a glance while the man locks eyes with me.

"You're wasting your time. No one here is going to tell you anything," he says. He's a good deal larger than the man we met in the hallway. I can see his muscles under his shirt, telling me he could probably break the table in half if he wanted to. His dark hair is cut short and clean, and he has a beard as well, but it's as dark as night. This place seems to have a very strict dress code, considering he's wearing a tie as well. I don't know who these men's tailor is, but he's good. These are some nice suits.

"Have a good evening," I say, backing away.

It's clear to me now this isn't a private club. Nor is it really a biker bar. This is some kind of mafia or gang-related outpost. It has to be. These people have some serious money, and in a town like Mardel, which is small without an established industry other than tourism, they stick out. That is, unless they all stay here all the time. But it's possible this is just one of many similar establishments, all meant to provide a boutique experience for its members. I think I need to have counterterrorism look into this place as well, just in case—

"Excuse me."

I turn to see a stunning woman, probably in her mid-forties, standing over me. She's at least six feet tall and wears a floor-length green gown with a slip that comes up to her mid-thigh. Her heels are a perfect match, giving her an extra five inches and her golden blonde hair is loose around the sharp angles of her face. She looks like someone going out to the opera, instead of a place like this. I'm starting to understand the extra security. Her dress is tight, and I can just barely make out the lines of a thigh holster on her right leg. I feel like I've stepped into the middle of a James Bond movie.

"You're the FBI agent," she says. Not a question, not an accusation, just a statement.

"That's right. Special Agent Emily Slate," I tell her.

"You're here to inquire about Brady Sanford." Again, not a question. I wouldn't be surprised if this woman has had eyes on us since we came up to the outside door.

"Actually, I'm here on his wife's behalf," I tell her. "She's… disappeared, and we were hoping someone here might know something about their relationship."

It's brief, but there's a small flash of something across her face. Surprise maybe. Though she doesn't strike me as the kind of person who is often surprised. "I see," she says.

"Did you know Brady?" I ask. She nods. I motion to Liam, getting his attention. He excuses himself from the table he was speaking to and joins us.

"What was the nature of your relationship?" I ask, as soon as Liam is in earshot.

"Perhaps we should go to my office," she says. "Where we can talk in private."

I almost blurt out *"Your office?"* but then I take another look around the place. All of a sudden I realize I've been looking at it all wrong. Almost all the tables have at least two men and one woman. Because of the entrance I had assumed this place had a certain type of organizational structure. Now I see that this place is much more female-friendly than I'd originally thought. "You run this place, don't you?" I ask. "Who are you?"

"Since you've ended up here," she says. "You probably know me as Isobella."

Chapter Sixteen

WE FOLLOW ISOBELLA UP A SHORT FLIGHT OF STAIRS OFF TO the side of the main area, out of the way and designed to be as inconspicuous as possible. When we reach the top, another man in an identical outfit as the bartenders and the one we saw at the door stands guard. With a flick of a finger from Isobella, he opens the only door to reveal an ornate office with a window that looks out over the entire area. There are a few couches in the room, low to the ground, along with a modern desk, which Isobella takes a seat behind as she motions for us to take the two chairs on the other side of the desk.

The man closes the door behind us, drowning out the noise from the bar.

"You'll have to excuse us; we have a band performing this evening and the crowd is larger than normal. But don't worry, you won't be able to hear them in here. We can discuss this in peace."

Neither Liam and I have taken our seats yet. "What kind of place is this?" I ask. "Your local police believe this is a biker bar of sorts. But to me, it's anything but."

A smile spreads across the woman's face. "Maybe thirty years ago it was a biker bar. But that was in my father's day.

He died more than a decade ago, leaving it all to me. And I wasn't satisfied with his kind of establishment. I wanted something more...upscale. Sandriders isn't that kind of establishment anymore. We provide a classy experience for our patrons and members. Something they can't get anywhere else."

I round the chair and take a seat. "In the middle of nowhere, Delaware? Wouldn't a place like this be better served in Philadelphia or Norfolk?"

She smiles. "You'd be surprised how many people in this area crave an experience like this," she says.

"And how do you fund something like this? I can't imagine it all comes from dues," I say. "Mardel isn't exactly known as a wealthy city."

"We manage to get by," she replies, a sly smile on her lips. And it's in that look that I know this is a front of some kind. It has to be. Whether they're moving opioids, cocaine or something harder, I am a hundred percent sure this is all just a cover for the real business. No wonder they keep it out here in the sticks, where the cops are too afraid to come in and no one else will bother them. I'd be willing to bet all those "patrons" down there are all shippers passing through. One thing I noticed was no vehicles anywhere out front. But I'd bet the back is full of trucks and shipping containers.

Liam clears his throat and I find he's staring at me intently. Am I that transparent that I'm thinking about the easiest and quickest way to take this place down? But I have to remember this isn't why I'm here. I need to let the local LEOs deal with this. My business begins and ends with Brady Sanford.

"So, Isobella," I say. "What can you tell us about Brady Sanford?"

"My real name is Demi Mosley. Isobella is an...alias. What's there to say?" she asks, holding up one hand. "He was a nice enough guy, but not very bright."

"What do you mean by that?"

"I mean it was extraordinarily easy to lure him into an affair."

I'm surprised by her bluntness. I thought it would take a lot more to get that out of her. But for some reason she seems determined to want to provide us with information, which makes me wary. I'm always a little suspicious of anyone who is *too* open with us. "So then you were sleeping together."

"We were, for almost six months," she replies.

"Was he planning on leaving his wife for you?" I ask.

She shakes her head. "I doubt it. Though he developed feelings for me quite early. But I don't think he had the spine to ever leave her. Especially not with their kids."

I have to admit, this is still puzzling. "How did you two meet?"

"An online dating site, of course," she replies. "I was looking for some fun, and apparently, he was bored at home. It was a relationship of convenience."

"You're being very forthcoming with us, Ms. Mosley," Liam says. "I assume you know Brady Sanford is dead."

"Which is exactly *why* I am being upfront with you. I thought this might come back to me once I saw what had happened." She folds her hands together on her desk, looking first at him, then back at me, all business. She clearly wants to answer our questions so we can leave her operation alone.

"Tell us about the money," I say.

She lets out a long breath and sits back in her chair. "I guess I shouldn't be surprised you know about that. But let me be clear, it wasn't my idea."

"What wasn't?" I ask.

"The payments," she replies. I continue to stare at her, trying to make her as uncomfortable as possible. Finally, she relents. "I may have implied to him that I was in need of money."

I look around the posh office. The place is done up nice, with a lot of expensive-looking furniture and fixtures. There's a lamp in the corner which I can't imagine costs less than a thousand dollars. "Seems like you're doing okay to me."

"Like you've never played a mark before," she says, resentment in her voice. "I just made the suggestion, I didn't come to him on my hands and knees, pleading. And he was more than willing to help me out. What am I going to do, refuse free money?"

"Were you aware that free money was bankrupting his family?" Liam asks.

She shrugs. "What do I care? If his wife was stupid enough not to know what he was doing behind her back, she deserved to lose her money."

"Really?" I ask, pinning her with my gaze.

Ms. Mosley takes a breath, spreading her hands out on the table between us. "That came out wrong. I just mean it wasn't my business where that money was coming from. He'd show up every third or fourth time we met with a bundle of cash, asking me if it was enough. I always thanked him properly, if you know what I mean."

"Yeah," I say. "I think I get it. And you never thought to tell him to stop paying you for sex?"

She chuckles. "You know, you can call it whatever you want. But the honest truth was, it was one friend helping out another. And that's it. We never made an arrangement, and we certainly didn't ever discuss a price. To be honest, the first time he showed up with a grand, I was surprised. I was expecting maybe a hundred bucks."

"How much did Brady end up paying you, in total?" I ask.

"Gifting, agent," she corrects. "It was all a gift. And I believe it was close to eighty or eighty-five thousand dollars in total."

"Where is that money now?" Liam asks.

"In various stocks and real estate holdings," she replies. "Like any responsible investor."

"So what happened the night of the sixteenth?" I ask.

She furrows her brow, and I see a genuine confusion come over her, which slips a small amount of doubt into my mind. Up until this point, I had been starting to build a case against her in my head. She certainly had the means to kill Brady and his wife. But as for motive and opportunity, I still need to uncover those.

"It was the night he showed up here," Liam says.

Her eyebrows shoot up and recognition comes over her. "Oh. Right. I must have mentioned in passing about this place. I usually don't slip up like that, but then again, I usually don't see anyone as long as I was seeing Brady. Regardless, he came here looking for me, and when he got inside—"

"—he saw you weren't as destitute as you'd made yourself out to be," I finish for her. "What was his reaction?"

"He was mad, of course," she replies. "He'd actually come to tell me that he couldn't afford to give me any more money, that his mother-in-law had cut them off? I don't know, I wasn't paying much attention."

"He wasn't upset that you'd been swindling him?" Liam asks.

"As I said, it was *his* choice to give me his money, not mine. But yes, he wasn't happy about it. He said he'd be going to the police but considering I didn't steal it off him and he gave it to me of my own free will, I told him he didn't have much of a case. It would be his word against mine, and since all the transactions were in cash, they were virtually untraceable." She takes a deep breath and examines the nails on one of her fingers. "Of course, he cut things off after that. Said he didn't want anything more to do with me. I was heartbroken." Her tone of voice suggests she was anything but. Considering she managed to sucker close to a hundred grand out of Brady Sanford for little to nothing, I'm starting to wonder if she had any ideas of retribution.

"So he cut you off," I say. "That must have stung."

"Agent, look around," Mosley says. "Do I look like I'm

hurting for cash? Brady's contribution was nice, but it amounts to very little compared to what I bring in a year. A drop in the bucket, one could say."

"So then why not give it back to him?" Liam asks. "Especially if you knew he'd been cut off?"

"Because that wasn't my problem. My father always told me I wasn't put on this Earth to solve stupid people's problems for them. He was dumb enough to do it, I figured he didn't deserve a second chance."

"When was the last time you saw Brady?" I ask.

"That night," she replies. "Hadn't seen or heard from him since. Not until I saw the news story."

"What about his wife, did you have any contact with her?"

"None." Her voice is flat, emotionless. I bet this woman is good at playing poker.

I take a deep breath and soak in the room a little more. A scent of a flower hangs on the air, but I can't identify it. I turn my attention back to her. "Here's what we're looking at, Ms. Mosley. Brady Sanford has been murdered, executed, really. His wife is...missing. And now I learn that just two weeks prior he met and broke up with you, cutting the payments he'd been giving to you for the past six months. You see how this looks."

"But I already told you, I didn't *need* the money," she replies. "I didn't care that he was cutting me off. I was getting bored with Brady anyway. I wanted someone new."

"Maybe you wanted a thrill," I say. "Or maybe you told one of your buddies down there about what happened, and he didn't like the idea of someone treating you that way."

A laugh bubbles up from her. "You've got to be kidding," she says. When I don't laugh along with her, the laughter dies in her throat. "Look. I've been very forthcoming here. I didn't kill Brady and I didn't do anything with his wife."

I lean forward again. "And yet, somehow, I don't believe you." I growl. I'm tired of this woman thinking she can jerk us around just because she believes she has some power here. "I don't really care what you think you know about the FBI, but let me tell you we do not stop until we find the person we're looking for. Someone put a bullet in the back of Brady Sanford's head, right in the middle of the street. And right now, you're looking like our best suspect."

"Okay, wait," she says, her eyes wide. She's rubbing her palms on her dress, like they've all of a sudden become clammy. "You can't just come in here and threaten me. I agreed to let you in because I thought we could settle this—"

I stand. "You *let* us in here? Give me one good reason I shouldn't have a dozen agents in here first thing tomorrow morning, tearing this place apart."

"Y-you can't do that, I have rights," she says.

"You're used to dealing with Quaker's men," I tell her. "They are puppy dogs compared to what those of us in the federal government can do. If I have cause to believe you murdered the man you were sleeping with, then I have broad authority to uncover any and all evidence relating to that crime." I'm pushing hard, and I know it. But get the impression if I don't, Mosley will think she can just walk all over us. The truth is there is very little I could do without some sort of evidence attaching her to the crime scene, but she doesn't need to know that part.

"Okay!" she says, holding up her hands. "You've made your point! What can I tell you that will convince you I had nothing to do with his death?" she asks.

"First, tell us where you were on Sunday evening," Liam says.

"I was in Austin," she says. "I didn't get back into BWI until Monday morning, and then it took me another three hours to get back here because of a wreck on the bridge."

That should be easy enough to verify. A simple call to BWI and a look at their security footage will tell us if she's telling the truth or not. "Who else knew about your relationship?" I ask.

She shakes her head. "No one. I don't exactly go around telling my employees I'm out trolling for ass on dating websites."

"No one here knew?" I ask.

She shakes her head. "Even if they did, they wouldn't dare do anything about it. They're all too afraid of me."

"Even if they thought it might get them in good with you?" Liam asks.

"No, I have a no tolerance policy. No cowboys. Everyone knows if they step out of line, they're out of the club. I don't have room for that shit here. The people here know it's a privilege."

I take a deep breath. Short of interrogating every single person down there in Quaker's station, there's not much more I can do to corroborate that part of her story. And without any evidence tying this place to Brady, other than the fact he walked in here once two weeks ago, my options are limited. But I'm still not convinced this place didn't have something to do with his death.

"Make sure you don't leave town again anytime soon," I tell her.

"I didn't have anything on the calendar anyway," she shoots back, regaining some of her composure. Liam stands and we head back for the door.

"And make sure you keep a low profile," I call back to her as we're leaving. "I'd hate to have to come back and investigate this place for anything else." The look on her face is positively delicious. I love making the corrupt squirm.

Once we're back outside and clear of the club, Liam turns to me, a smile on his face. "What?" I ask.

"Nothing. I just never knew you could be so ruthless."

I want to quip with him but restrain myself. Instead, I look straight ahead. "Sometimes it just comes with the territory."

Chapter Seventeen

AFTER LEAVING SANDRIDERS, WE DECIDE TO CALL IT A NIGHT and head back to the hotel, where I finally get a shower and manage to get some of the stench from the club off me. Liam proposed dinner but given I'm still feeling that natural pull toward him, I opted out, making something up about being too tired and needing some extra rest.

Instead, I sit in my room, going over what little we have so far. I'll call Caruthers back at HQ tomorrow and see if he can't verify Demi Mosley was on a flight from Austin to BWI Monday morning. And this time, I'll make sure we get *visual* confirmation. I don't need another Victoria Wright situation on my hands.

But something in my gut tells me she's not my killer. This all feels different than a revenge killing, but I'm not sure why. I think I'm so turned around about what's going on at home and what I'm dealing with regarding Liam that I'm just not feeling like myself. That stunt in the club, for instance. I *never* used to go off on people like that, but I feel like these days I'm living every minute on the edge of a knife, like the world will cleave itself in two if I don't maintain perfect balance.

Of course, I'm not that narcissistic. I know that even if

everything falls apart for me personally, it's a small drop in a very big ocean, relatively speaking. And at the moment there's very little I can do about it. Instead, I have to trust Janice and Zara to do their jobs while I stay here and do mine.

Now that both Summer and Brady have been found dead, we need to change the direction of this investigation. First thing tomorrow we'll go through the Sanford home; maybe there will be something there after all. And I need to interview Adelaide again and find out what was going on with the money. Was she supporting them? Or just supplementing their income? And if so, did she know about Brady's infidelity? Perhaps that was why she cut them off, because she didn't want to continue to finance that. It makes sense.

As I lay my head down on the pillow, I still can't get over what this case has become. It was just supposed to be a simple murder, that was it. Now I'm out here negotiating with drug lords and have somehow inserted myself into the middle of a jurisdictional feud. It's times like these when I really wish Zara was here.

But as my mind begins to drift, I find myself thinking of Liam again, not more than ten feet away from my exact position. How difficult would it be to go over there and just talk with the man? Would that be so bad? I try to imagine how that would go, and every time I do, I can only come to one inevitable conclusion: I'm attracted to him. And not just in a physical capacity, but all of him. Part of me wants to revel in it, while another, more reasonable part, shuts me down, scolding me for even thinking such things with my husband barely gone seven months. What would he think if he knew I had feelings for someone else? I know he'd want me to be happy, but I'm just not sure I can ever do that. How am I ever supposed to be with someone else and not see his face? Or feel his lips on mine? Matt and I...we were soulmates, not that I actually believe in such a thing. But if it did exist, we were it. We fit together like two puzzle pieces, perfectly matched.

When he died it nearly destroyed me. And here I am, seven months later, already thinking of someone else? What kind of person does that?

And yet…he lied.

I turn over in frustration, pulling my covers to my chin. This case is complex enough, it should be holding my attention. But I just can't seem to keep my mind from wandering. But as I lay in bed, I make a silent promise to myself: that I will not let anything get in the way of me solving this case. Not Liam, not the assassin, not even Chief Quaker or Sheriff Black. I am going to find out who killed Brady and Summer Sanford if it takes everything I have and everything I am.

That's a promise.

I awaken refreshed and invigorated, feeling like I've had my best night's sleep in a month. But also, I wake up starving since I never ate dinner, just had a few crackers from the vending machine and some water. After a quick shower and trying the coffee from the crappy machine in the room, I opt for the hotel's breakfast.

Unfortunately, it's not much better. Their offerings are mostly cold cereal and a selection of muffins.

"Sleep well?"

I turn to see Liam coming over from the lobby. "I did, I just wish we could get a decent breakfast," I say, not even bothering to find out if the muffins feel as hard as they look.

"We could always try the Barrell," he suggests.

"And run into Black again? No, thank you," I reply. "There has to be somewhere else to eat in this town that's not fast food." My stomach seems to grumble in agreement.

"I've got an idea," Liam says, "Come with me." Intrigued, I follow him out to the car. "Keys?"

"Where are we going?"

"Are you one of those people who likes to ruin the surprise before it happens?" he asks and I find it difficult not to smile.

"No, I'm just…" I don't know what I'm doing anymore. Frustrated, I toss him the keys and get into the passenger side of the car.

"Just…?" he asks as he turns the engine over.

"Nothing," I say. "I was thinking more about the case and I'm confident Mosley's alibi is going to hold up." I have to keep the conversation—and my mind—focused on the facts at hand. The time for distractions is over.

"What about all those other people in there?" he asks. "Just because she thinks she's got them all under her thumb doesn't mean she really does."

I've been giving that some thought too, but I'm just not sure it lines up. "Let's say someone that works for or with her knew about her relationship with him. Why kill Brady? It was clear Demi was getting tired of being in a relationship with him, so it wasn't like he slighted her. And she's right, she didn't need the money, which is probably the most tragic part of all of this. Brady was just spending all his money on this woman who didn't even appreciate it, bankrupting his family in the process."

"Guys are nothing if not incredibly stupid when it comes to women," Liam says. I feel like I detect a hint of self-depre-cating humor there, but I don't say anything. He pulls the car out onto the main highway that leads out of Mardel.

"So let's table that aspect for now. I've already put in a call to HQ to verify her alibi, but I don't think Mosley is stupid enough to give us an alibi that could be so easily debunked."

"Where does that leave us then?" Liam asks. "Who else has a motive?"

I let out a sigh. "I'm really not sure. Maybe when we go through their house, we'll find something tangible, but at the moment it looks like we're right back at square one."

We ride in silence for a bit as Mardel falls behind us. I

have no idea where we're going or how far away it is, but really, I don't care right now. I just want to figure this out so we can catch this bastard.

"Is it always like this?" Liam asks out of the blue.

I turn to him. "What?"

"This job. It is always like this, chasing down killers, always on edge about the next bad thing happening? How are you supposed to live a normal life?"

"It's not always like this, no," I tell him. "Usually, I'm sitting behind a desk doing background checks or out knocking on doors looking for witnesses." At least, that's how it used to be. But it seems like ever since Matt died, I've been on a treadmill that won't stop, or even slow down. "Though I'll admit, things have been more hectic than normal, lately." I grin. "Why? Starting to regret your decision to join?"

"Not at all," he says. "I believe in the Bureau's mission and I want to protect the public. I just didn't realize how…intense it all is."

I watch as we cross the state line back into Maryland, headed in the direction of Sheriff Black's offices in Fairview.

"Most agents can tell if they're going to stay with the Bureau long-term within the first month," I tell him. "And it's rarely a hard decision. They're either all in, or completely out."

"Is that how it was for you?" he asks.

I shift in my seat some. I'm not used to talking about myself so much. The nice thing about Zara is she knows all this already, so we never have to talk about history. And I usually don't work with anyone else. So telling someone about my past is something of a new experience for me. Or, at least, it's an experience I haven't had in a while. "It was," I say. "I knew after the first day I was never going to do anything else. Which was why it was so hard when they almost fired me."

He shakes his head. "I still don't see how they could have done that. You saved those kids."

"My recklessness got another agent shot. Despite the fact he was an asshole, he didn't deserve that. I almost blew the entire thing. I almost killed a kid." I find it's all pouring out of me even though I had no intention of ever talking about any of this ever again. There's just something about Liam that makes it easy for me to open up to him. And that scares me as well.

"Still," he says. "Seems unfair."

"Sometimes that's how it goes," I say. I'm not naïve. Standing around complaining about how life isn't fair doesn't do anyone—least of all me—any good. Instead I need to focus on doing better, on solving my cases and bringing criminals to justice.

"Here we are," he says as he pulls into the parking lot of a small building that looks like it's about one grease fire away from going up in flames.

"Biscuit Town?" I ask, looking up at the sign that's probably older than I am.

"Yep."

"They don't even look open." That isn't true, of course. The lights are on, though there aren't any other cars in the parking lot. The building looks like it used to be someone's house that's now been converted into a restaurant of sorts. A smaller, more commercial section looks to have been built on to the back of the building.

"Trust me," he says, getting out of the car. I follow him to the door which sticks as he pulls on it, causing him to grunt a bit as he gets it open. When we get inside, I can still see the original layout of the house as it once was. The living room is in the front, though it's all been opened up, and there's a small podium right inside the door, probably where the old foyer used to be. The building opens up to more seating in the back, out into the extended section. The kitchen sits off to our right, taking up that entire side of the house.

I try not to be a snob about where I eat, but I can't help

but feel like I've stepped into someone's home, which I find somewhat odd.

"Here," Liam says, and leads me over a small table by what used to be the house's front windows. It looks like they still might even have the original blinds.

A woman in her sixties comes over, a pen behind her ear and her hair pulled back. She's wearing a stained apron over jeans and a t-shirt and the lines around her mouth and her yellow teeth tell me she's probably been a life-long smoker.

"Mornin'," she says without much enthusiasm. "Coffee?"

"Two," Liam says. "And we'll have the special."

She grunts and heads back to the kitchen where I hear people working. "What is this place?" I ask, looking around. No other patrons. No other activity. It's like we've stepped into another dimension void of people.

"Biscuit Town, everyone knows Biscuit Town," he says easily, like it's the most obvious thing in the world.

"Liam…" I warn.

"Trust me," he says again. "You're gonna love this."

A minute later the waitress brings back two cups and fills them both from the pitcher she's carrying. The aroma hits me immediately and I swear a little drool escapes my mouth before I can suck it back in. Liam stares at me with a satisfied look on his face. "How did you know?" I ask.

"Just wait," he says, pulling his own cup to him and taking a sip. He closes his eyes and relishes the taste while I do the same. It's heavenly, probably the best cup of coffee I've ever had.

The waitress is back in less than a minute with two plates, both with two biscuits that have been split down the middle covering the plate. "I guess this is why they call it Biscuit Town, huh?" I ask.

Liam only grins, like he's in on some secret. How did he even know about this place? I go for one of the biscuits, but he reaches out and stops me, our hands touching for a brief second. It's like a surge of electricity pulses through my arm even though I know it hasn't, and I pull my hand back.

"You're impatient," he teases. Did he just feel the same thing I did? Or was that all in my head?

The waitress returns one last time with a massive ceramic pitcher. I look down at my cup, which is still mostly full; there's no need for a refill yet. But instead of pouring us more coffee, she tips the pitcher over the biscuits, smothering them in thick sausage gravy until I can't even see the biscuits anymore.

"Enjoy," she says and heads back off for the kitchen.

The smell of the sausage gravy really does make my mouth water and this time I make sure to keep it closed.

"Okay, *now* you can eat it," Liam says.

I don't even bother asking any questions, instead digging right in. The biscuit is just the right fluffiness, and combined with the gravy, which is thick but not too heavy and full of spice, makes me want to moan right here at this table. Fortunately, I still have some of my capacity left. "How did you find this place?" I ask, my mouth full of biscuit and gravy.

"After yesterday's breakfast fail, I did some research," he says. "This place isn't even on yelp. But everyone I talked to said this was the place to come get a good, hearty breakfast. They pride themselves by staying off the map. Sort of like a local secret."

"Mmm," I hear myself say, even though what I want to say is *thank you*, but I can't quit eating. It's just that good. This is exactly what I needed. Too often I skip breakfast because I'm too busy and end up running on fumes all day. But this has to be one of the best breakfasts I've ever had. And I can't help but think how thoughtful it was of Liam to do some reconnaissance to find it. I never would have put that much effort into something like this. I probably would have just ended up with another fast food option.

"I kind of don't want to leave now," I finally manage to say. "We're doing this every morning we're here."

He raises his cup in a toast to me, grinning like an idiot the whole time.

As I'm halfway through my second biscuit, my phone buzzes in my pocket. I chew fast and pull it out. "Slate."

"Agent Slate, this is Sharon, from the scene yesterday."

"Good morning," I say, my pulse quickening. "What can I do for you?"

"I'm done with the autopsy on Summer Sanford. I thought you'd like to go over my findings."

I motion for Liam to hurry. "Absolutely," I say. "We'll be right there." As soon as I hang up I look across the table. "Get a bag. We're taking the rest of this to go."

Chapter Eighteen

"GOOD MORNING, AGENTS," SHARON SAYS AS WE ENTER THE Mardel medical examiner's office. She's dressed in smart scrubs, with a white coat and holding an iPad as we enter. I see no sign of Metcaffe anywhere.

"Morning," I say. "Working alone this morning?"

"All night, actually," she replies. "I wanted to get this information to you as soon as I could. And it took some work convincing Chief Quaker we didn't need to wait for Metcaffe to return from his vacation."

"He's on *vacation*?" I ask, incredulous. What kind of man goes on vacation in the middle of a murder spree? Not only was he lackadaisical with Brady Sanford, but he didn't even bother to stick around in the event we needed something.

"The man does not like for his schedule to be interrupted. By death or any other inconvenience," she replies wryly. I like Sharon a lot more than her boss.

"Thank you for jumping right on this," I say. "We really do appreciate it."

"Of course," she replies. "My original assessment was off by only a little. It looks as though she died between midnight and eight a.m. on Monday morning."

"So then probably within twelve hours of her husband's death," I say.

"More or less," she replies. "And whoever killed her was sloppy. The ligature marks around her neck indicate strangulation was the primary cause of death, but I was able to pull a lot of organic material from under her fingernails. Looks like she gave as good as she got before she died. You're looking for someone with fresh scratches. I've already sent the material off for DNA analysis, but who knows if it will come back or not."

"Fingerprints?" I ask.

"Sloppy, but not completely inept," she replies. "The killer wore gloves of some kind. I believe them to be either workman's gloves or maybe even something softer, like gardening gloves. Not rubber gloves by any means, the marks are too rough."

"Wonder why they didn't just shoot her, like they did her husband?" Liam asks.

"That's the other part," Sharon says. "She was sexually assaulted."

"Don't tell me you got a sample," I say.

She grins and gives me a nod. "I've already sent it out for analysis too. It looks, from the way the blood has pooled in the body, that she was probably alive for the assault. Or she could have possibly died during, via strangulation."

"Jesus," I say, the gravy in my stomach doing a small lurch. "So the killer came up on them, shot Brady in the back of the head, and kidnapped her, only to assault her and kill her too."

"What are you thinking?" Liam asks.

I'm not sure yet, I'm still trying to understand this killer. Was this a crime of opportunity? Or was it something personal? It certainly feels personal and given there haven't been any other crimes of a similar nature I have to assume that the killer knew his victims.

But who else would have had it out for them? Who could have been watching and waiting to take their opportunity?

"Did you find anything else?" I ask.

"Her clothes, ID and purse were all missing from the scene," Sharon says. "And weren't recovered anywhere within a five-hundred-yard radius. Someone carried her out there, as there were no drag or wheel marks, but we couldn't get any good footprints. Regardless, you're looking for someone strong enough to take a woman out into the middle of the woods and dump her."

I extend my hand and take Sharon's. "Thank you. Really, this is such a big help."

"I just hope you manage to catch whoever did this," she says. "I'll let you know as soon as we hear back on the DNA and semen tests."

Liam and I head back outside. Given all this new information, I need some time to build a new profile. We're looking for someone who isn't as professional as I first thought, otherwise they would have been smart enough to wear protective gear and a condom to prevent any of their DNA from coming loose. But just because we have it, doesn't mean we can match it to anything. If the killer isn't in the system, then it will take a lot longer to track them down. But then again, we might get lucky.

As Liam and I make our way to the car, I notice a Nanticoke county sheriff's cruiser parked out front. Just as I'm processing what I'm seeing, the door opens and Sheriff Black steps out, a sour frown on his face, causing his large beard to droop.

"What now?" I say under my breath.

"Agent Slate!" he calls out, storming his way up to us. "What the *hell* are you playin' at here, little girl?"

"Excuse me," I ask, immediately on the defensive. "Watch your tone, Sheriff."

"I'll speak as I please," he says. "Especially when my own men are bein' investigated by your new pal."

"What are you talking about?" Liam asks, squaring his

shoulders. Black looks like he's about to take a swing at one or maybe both of us.

"Don't play dumb with me," he says. "You know exactly what you're doin' and I can tell you right now, I won't stand for it. You feds think you can come in here and throw your weight around just because you happen to work for the government but that ain't how it works here. These people are under *my* jurisdiction, and if you want to file a complaint, you do it the right way, instead of goin' behind by back and startin' some kind of witch hunt."

"Sheriff," I have to yell. "I don't know what you're talking about," I say. "Now slow down and explain what is going on."

He screws up his features and glares at me with a hatred I'm not used to seeing from another human. Even with Burke it wasn't this bad, but Sheriff Black seems to have a real distaste for us, regardless. "I'm talkin' 'bout the investigation Chief Quaker has opened into four of my deputies," he says, his tone filled with bile. "Let me guess, you didn't put her up to it."

"I don't know anything about that," I say.

"Funny. 'cause it seems like ever since you got here, my people have been under extra scrutiny."

"They missed the Sanford's vehicle in the lot, Sheriff," I say. "It was right there in front of them."

He works his jaw. "I know it's common for people to get killed in D.C., but out here, we don't see that many murders. My guys did the best with what they had. I won't apologize for it."

"No, but you need to take responsibility for it," I shoot back. "That is a major piece of evidence. And it was a rookie mistake. I expect better of you, Sheriff."

That really seems to set him off as his eyes flash and he grits his teeth. "Now listen here, I—"

"Okay," Liam says, getting between us. "I think that's

enough. Sheriff, you've made your complaint. We'll speak to Chief Quaker about her investigation."

"You better," he replies. "Unless you want to be the subject of a criminal suit—misappropriation of power and resources. I have a lot of pull in these counties, and I know every single one of the judges that sit on the benches."

"Is that a threat, Sheriff?" I ask.

"Just makin' sure we're all on the same page," he replies. "Take care of it. Now." He turns and heads back to his car and pulls away before I can get myself fully under control again.

"Blowhard," I finally say once I stop shaking with anger.

"Chief Quaker wouldn't really be that stupid, would she?" Liam asks. "I know she said she thought they were negligent, but to open up an investigation while we're in the middle of trying to find a killer…"

I shake my head, dumbfounded by it all. "People have some screwed up priorities sometimes," I say. "And Chief Quaker strikes me as someone who will do whatever it takes to ensure her own future. Same with Black. Ironically, they're probably more alike than different."

Liam crosses his arms and stares in the direction Sheriff Black just drove off. "So now what?"

"Now we call Quaker. We have a house to inspect, and I don't have time to play babysitter." I might have no choice but to sideline both of them until we can find out what really happened here.

Chapter Nineteen

WE'RE SITTING OUTSIDE THE SANFORD'S HOUSE, WAITING FOR Chief Quaker to show up with the set of keys from Brady Sanford's personal effects. The whole way over here I couldn't stop thinking about this feud between her and Black, and how much it's interfering with this investigation. It's amazing to me that they can't seem to put things aside and work together, and if this goes on much longer, it has a good chance of derailing us entirely. I need to put a stop to it right now. Even if Black's men did miss the car, I don't think they did it on purpose. I just get the sense that when you sign up to be a Nanticoke county deputy you figure you'll be dealing with domestic disputes and thefts rather than cold-blooded murders. But my thoughts about the case keep getting interrupted by other things. And if I don't excise this now, I'll be thinking about it all day.

"I never said thank you," I blurt out. Liam turns to me. "For breakfast."

"You're welcome," he says with a smile. "I'm just glad we finally found a reputable spot. So how do we proceed from here? Now that we know we're looking for someone who maybe isn't as professional as we first thought."

Internally, I breathe a sigh of relief. *Now* I can focus. "I'm hoping we find something in that house," I say. "The shot to Brady was so clean, I was sure we were working with someone who had done this before, but now I'm not so sure. The way Summer was left makes me question if maybe our killer just happens to be a good shot, but not very smart in other areas."

"Then we're looking for someone with experience firing a weapon," he says.

I nod. "And good luck picking them out of this crowd. Probably every man in this town has a license to hunt when the season starts. I'd be willing to bet half of them got their first rifle as a Christmas present."

"But what's the motive?" he asks.

"I'm not sure. I want to speak to the grandmother again." Out of the corner of my eye I see Chief Quaker's car come beside us, then pull up in front along the street. "Which reminds me, I need to ask the chief if the boy has started talking again yet." Thankfully, Quaker informed the family yesterday of what he'd found out in the woods, though I don't know if they've told young Ashleigh yet. I do know that Elliott is going to be scarred for life. What were the odds he would be the one to find his own mother? There's something about it that doesn't sit right with me, but it's not like I think he killed his own parents. He doesn't have a driver's license and he's not a big enough kid to have carried her body all the way out there.

But I do plan on seeing just how many guns this family has in here. We'll need to catalogue them and test them against the bullet recovered from Brady Sanford's skull.

"Chief," I say, getting out of the car at the same time as Liam. Quaker is fumbling with the keys in her hand after exiting her own car.

"Thanks for not forgetting about me," she says. "I've been looking forward to looking in here ever since we found out who the victim was."

"Why is that?" I ask.

"It's exciting, isn't it?" she replies. "Who knows what we'll find in there. I'm not sure this town has ever seen a double homicide, at least not since back when it was nothing more than a railroad town."

"Chief," I say in the sternest voice I can muster. "I'm not sure you realize the gravity of this situation. Two children have lost their parents. This is not exciting. And I shouldn't need to explain that to someone in your position."

She pulls back like I've slapped her. "Well, I just mean—"

"And did you open an investigation into Sheriff Black's deputies?"

The accusation flips something in her. "And if I did? What business is it of yours?"

"Given that both of you are vying for jurisdiction on what has now become a double homicide case, I think it's a conflict of interest," I say. "Not to mention you are potentially jeopardizing the validity of this case. The crime scene is still in Black's territory. Accusing him of incompetence—however accurate—isn't going to help us find out who killed the Sanfords." Now that I'm saying it out loud, I really can't believe she would be this petty as to try and pin something on Black and his men.

Quaker shakes her head. "No one is above the law. Big John's men missed a lot. And I'm not sure they didn't do it on purpose. But don't worry, I'll be discreet."

"No," I tell her. "You'll drop this, at least until our killer is found. I don't need some internal grandstanding screwing up my case. Black is threatening to bring legal action against both you and the Bureau. He thinks we're involved."

Quaker adopts a haughty stance. "I would have thought you'd want corruption rooted out."

"There's a time and a place, Chief, and now isn't it," I say. "When we have a suspect in custody and a confession on paper, *then* you can go after him all you like."

She scoffs. "You feds, you're all alike. Metcaffe said I shouldn't trust you, but I was willing to give you a chance because you were on our side. Looks like he was right."

I press my fingers to my temples. "You've got to be kidding me. We're not on anyone's side here."

"You might have control over this case, Agent Slate, but you don't have the authority to direct how I run my town. If I feel an investigation is warranted, then I'll proceed with that investigation, no matter what. Understood?"

"And if all this internal squabbling allows the killer to slip away? Then what? What do you tell Ashleigh and Elliott? That we didn't catch the person that killed their parents because we thought it was more prudent to go after each other?"

She purses her lips, then draws them into a line. "You know what, perhaps I should leave this investigation to the *professionals*. I have other matters that need my attention." She tosses me two keys on a small ring.

"Chief, are we going to have a problem here?" I ask.

"Not at all," she replies and heads back to her car. "Oh, I forgot to mention. We have some work crews coming in to do some scheduled repairs to our HVAC system. But the access is around the terminals you were using. I'm afraid we won't have space for you until the work is complete." She smiles, then gets back in her car.

"Repair work my ass," I say under my breath.

"Whatever we're going to do, we better do it fast," Liam says. "Otherwise, I think you're right. This tiff between her and Black could derail the whole thing."

"And now we can't rely on either one of them for backup," I add. "Great."

"It was the right call, confronting her," he says.

"I could really care less about how she runs her operation here, as long as it doesn't get in our way. And right now, it's a herd of cows on the train tracks."

Liam arches an eyebrow at me.

"What? It's something my dad used to say."

"You've got a lot of funny colloquialisms," he says.

"And you don't? Having a family from Ireland you must have heard some good ones from your parents."

He scoffs. "Only when they're drunk and then they'd usually come out in Gaelic."

I smile. "C'mon, let's get in there. Grab some evidence bags from my trunk. No telling what we might find inside."

As Liam heads to the back of the car, I approach the house, fingering the keys in my hand. One is heavier, more likely for the deadbolt. The walkway is short to the front door, though it looks like a nice, middle-class house. Two floors, brick façade on the front and siding on the sides and back. The door has a large oval window built into it and can only be reached by climbing three stairs to the porch. When I get up to the door I unlock the deadbolt first, then the second lock before I pull on gloves and small booties for my shoes. We're just looking for anything out of the ordinary for right now. Depending on what we find, we may send tech services back out here to do a thorough inspection.

"Got 'em," Liam says, heading up the steps as he pulls his own gloves on. He stares at the open door. "No security system?"

I point to the keypad right inside the door, but it's in shadow. "The grandparents already disabled it."

"Then lead the way," he says.

Inside the foyer is dark, so I flip on the closest light, illuminating a large chandelier above us that sits right beside the staircase up to the second floor.

"You take this level, I'm headed upstairs," I tell Liam. As I head up my first stop is the primary bedroom. It seems normal enough. Queen-sized bed, nice furniture, which all looks like it was purchased at the same time. The bed remains unmade from the last time the Sanfords slept here, which strikes me as profoundly sad. They had no clue when they woke up Sunday morning it would be the last day they ever got up together.

Unless, of course, I happen to find out one of them really did orchestrate this madness and it backfired on them.

I take a minute to look through the bathroom, finding nothing of note other than a few medicine bottles out on the counter. But it's nothing more than strong prescriptions of ibuprofen, nothing that would indicate a serious issue anywhere.

Next, I head for the closets and spend a few minutes observing everything. It doesn't take long for me to find the safe at the bottom of one side, still locked. I assume the guns registered to the Sanfords are still in there, but we'll have to get a locksmith out here to open it for us. Other than the safe, there's nothing of note in the closets. No secret stashes of notes outlining the details of an affair, or any proof at all Summer even knew what was going on. All their luggage is stored in the back of the closets, empty. No one was planning on leaving.

I head back out and check the nightstands on either side of the bed. Nothing in either. Underneath the bed are a few totes filled with winter clothes, but nothing else. So far this is looking like a bust.

I head back out into the hallway and turn left into one of the kid's rooms. This one is done up in neutral colors, and building toys are scattered all over the ground. A couple of stuffed animals sit on the bed, but there are obvious spots where ones are missing from the group. No doubt Ashleigh took them with her when she came to get her stuff.

I leave her room and go across the hall to Elliott's room. The colors in here are darker, and he's got more posters up than his sister does. Though, I notice they're not the typical posters I would expect to see in a teenage boy's room. Usually I'll find sports stars, cars or bands. But Elliott's posters are all copies of famous works of art. Not that it's *that* unusual, it just strikes me as odd that a kid Elliott's age would appreciate something like that. Maybe he's just advanced for his age; I typically see these kinds of posters in college dorms or shared housing. It's the normal stuff, M.C. Escher, Le Chat Noir, Starry Night, etc. that you see on college campuses every-where. He has a desktop computer in his room which his sister does not, though it's off. And since the warrant doesn't cover electronics, I have to leave it for now.

The rest of his room is something of a mess. He has old video games stacked in a corner as well as a box of toys from his younger days shoved under his bed. I don't expect to find anything scandalous; kids are too smart for that these days. Whatever Elliott is looking at, it's confined to his computer. There are also piles of clothing scattered around the room. As best I can tell, neither child plays any sports, which is a little strange for two middle-class kids. But perhaps they never had any interest, or the parents just didn't want to pay for it. Either way, there's not much here.

After checking the few remaining rooms, I head back downstairs to meet up with Liam. "Anything?" I ask.

He's in the kitchen, searching through the cabinets. "Not really. You?"

"Safe upstairs, but it's locked. I'm willing to bet their guns are in there. Where else can I check down here?"

"Haven't done the living room yet," Liam says.

I head into the main room where the large TV hangs on the wall above the fireplace. A lone backpack sits at the foot of the couch, slumped over and half-open. I reach in and pull out a notebook, flipping through the pages. From the subject matter I gather this is probably Elliott's backpack, since I doubt Ashleigh is working on geometry in the fourth grade. But when I flip to the back of the book, I notice some doodles on the last few pages.

Furrowing my brow, I take the notebook back to Liam. "What do you make of this?"

He pauses his search and takes the notebook from me, flipping through the last few pages. He then flips to the front again and examines it from page one. "This is Elliott's?" he asks. I nod. He closes it up and hands the notebook back to me. "Then it looks like he has a crush on some guy named Jay."

I flip to the back pages again, looking at all the doodles. Some are just names, some are a combination of names, others are actual drawings of a guy with his shirt off. "I wonder if his parents knew?"

"You think it's relevant?" Liam asks.

"Probably not," I say. "But if he'd just come out to them, it could have created additional stress in a home that was already dealing with money problems and an affair. But then again, he might not have told anyone yet. In which case it's irrelevant." I return the notebook to Elliott's backpack, placing it back the way it was.

Off to the side of the living room is a small office, which houses another computer and a few filing cabinets. I take a few minutes to rifle through them, looking for anything that might give us a lead. "Hey, Liam," I call after finding some of the printed bank records.

He pops his head in the doorway. "Yeah?"

"Look at this." I hand him a series of bank statements. There are two large deposits in their shared account, both for twenty-five thousand each and three months apart. Both are highlighted and marked with an "A".

"A for Adeline?" he asks.

"Could be. So she was giving them money. But Summer's coworker said she'd recently cut them off. I wonder if she figured out what Brady was doing."

"You think she ordered a hit?" he asks, handing the papers back to me.

"Probably not. But then again, she didn't seem too upset when we mentioned his death. Maybe she got into something she didn't know how to control, and the killer decided they'd rather have Summer than the money for taking out Brady."

"I don't know, Em. That seems like a stretch," he says.

I nod. He's right, it is. Adeline doesn't strike me as the killing type. She'd cut them off, sure, but to go as far as to hire someone to kill her daughter's husband? The father of her grandchildren? "Yeah, you're probably right. I was just thinking out loud." If it looks like we don't have any other leads, I may start an investigation into her and her husband, but right now, I'm not going to consider them suspects. Especially considering this is turning out to look like Summer was the real target. Brady was just collateral damage so the killer could get to her.

"I don't think we're going to find anything else here," Liam says.

Unfortunately, I have to agree. There's little of interest in the house, and nothing that points to anyone looking to kill the Sanfords. "I'll get in touch with a local locksmith, see if they can't crack that safe for us. I still want to get hands on the weapons registered to them. If they're not in that safe, we'll send the techs back out here to do a deep dive."

Liam lets out a frustrated breath, heading back to the foyer. "Now what?"

I don't see any other choice since we have virtually no evidence. "Back to square one."

Chapter Twenty

As Liam drives, I watch the landscape fly by from the passenger side window. It's an overcast day, shrouding the landscape in a dreary gray that seems to go on forever. I realize I'm starting to get used to him driving all the time, which both annoys and frustrates me. He's only here because of a perceived threat to my life, but we've been here three days so far and there's been no sign of anyone looking to target me.

Personally, I think the whole thing is overkill. If the woman who killed my husband had wanted me dead, she would have done it already. But it's nice having someone here to help me try to unravel this mystery. We have a very dangerous person on the loose and unless some new piece of evidence turns up, we're going to be dead in the water.

"Do you really think we'll find anything new out there?" Liam asks. I don't look over. Right now, I'm running out of ideas, and this is the best I have to offer. Part of me feels incompetent at not being able to piece this together better. I try to allow myself some grace, given the fact that I'm so distracted from what should be my primary concern, but I know that this case is stumping me when it should not.

"In the absence of any new evidence, returning to the original scene is the last recourse for the desperate," I admit.

He turns to me. "C'mon, it's not that bad."

"It's not good, either. I really thought the mistress angle would pay off." I know by now I should have called Janice with an update, but I don't have any news for her. It isn't like I'm going to call her just to tell her I don't have anything to tell her. Still, I feel like we should have made *some* headway by now.

"Maybe we'll get lucky and find the murder weapon lying in a ditch," Liam laughs.

I have to chuckle. Given the ineptness of Black's deputies, I wouldn't be surprised.

Fifteen minutes later, Liam pulls to the other side of Basil Avenue, the street where the crime took place. The tape is still up, but the scene has been abandoned by Black's men. The empty lot at the end of the block shows no signs of anyone parking there and the lights to the restaurant on the other end are dark. Apparently, they don't open up until dinnertime. Though I do have to wonder how people eating there feel about having to walk around the taped-off crime scene. I'm sure it hasn't been good for business.

A brisk wind blows in from the east, off the coast, chilling the air, despite the fact it's close to eighty-five out. With the sky looking as it does, I'd be willing to bet a storm is moving in. We better make this quick.

I cross the street and duck the tape, standing right where Brady Sanford was when he was shot. What's left of the bloodstain still colors the concrete at my feet. I turn, looking in the direction of the parking lot. According to Metcaffe, he was shot in the back of the head, so then whoever killed him came up behind him. And since no one reported seeing anyone dragging Summer Sanford away, I have to assume whoever killed Brady was in a vehicle.

I turn and look behind me. The street is empty of traffic,

but I could see how a vehicle could come right up on them here. I return to the street and walk a few yards down, then turn around and walk up to the spot again.

"What are you doing?" Liam asks.

"Trying to re-create the whole thing in my head," I reply. "Let's assume Brady and Summer were walking back from the restaurant. They'd just had an argument. What happens when you have an argument with your wife and you have to get somewhere?"

He shoots me a quizzical look for a second before it dawns on him. "Right. Usually, you aren't holding hands and smiling."

"Yes," I say, pointing to him. "So Summer was more than likely walking ahead of Brady, leaving him bringing up the rear. He's walking along, and now imagine a vehicle comes up behind him, pops him in the back of the head, he goes down." I mimic Brady falling to the ground. "Summer turns at the sound, only to see a gun pointed in her face. The gun that killed her husband. She's either too scared to move or is frozen by shock. Either way, the perpetrator grabs her, throws her into the vehicle, and drives off to rape and kill her later."

"Pretty brutal," Liam says.

"Extremely." I turn around again, then crouch back where the vehicle was. "Give me the keys," I say.

"What?"

I hold out my hand. "Keys." He tosses them to me. I run back to the car and get in. Liam catches up just as I'm starting the engine. I peel away from the curb and gun it down the street.

"What are you doing?" he yells.

I pull the parking brake at the same time I turn the wheel, causing the vehicle's wheels to lock and drift, spinning us a hundred and eighty degrees. I then drop the brake and slam on the gas again. "Emily!" Liam yells.

I pull close to the curb, keeping the car at about thirty as

I roll down the passenger window. I then point my fingers like I'm pointing my weapon and lean across Liam as I'm aiming out the window, but it's too chaotic. I have to slow down even more, to around fifteen miles per hour before I'm confident I could get a clean shot. And if this guy is an amateur, he would have to slow down even more, maybe to five or ten.

"He would have had to have been driving slow," I say, leaning back to my side as I stop the car. "To get a clean shot on Brady he couldn't have been going more than ten miles per hour. Fifteen if he is an excellent shot."

"How does that help us?" Liam asks.

"Look at the angle," I say. "From down here, I would have had to shoot up to hit Brady in the head. But a taller vehicle would have changed the angle of entry for the bullet. We need Sharon to take another look at Brady's wound. It might help us figure out what kind of vehicle we're looking for."

I pull the vehicle to a stop right beside the crime scene. "Still, that doesn't give us much. It tells us, what…it's either a sedan, or a van or truck."

I shrug. "Something is better than nothing. If we at least know what size vehicle we're looking for, someone might remember something."

"Okay. I guess," he says.

I'm not surprised by his reluctance. But right now this is all we have. "He also would have needed to put the car in park to get out and grab Summer. Which would have needed to be quick. I'm willing to bet we're looking for a larger vehicle. Something where a person can be tossed inside without much fuss. Nothing so large that you need to step up into it, but not so small that you have to pull the seat forward to get in the back either." I pull out my phone.

"I guess that's something," Liam says.

I try to ignore his lack of enthusiasm. Dialing Sharon's number, I put it on speaker so we both can hear.

"Agent Slate," Sharon says. "This is good timing; I was just about to call."

I glance at Liam. "There's no way you have a DNA match already," I say.

"Not at all. But I did manage to get that semen sample analyzed. I don't know who it belongs to, but I can tell you we found two different samples inside Mrs. Sanford."

"Her husband?" I ask, thoughts of them having some kind of angry sex in a restaurant bathroom flashing through my head.

"No, neither are a match for Brady Sanford. And both have basically decayed at the same rate. I believe you're looking for two men, not just one."

My eyes go wide. What if there were two of them in the car that night, not just one? It changes my entire theory.

"Agent Slate, are you there?" Sharon asks.

"We're here," I reply. "I just...I should have anticipated that."

"What is it that I can help you with?" Sharon asks. I look over at Liam. We still need the information, but this changes how my theory is structured.

"Can you re-examine the body of Brady Sanford for us? I need to know the angle of entry for the bullet wound to the back of his head."

"Sure, that shouldn't take long. I'm surprised Metcaffe didn't mention it," she says.

"Seems like people around here miss a lot," I say. "Present company excluded."

I hear a scoff on the other side of the line. "You're not wrong. Let me work on that and get back to you." The phone cuts off as she ends the call.

If we're dealing with two unsubs instead of one, it changes things. "Okay, time for a little roleplay." A quick glance behind me and I throw the car into reverse, backing up all the way until we're in the front of the restaurant. I put it back in drive again and keep it around ten miles per hour. "Pretend like you're going to shoot Brady Sanford," I say.

Liam points his finger out the window and I can see it happening in my mind's eye. Except the killers had a rifle. But it's the same concept. With one driver and one shooter, it makes killing Brady much cleaner and easier.

"It's a smooth shot," Liam says, drawing his hand back in.

"And now I don't have to put the car in park. I don't even have to stop if I don't need to. You can jump out, grab Summer and then toss her in the back all while I'm keeping the car moving along the side of the road, looking for trouble."

Liam gives me a triumphant grin. "So now we're looking for two people," he says.

"Two people who were stupid enough to leave their DNA behind," I say. "Who do you think would be dumb enough to fall into that category?"

His eyes narrow. "People who think they're invincible. Untouchable."

I nod. "Exactly."

Chapter Twenty-One

FORTUNATELY, SHARON WAS ABLE TO GET BACK TO US WITHIN the hour, just enough time for a fast storm to move in and soak the place, washing away what little remained of Brady Sanford off the concrete. She confirmed that the bullet had gone in at a slightly upward angle, instead of a sharp upward, which tells us we're looking for a vehicle where the passenger sits almost at or just below a five-foot-eleven man. More than likely we're looking for a pickup or perhaps even a van of some kind.

The storm passes through quickly while Liam and I run through a couple of possible options for what might have happened to Summer during and after she saw her husband die. I feel like, given what her mother told us about her, she was probably too scared to do much of anything and had to be dragged or carried into the vehicle. Whoever took her was reckless enough to have sex with her without a condom, which means as soon as we have a suspect all we'll need to do is a mouth swab and find a match. But the trick will be finding a pair of suspects. And I can't forget what Sharon said about the scratches. We're looking for two men with recent wounds, maybe on their arms or even faces.

And these two men are either very stupid, or very brazen. I'm not sure which, yet.

As much as I want to get these men off the streets, I know there isn't much we can do until we manage to narrow down the suspect pool from virtually every man in the county. Which is part of the reason we stayed out here, even through the storm, because I'm not convinced Black's men did enough that night and I want another crack at anyone who might have seen anything.

Once the rain stops, I start patrolling the side roads to where the crime took place, looking for anyone we might be able to question. Off the main road it's mostly single-family homes that aren't in the best condition, which leads me to assume the people in this neighborhood probably aren't eager to help the police, if it's about a murder or not. A total of four streets branch off from the main road where Brady was shot, though only three of them are close enough to have seen anything. I park at the first house and give Liam the other side of the street while I take the near one. But either no one wants to talk or they're really not home as the entire block is a bust.

Coming back up the next street I see a woman sitting out on her porch, smoking. Her house is about three down from Basil Avenue, which is close enough, in my opinion. I pull the car over and get out, giving her a friendly wave. She just stares back at me as she finishes her cigarette.

"Afternoon," I say, approaching the house while Liam stays with the car. "I'm Agent Slate with the FBI."

"Don't want nothin' to do with no cops," the woman says, and puts the cigarette out under her shoe before heading back inside.

"Please, ma'am, this is regarding the murder that took place just a few—" She slams the door before I can finish. I consider going up to the door and knocking, but in my experience, if someone is adamant about not talking to us, there's little I can do to change their mind, unless they're a suspect.

I head back to the car with a sheepish look on my face. Liam does his best to hide a smile as I get back into the car. "Shut up." I give him a small shove.

"Did I say anything?" I bring the car up to Basil Avenue again and park.

"Same deal," I tell him. "Evens are mine. Odds are yours."

"Yessum," he replies and we go through it all again. I get a few people who actually answer their doors this time, but no one was home or is willing to admit they were. It's another bust.

The look on Liam's face when we return to the car tells me he hasn't had any more luck than I have. We drive down to the third street off Basil and park again. But as I'm stepping out, I spot movement at one of the blinds in the second house.

"There," I say. I head up to the door and give it a firm knock. "Anyone home?"

A moment later the door opens still on the chain and a young face peers out at me. She can't be more than fifteen or sixteen years old. A jolt of anxiousness runs through me but I immediately tell myself to calm down. This isn't a little kid, and there is no danger here. I can handle this. "Hello," I say. "Are your parents home?"

"They don't live here anymore," she replies.

"I'm Agent Slate, with the FBI," I say, trying to keep the tremble out of my voice. This is ridiculous. This kid is almost an adult, but she's still young and that just gets all of my senses firing. "Were you home on Sunday night?" Technically I'm not supposed to question a minor without an adult or guardian present, but this isn't an interrogation. I'm just looking for witnesses.

She nods. "Me and my brother."

"Where's your brother?" I ask.

"At work. Down at Woodie's Auto. He's there most afternoons."

I glance down to Basil Avenue from the porch of the house. They have a pretty good view of the road, and while I can't see the restaurant from here, I can see the parking lot where the Sanfords' car was found. "Do you know about what happened that night?"

"Saw it in the news," she says.

"Did you see anything else?" I ask.

She looks nervously to the side, then back at me. "Like what?"

"Like a truck or a van that night. Out there." I point out to the road.

She shakes her head. "When I heard the shot I got under my bed, like Olly told me. He says this neighborhood keeps gettin' worse and worse." This girl certainly doesn't act like the typical teenager in my experience. She comes across to me as younger, like she hasn't matured as much as some of her peers. I should have assumed that she wouldn't have looked out and seen anything, who would? Any kid with half a brain would duck and cover or run.

"Okay, well thank you for your help," I say, and turn to leave.

"*I* didn't see anything," she adds. "But my brother did."

"I'm looking for an Orlando Stout," I tell the man half covered in grease as he attempts to wipe some of it off on a red rag. He's wearing overalls that only accentuate his considerable belly, and a camo trucker hat with the words "Get R Dun" emblazoned across the top.

"Yeah?" He asks. "He in some sort of trouble?" The man gives me and Liam a smirk as if he's hoping for something of a confrontation.

"That's not your concern," I tell him. "Just let him know we want to speak to him."

"The hell it ain't," the man replies. "If he's in trouble with the law, I got a right to know. I ain't gonna employ hoodlums or criminals in my business. I'll fire him right here, you watch."

I level my gaze at him. "Mr...Duffy," I say, looking at his embroidered name on the overalls. "Orlando isn't in any trouble, but he may have crucial information about a recent crime. We just need to speak to him for a minute. He hasn't committed any offenses."

Duffy's face falls just a little, then he grunts and heads to the back of Woodie's Auto shop. I give Liam a "can you believe this guy" look to which he grins and turns away. A moment later, a tall, skinny kid comes in from the back. He's got on a pair of overalls as well, except the top half is folded and tied around his waist and his toned chest and stomach are completely exposed and half covered in grease. He also has a bandana around his head that's covered in oil. It looks like the kid has been working underneath cars all day. He gives us both a skeptical look.

"Mr. Stout?" I ask.

"Yeah?" he says, wary.

I show him my badge. "I'm Agent Emily Slate, with the FBI. This is Agent Coll. Can we ask you a few questions about the incident this past Sunday night?"

I see him glance at the door, like he's trying to decide if he should make a run for it. I understand he might be skittish, especially when people come around asking about a murder.

"Let me be clear, you're not under suspicion here," I add. "But we think you may have seen something that could help our investigation."

"Oh," he says, though he's still a little on edge. I catch Duffy standing on the other side of the door, a few feet away.

"How about we go outside to talk about this? I'm sure you could use the air after being in the garage all day."

Duffy steps forward. "Hey he can't go on break until—"

He stops talking when he sees the glare I'm giving him. "I mean…five minutes Orlando. No more."

"Yes, Mr. Duffy," Orlando says, then turns back to us. The look in the kid's eyes tells me he thinks he's going from the frying pan right into the fire.

We head outside and find some shade on the side of the building. The storm pushed the gray clouds from this morning off and now it's hot and sunny again. Orlando takes off the rag around his forehead and flips it over, wiping his face with it, which does little to remove the grease and oil.

"Nice boss," I tell him, once we're out of earshot of Duffy.

"Guy's an asshole. But a job's a job. Especially in this town," Orlando says. "What do two FBI agents want with a drive-by?"

"Seems like you already know something about it," Liam says.

"A man got shot a hundred yards from my house, of course I know something about it," he shoots back. "I ain't stupid."

"And this isn't as simple of a case as it might seem," I tell him. "We spoke to your sister earlier today. She says you were both home when it happened."

He pinches his face and turns away from us, kicking at a rock at the ground. I'm thinking he was hoping he could deny having any knowledge about it, but because his sister already pinned him on it, he's got nowhere to go now. "Yeah, we was," he finally says.

"She says you ran outside when you heard the shot."

"Now wait a second," he says, turning back to us. "You said I wasn't in no trouble."

"You're not," I say. "Unless something happened that you want to tell us about."

Orlando leans back against the cinder block wall. "Cops, man. You're all alike. Nothing but lies."

"It's not a lie," I tell him. "If you have information about that night, we need to hear it. We're trying to get a killer off your town's streets."

He looks the other way again, clearly avoiding eye contact. "I dunno, man."

"Orlando," Liam says. "What are you afraid of? Did you see what happened?"

The kid works his jaw, squinting again. I can see he's clearly uncomfortable, but he hasn't completely dismissed us yet. That tells me he wants to help; he just doesn't know if he can trust us. "That night, did the cops come to your door?"

"Yeah."

"And what did you tell them?" I ask.

"Look, I've been takin' care of my sister ever since our moms ran off three years ago, okay? Without me, she's got nobody to help. She's on the spectrum, all right? Which means she has a hard time with people. Now if I tell you something other than what I told them, how do I know that doesn't come back on me? I can't be in no county jail for two weeks."

I hold up one hand. "Orlando, it's okay. I get that you may not have wanted to tell them the truth because you were scared and didn't want to get involved. That's fine. If you tell us what really happened, I promise none of this comes back on you, okay? You're not who we're looking for." As I say the words, I immediately regret them, because I don't know Orlando *wasn't* involved somehow. I'm just hoping that I can convince him to tell us what really happened. Unfortunately, he fits the possible profile.

"*Aight*," he finally says. "Look, we was just sittin on the couch, watchin' that dumb dog show she likes so much when I heard the shot. I figured it was someone in the neighborhood either screwin' around or it was a legitimate threat. Either way, I grabbed my gun and ran out to check. I'm not about to get robbed by some meth-head with a piece."

"Okay," I say, waiting for him to continue.

"Anyway, I go outside, gettin' ready to scare 'em off, when I see this truck pullin' away from the curb down by that restaurant."

I exchange glances with Liam. I imagine the surprise on my face must look similar to his right now. "A truck?"

"Yeah," he says. "Got out of there quick too. Couldn't see much else. I didn't think anythin' of it until I saw the report on the news. I just figured someone was in a hurry. I didn't see anyone else lurkin' around our place, so I went back inside and had to get Jenna out from under her bed. Took me a good half hour to calm her down."

"You didn't notice the dead body lying on the sidewalk when the truck pulled away?" Liam asks.

Orlando looks at him like he's crazy. "Man, there ain't no streetlights out there. And it's a hundred yards away. Can *you* see a lump on the ground at hundred yards at eleven o-clock at night?"

"I guess that means you didn't get a license plate," I say.

He shakes his head. "If I couldn't see that poor man, I sure as hell couldn't see no plate."

He saw a truck, but no plate. At least it's a start. "Why didn't you tell any of the police this when they asked?"

"My gun ain't registered," he admits. "I got it from my uncle a few years ago. I dunno where he got it, but it probably wasn't good. I didn't want them nailin' me for it."

I decide to leave that thread where it lies. "As far as I'm concerned, that's a weapon you only use for self-defense, am I right?" I ask, pinning him in place with my gaze.

He has difficulty looking away. "Y-yes ma'am."

That's good enough for me right now. I'm not about to berate some poor kid for just trying to protect himself and his sister. An unregistered weapon is way down on my list of priorities. "Good. Now as far as this truck. Do you know what kind? What color? Could you pick it out of a bunch of other trucks if we showed you a lot of them?"

"No need. It was Zach Dempsey's truck. I know because he's had it in the shop a few times to try and fix that fucked-up transmission of his. Thing is a piece of crap, yet somehow it still runs."

It takes me a second to catch up. "You know this Zach Dempsey?"

He nods. "He was a year below me at school. He's a senior now. Asshole thinks he's better than everybody else, but we all know the truth. He's cut from the same cloth as the rest of us, even if he don't wanna admit it."

"Did you see him driving?" Liam asks.

"Nah, I couldn't tell that far away," he says. "But I've never seen anyone else drive that piece of shit. Doubt they'd be caught dead doing it."

"Where does Zach live?" I ask.

"Somewhere over on the other side of Fairview," he says. "I'm not sure where. We didn't cross paths much back in school."

"This has been really helpful, Orlando, you have no idea," I say.

He holds up his hands. "Hey, just keep me and my sister out of it, okay? We don't need nobody else to come snooping around."

Thankfully, we shouldn't need to bother Orlando any further. If we can get a sample of Zach Dempsey's DNA, then that will be all she wrote. The evidence will be so strong there won't even need to be a trial. Any lawyer worth his salt would plead for a deal. "We're all good," I say. "You take care and tell that boss of yours the FBI say to lay off or they'll start poking around his business."

That gets the first laugh out of him that I've seen. He's got a nice smile that really lights up his face. "That's a good one. Yeah, I'll go back and tell him right now." He heads off, still laughing like that's the funniest thing he's ever heard.

I turn to Liam once he's back in the garage. "Let's go get the bastard."

Chapter Twenty-Two

ZARA FOLEY STARES AT THE SMALL, FIVE-STORY BUILDING THAT sits in the one of the most unassuming parts of Washington D.C.: Quincy Heights. It's a small commercial section of the city but it's not near any of the big tourist destinations or even any of the famous intersections. It's like the corner of the city that history conveniently forgot.

She's been on the hunt ever since Emily and Liam left for Delaware, and her hunt has led her here.

She wasn't kidding when she said she was going to do everything she could to find out the truth about Emily's husband and his supposed boss. After receiving the glut of information from the assassin while they were still in New York, Zara has been pondering the situation in her mind, over and over. Her job in New York was to assuage her friend's mind, to keep them on task. Which meant not buying into any of the bullshit that assassin emailed her. In truth, she didn't believe a word of it at first. But as time has gone on and she's had a chance to do a deep dive into some of the documents, she's begun to have serious doubts that Matt really was who he said he was. She doesn't want to voice her concerns to Emily just yet; Emily still believes it was a discrepancy of some kind.

After all, Zara was the one who tried to convince her of that fact. But given what she's been able to find out so far, it's clear Matt was lying after all.

Take the stack of documents the assassin emailed, for example. While they might not explicitly say that Matt was being deceptive, Zara hasn't been able to find any documentation that disputes them. So far, all his employment records with Covington College have turned out to be forgeries and his "office" at the same college was nothing more than a broom closet, full of brooms.

Emily said she'd never visited him at work as she'd never had the time. And Zara gets it. The Bureau requires a lot of time, especially when you're a SA. And it seems like Matt took advantage of that by conveniently omitting the fact that he didn't really work where he said he did. At the time Zara had never questioned it because back then she and Emily weren't as close as they are now, and Matt had seemed like a perfectly normal, reasonable person. Who would have suspected he was actually lying about his job the entire time?

But that hasn't been all. Matt brought in a steady paycheck. And from what Zara can find, that check was issued by the college itself. But when she double-checked the college's records with those of Matt's pay stubs, nothing matched up. It was like someone had forged all of his documents from the time he had started "working" there until his death.

Needless to say, the college was as confused as she was.

Hitting nothing but a dead end there, Zara decided instead to focus on the only other person that might have known anything about Matt: his boss, Brian Garrett. And other than a semi-blurry picture of him at a Christmas Party a few years back, all Zara had of the man was the one thing he shared with Matt: a phone number for their shared office at the college.

It took two days, but she managed to work with Caruthers down in communications to trace the phone number. While the signal originally appeared to derive from Covington College, there was actually an elaborate signal bounce that caused the line to only *look* like it originated from there. In reality, it pinged a few other places across the country before landing right back here in D.C., on the fourth floor of the building she's been staring at for the past twenty minutes. And Zara knows it takes some serious equipment to pull something like that off.

Part of her thinks she should go ahead and loop Janice in on this. She has clear evidence of subterfuge, and it would only strengthen Emily's case against these people, whoever they are. But at the same time, she's afraid if she doesn't do this right now, it might all disappear. They are dealing with some very professional people here, and she has no doubt that if they get wind that an FBI agent has managed to track them down, they will disappear into the wind.

Her hope is she can surprise Garrett, and force a confession out of him, and get him to admit he conspired to cover up the truth from Emily and everyone at the FBI. The FBI does extensive background checks on spouses of agents. How they could have missed this is unthinkable.

Resolve steeling her veins, Zara gets out of her car and heads across the street to the building. She flashes her badge and the security guard at the door opens it, letting her in and she heads straight for the elevators, bypassing the front desk. The elevator doors open, and she presses the button for the fourth floor, her heart racing. There's no telling what she's going to find up here, but she knows she must be strong, quick and decisive. She would love for Emily to come back to find they had Garrett in custody and had already squeezed a confession out of him, explaining all of this. Then maybe Emily would finally be able to move on with her life.

The elevator dings and the doors open on a marble foyer, which Zara steps into cautiously. She's not sure what to expect here, other than the fact that this entire floor is leased out to a

Caribbean company that—as far as she can tell—has no real presence anywhere in St. Thomas or any other island. For all intents and purposes, it's a shell company that leads to another dead end.

There's a glass wall separating the elevator bank from the lobby of whatever this business is, and Zara is surprised to find the glass door inset into the wall swings open without a keycard. Ahead of her is a half-moon-shaped desk, where a woman with light blonde hair sits, typing away. She looks up at Zara and smiles as she approaches.

"Good afternoon," she says, turning from her computer and folding her hands in front of her. "How can I help you?"

Zara is thrown by her friendly nature. She'd expected to come in here and be stonewalled. But she's not about to let her good luck go to waste. "Good afternoon," she finally says. "I'm here to see Brian Garrett."

The woman furrows her brow, though a smile remains on her face. "I'm sorry, who?"

Either she's playing dumb or she's not part of his cover. Either way, Zara isn't about to give up. She fishes her phone from her pocket and slides the photos until she comes to the one from Emily's Christmas party. "Sorry," she says. "We met on a dating app. I know sometimes people don't always give their real names on things like that." She shows the secretary the image.

"Oh! That's Mr. Renquist," she says, leaning forward. "Personally, I never give my real name on those things. You never know what kind of creepers are out there. I need at least three dates before telling them who I really am."

Zara smiles conspiratorially. "I know what you mean. Is he in? He left my apartment rather quickly the other night and I just wanted a chance for closure."

"Oh, I totally understand. It's so upsetting when they don't call back," the secretary says, putting her phone to her ear. "Who should I say is here?"

"Just tell him there's a package," Zara says. "I don't want to spook him."

The secretary winks. "Got it." She dials a five-digit code. "Mr. Renquist. A package has just been delivered for you sir. It's a little too large for me to carry back. Yes, sir. Thank you." She hangs up. "He'll be right up."

Zara's heart nearly jumps up in her throat. She's about to find out what is behind all of this, everything from the assassin to Matt's death seven months ago. Emily really should be here to help her with this, but Janice was clear. She doesn't want Emily anywhere near this, she's too close to it. This is Zara's case now, and she's not about to screw it up.

A moment later, a man appears from around the corner. He doesn't look much different from the picture Emily emailed Zara from her party. He's in his mid-forties and sports a neat moustache and beard and wears a designer suit with pinstripes. He's also wearing a pair of trendy glasses. He's all smiles until he sees Zara's face and then he stops cold.

"Hey Brian," Zara says. "Remember me? From the Christmas Party?"

Brian Garrett, or Mr. Renquist as he's known here, turns and bolts down the hallway. Zara takes off after him, ignoring the cries of the secretary. She's willing to bet she'll call security, but at this point, that would be a bonus. Anything to slow Garrett down.

Unfortunately, he's fast. Zara could tell he fit from the way he carried himself, but now it's really showing as he begins to outpace her down the hallway. He doesn't go for any of the offices though, instead heads straight for the stairway exit sign at the far end of the hallway.

"Stop!" Zara yells. "FBI!" But it does nothing to slow Garrett down. He barrels through the door into the stairwell and by the time Zara reaches the door herself, he's already half a flight down. She stays in pursuit, though she doesn't draw her weapon yet. She can't risk accidentally shooting him, especially not in such an enclosed area like this. With all these concrete walls there's a chance the bullet could miss and rico- chet. "Garrett, it doesn't have to be like this."

He doesn't reply, only continues to take the steps two at a time, then jumping to the nearest landing when he's close enough. Zara is forced to take the same measures. Because he's got some height on her, if they get out in the open, she'll never catch him. She needs to find a way to stop him in here.

"What are you a part of, Garrett?" she adds, hitting the landing for the second floor. "Why are you doing this to Emily?"

All she can hear is his breath, hard and fast below her. She doesn't have a choice. If she's going to catch him, she has to do something drastic.

Zara climbs over the railing and after a quick look, drops down the remaining two floors, though her body slams into the last part of the railing on the way down and she hits the floor hard and with a grunt. Garrett, still above her, stops short on the final landing. She's all that stands between him and the exit door.

She's on her hands and knees, and her side really hurts, but Zara manages to pull her service weapon, wincing. "Enough running," she says. "Time to talk."

"You don't know what you're getting yourself into," Garrett finally says.

"Yeah, I know," she replies. "That's the whole reason I'm here. To find out."

He shakes his head. "No, you *really* don't know. Let me go. I can't let you take me in."

"You falsified your entire life, your profession," she says. "You conspired to keep the truth from Emily, with her husband." She points the gun at him.

Garrett raises his hands. "Last time I checked, lying to your wife isn't a crime."

"No, but lying to the federal government is. Matt was

never a teacher with Covington College. And neither were you. We know Matt's death was no accident. And we know that the woman who killed him is now threatening Emily. You're going to tell me why."

Zara can see his mind working, his eyes darting back and forth, weighing his options. She doesn't like the desperation she sees in his face, the fear. This is a man who is unlikely to ever break, not unless they can offer him something he doesn't already have. Because right now, he's scared to death.

"Tell me what's going on," she says. "We can help you. We can protect you."

"You couldn't protect Matt and you won't be able to protect Emily," he says. His eyes flash and he darts back up the stairs. Zara curses and begins running after him, afraid he'll just exit out on the second floor and find another stairwell to leave through. But as soon as he's at the second floor landing, he does exactly what Zara did, only better. He jumps down to the ground level and lands perfectly, then pushes out through the door, causing a fire alarm to sound.

"Son of a——" Zara says as she turns and heads after him, the afternoon light blinding her for a second as she exits the building. She catches sight of him running across the nearest street, past where she's parked. Zara takes off, pursuing as fast as she can, and pulls her cell as she does, hitting her fast dial. "Agent in pursuit, I have a suspect in sights, Caucasian male, dark hair, dark blue pinstripe suit, headed east down Atlantic on foot. Requesting immediate backup by anything in the area!"

"On it," dispatch says on the other side. "Local units on the way. Dispatching the closest agents. Two minutes."

Zara pumps her legs as fast as she can, doing her best to keep up. This is the first time she's ever had to pursue someone like this, and it's a bit different than she'd imagined. Running on the treadmill is one thing but sprinting after a suspect is something completely different.

"He's headed into the metro," Zara yells into her phone. "Georgia-Petworth station."

"Stick with him, locals have been informed," the dispatcher tells her. Zara hangs up and pockets her phone, doing everything she can to keep up with Garrett, but he's outpacing her quick. He disappears into the mouth of the station and by the time she reaches it, she realizes he's already at the bottom, having slid down the center of the two escalators.

"Dammit," she mutters and jumps on them, sliding down as well. People gawk at her as she reaches the bottom and loses her footing, tumbling ass over head on the ground. Someone tries to help her up, but she ignores them, pushing herself up and turning left toward the trains. Garrett is nowhere in sight, but the station is small, and doesn't have many places he can hide. She jumps the turnstiles as she comes into the station proper, with its arched interior. Fortunately, both lines run off the same platform and she has to descend another set of stairs to get down to it. Once she finally reaches the platform itself, she's dismayed to find it full of travelers, most of whom are staring at her, huffing and puffing. She pulls out her badge. "Official FBI business, move aside," she manages to say. Most people part for her to get through. But there's no sign of Garrett.

It's a long platform, and Zara scans the crowd, looking for any sign of the man. The rumble from one of the tunnels tells her a train is approaching, which means she might lose him forever if he makes it on board. She thinks she catches sight of the top of his head over on the right side just as a blast of air announces the train coming into the station. It stops, allowing a large group of people to exit, which only makes the crowd worse and forces Zara to stay back. She tries calling out again, but as she does, another train pulls into the station on the other tracks, drowning her out.

Now she's not sure which one to go for. Both are open and

loading and unloading passengers. She hesitates a second too long and the doors of the first train close, filled with passengers. She decides to cut her losses and gets on the other train just before its doors close. But as they do, she catches sight of Garrett, standing at the window of the other train, looking directly at her as it begins to pull away.

"Dammit!" she yells, then tries to force the doors of her train back open, but they won't budge. The other train is already on the move and the last thing she sees is Brian Garrett glaring at her as the train disappears into the tunnel.

He'd known where she was the whole time. And she's just lost her best lead.

Chapter Twenty-Three

AFTER A QUICK SEARCH, WE MANAGED TO FIND THE RESIDENCE of one Zachary Dempsey, a senior at Fairview High School and captain of the basketball team. Liam and I wasted no time coming out to the house, though we're keeping our distance for now. We have one eyewitness testimony, but it was dark and without a positive ID on the person himself, all we know is Dempsey's vehicle was there that night. We need a DNA sample before we'll be able to definitively say that he was the one that either shot Brady Sanford or raped and murdered Summer Sanford, or both.

We also don't know who our second unsub is. It's possible Zach was only driving, in which case we might be able to get him to roll on whoever was with him in the vehicle, but then again we may not. I would rather keep an eye on his movements for a while before we go in for the kill. If we've only got one shot at this, I don't want to miss.

"Nice house," Liam says, looking through the small binoculars.

"Expect anything else from the captain of the basketball team?" I ask, sarcasm tinting my voice.

He lowers the binoculars. "Let me guess, someone wasn't very popular in high school."

"How about you shut up about it," I say, reading over what little we've found on Dempsey. His social feeds are little more than selfies of him in the gym or with a bunch of different girls. But even from his pictures, and more so the comments on his pictures, I can tell he's the kind of guy who isn't used to people saying no to him. He's privileged, which means he fits my profile perfectly. The kind of person who thinks they can get away with anything and be celebrated for it. Though I'm not convinced he was the actual killer. It's possible he became mixed up with someone older and more dangerous. Then again, he could have conceived the whole thing, and I'm looking at a sociopath here. One thing's for sure, he likes making himself the center of attention.

"What's the play?" Liam asks. "Doesn't look like anyone is home right now."

I check the time. It's almost four in the afternoon. "Let's stick around a while, see if he shows up. He's obviously not in school, but he could have a summer job. My gut says he likes to keep Friday nights free, so maybe he'll show up to primp, then head back out."

Liam chuckles. "Wow, you really don't like this guy."

"I don't like what he represents," I say without looking over. "More power for the powerful. Someone at the top who gets to make all the rules. I've been dealing with people like Zach Dempsey all my life and they're all the same. They believe the world revolves around them and that's the correct order of things. No one else can have or gain as much as them, otherwise things are 'unfair' or 'rigged' against them. They're the first to take advantage of people and the first to cry foul when something doesn't go their way. The world is built by people like him *for* people like him, and I won't tolerate it."

"Next time, tell me how you really feel."

I look over to see him grinning and I can't help but crack a smile myself. I didn't mean to go on a tirade there, but I always get worked up when I find people like this guy. The Zach Dempseys of the world have every advantage at their fingertips, while the rest of us have to work twice as hard to get half as far. "What, don't you have any strongly held beliefs of your own?"

"Oh, I definitely do," he replies. "But they tend to revolve more around planetary scale stuff."

I cock my head at him. "Are you saying your concerns are more important than mine, Coll?"

He eyes me like he's not sure if I'm serious or not. "What? No, of course not. I just meant when people start destroying animal habitats to drill for oil or huge corporations won't cut back on the toxic fumes contributing to climate change is where I get peeved. But they're one and the same, aren't they? The same people that get on your nerves are the ones running these companies that seem to believe they can have unlimited growth at everyone else's expense."

"Nice save," I say, finally revealing my smile. "I was just giving you a hard time, anyway." He seems to let out a breath he didn't know he was holding. "So when did you become an environmentalist?"

"I wouldn't call myself an environmentalist, per se," he says. "It's not like I'm about to go sign up with Greenpeace. I just think we all have to share this planet and no one person or group of people can operate in a vacuum. What one does affects all of us, good or bad. Some people just don't seem to get that."

"No, they don't," I reply. "Or they just don't care, which is even worse. At least if you're ignorant you can work to rectify the problem, but if you're willfully destroying on purpose, killing innocent people for example, then you have to be stopped."

"If I had a beer, I'd clink your glass, Slate," he says,

holding up a mock mug. He then turns his attention back to the house, but there's no activity over there. It's all quiet on the Dempsey front.

"Hey, while you're looking, make sure you keep an eye out for any assassins," I say before I realize what's coming out of my mouth. I pause, and take a breath. "I'm sorry. I didn't mean that the way it came out. It's just—"

"You think this whole thing is unnecessary," he says before I can. Though he's a lot more diplomatic in his words.

"Isn't it, though? A bodyguard? Not that I don't like having you around, but I think I can take care of myself. And if I can't, I don't think I'd even see it coming. She's a professional. If she wanted me dead, I would be."

He turns back to me, his eyes turned down, sort of sad. "You're kind of a fatalist, aren't you?"

"Can you blame me?" I ask. "Given everything that's happened." I shake my head, my eyes focusing on my lap. "Part of me wants to believe I can make a difference, that I can really change someone's future. But that only seems to extend to other people. I don't think I can change my own fate. And if it's my destiny to die at the hands of someone just like Matt, then there isn't much I can do about that."

"I'd beg to differ," Liam says. "Why do you think you're different than anyone else? Don't you deserve to have a different future too?"

I rub my fingers over my thumbs a few times. "I don't know. It just seems like if I was an effective agent, I should have seen it coming. I should have been able to save him. But I was too close to see the big picture. That's why I don't like getting close to the people in any of my cases, it allows me to keep a bird's eye view of everything. I can see the threats before they happen. I just can't do it for anyone I'm close to. Or myself."

"Sounds like you're making excuses to me," he says and goes back to watching the house.

I look up. "What's that supposed to mean?"

"I mean it looks like you're looking for a reason why you shouldn't have a future, instead of accepting your mistakes and moving on."

I feel my pulse quickening. I don't like the fact he's questioning my guilt. "Easy for you to say. You're not in my position."

"No, and I'm not trying to be. I'm just saying that you seem like you've already made up your mind about your future and there's no way to change it. And because you can't change it, you can't be held at fault when something goes wrong again. You're absolving your responsibility to yourself."

His words hit me like I've been slapped. Suddenly my palms are clammy, and I can't seem to get my breathing under control. "How dare you," I growl.

"Tell me I'm wrong," Liam says, dead serious. "You screwed up, and it cost you the most important part of your life. You're afraid if you screw up again, you'll be next. So you've just decided that there's nothing that can be done about it. It's convenient…and easier to live with."

"You know what? Fuck you," I say and open my door, stepping out into the afternoon sun. I storm down the sidewalk across from Dempsey's house, my worries about his schedule having been shoved to the back of my mind. I can't believe Liam just called me out like that. Who does he think he is, trying to psychoanalyze me? He might as well have just called me a coward.

"Emily, wait," he calls but I ignore him. I don't care if he's worried about his duty to keep an eye on me. I don't even care if Zach Dempsey drives up right now and sees us. All I can think about is seeing Matt's dead body slumped over on our floor, unmoving. About how I thought it was all a terrible accident, only to learn that he'd been targeted—killed by some unknown person for some unknown reason.

I flex my fists as I think about how she tried to tell me he wasn't the man I thought he was, that he'd been lying to me for our entire relationship. And part of me hates that I believed her. That I still believe her, even if the emotional part of my brain doesn't want to admit it.

All of that means that not only did I not protect him like I should have, but he was playing me for four years and I never suspected a thing. I couldn't even do the one thing I was trained to do, which was look someone in the eye and tell if they were lying or not. I spot a branch on the ground and pick it up, then bring it down again, slamming it against the concrete, over and over until it breaks into tiny shards. By the time its little more than a handle in my hands, I'm out of breath and my face is burning up.

"Emily…"

I spin to find Liam standing there, his arms heavy and his shoulders pulled low. His brows are knitted and there's a pained expression in his eyes. "I didn't mean—"

"It's fine," I say, throwing away what's left of the branch. It hits the underbrush and disappears.

"No, I shouldn't have said those things."

I stare at him, making sure I catch his eyes. "I'd rather you always tell me what you're really feeling, than tell me a lie that you think will make me feel better. I've had too many people in my life lie to me, and I don't need any more of that." I turn and walk a few more steps before finally just sitting down on the concrete sidewalk and drawing my legs up to my chest.

Liam comes and squats beside me but doesn't sit. "Still. I didn't mean to be cruel."

I turn away from him. "You weren't cruel. You were right."

"What?"

I turn back and can't keep my eyes from welling up. "You don't think I know what I am? It's not in the reports yet, but she emailed me, when we were in New York. Sent a bunch of documentation showing that Matt wasn't who he said he was.

Zara told me to ignore it, but I could see in her eyes that she
had doubts once she looked it over. And the worst part was I
didn't even consider Matt wasn't who he said he was up until
that moment. I already know that I'm a fraud. Because any
agent worth her salt would have seen that a mile away."

"You're not a fraud. A fraud wouldn't have figured out
Gerald Wright was a serial killer. Or found Hannah Stewart,
alive and well. Or uncovered the truth behind all those fires
down in Charleston."

I look up, surprised. "You've been following all my cases?"
I ask.

He nods. "A fraud wouldn't have found out who killed that
FBI agent and brought her to justice." He points right to the
center of my chest. "Because you're *not* a fraud. Everyone is
allowed to make mistakes, Em. It's how we improve."

I scoff, wiping away a few tears. "Pretty big mistakes."

"That's what makes you one of the best. You wouldn't be
where you are if you did everything right the first time."

"Thanks," I say, laying my head on my knees. I'm so
conflicted. Something is pulling me toward Liam like the
world's strongest magnet, but at the same time, I still feel a
loyalty to Matt, even if he did lie. And given that I'm taking
the word of a known assassin as the basis of my belief, maybe
I should reserve judgement until we find out the real truth. At
least one thing is for certain, I can trust Liam to be honest
with me, no matter how hard that honesty is. And that in itself
is invaluable.

I take a deep breath and push myself back up, Liam
standing at the same time. "I think I need a drink."

"You and me both," he says. "Once we get hold of this
guy, I'll buy you a round."

I wipe my eyes again and recenter myself. "Sounds good
to me." We both head back to the car, walking over the splin-
tered remains of the tree branch. I haven't lost control like
that in a long time, but it felt good to let loose.

"Guess it's a good thing Dempsey isn't a homebody," Liam says, "Otherwise he might have witnessed that whole thing."

"I doubt it," I say. "He probably wouldn't leave his mirror unless a nuclear bomb went off beside his house."

Liam chuckles. "I can't wait until we meet this guy, and he turns out to be the sweetest, most caring and thoughtful person you've ever met. I'm gonna make you eat whatever picture you've built up of him in your head."

"Fine, don't believe me," I say. "But you just wait and see. He's gonna be a self-centered, egotistical meathead. No question."

Liam gives me a sly look, telling me he's got something up his sleeve. He pulls out his phone, opening up what looks like a betting app. "Okay Slate. How about we make this interesting?"

I'm not a gambler. Not usually anyway. But in this case, I'll make an exception. "You're on."

Chapter Twenty-Four

IT ONLY TAKES TWENTY MORE MINUTES FOR ZACH TO SHOW UP at his house, driving the vehicle Orlando described to us. Since we're parked a few houses down and are mixed in with other cars parked on the street, I'm not worried he's looking for us.

"Looks like a 2015 Ford F150, maroon," Liam says more for his own benefit than mine. I got the DMV records while we were waiting and found out that his mother originally purchased the truck, then transferred ownership to him when he turned eighteen. I'm willing to bet he didn't pay a dime for it.

"Nice too," Liam adds, looking through the binoculars. "Custom trim, rollbar in the back. Seems Zach is putting all his extra dough into his truck."

"I can't wait to get a look inside that thing," I say. "Odds are we find evidence of Summer inside. Probably a hair or maybe even skin cells." From what I can tell he's a strong-looking kid. Strong enough to haul a body out into the middle of the woods. And according to the locals, the spot where she was found is a known hang out for teenagers who like to have fun on the weekends, so it would have been a place he knew.

"He's getting out." Liam leans forward with the binoculars.

"Does he have any visible cuts or scars?"

He shakes his head. "Can't tell from here. He's facing away from us. Maybe when he comes back outside again."

It doesn't take long. By five-thirty Zach appears at the door to his house and locks up, headed back to the truck. "Don't see any scratches from here," Liam says. "At least none that are visible."

"Did he just pop his collar?" I ask, squinting.

"Um…yes, I believe he did."

"Okay, that's it," I say. "I'm calling the D.A. We need the warrant."

Liam arches his eyebrow at me. "Because of the popped collar?"

"That was just the straw," I say. "I don't like the idea of him driving around out here thinking he got away scot-free. He may lead us to his partner, and then again, he may not. I'd rather have him in custody and squeeze him than let him roam free all night. Who's to say he doesn't go out and do it again?"

Liam nods. "Fair point."

It takes me a minute to call the local D.A., who just happens to be on his way out the office for a weekend off. Thankfully, with Orlando's testimony, I'm able to convince him that an expedited warrant is not only necessary, but prudent at this point.

While I'm waiting on the phone, Zach backs out and roars down the road, completely ignoring us. Liam follows at a reasonable distance, just far enough so that he doesn't suspect anything. By the time the D.A. calls me back telling me we have the go-ahead, Zach has crossed over into Delaware, and is in the middle of Mardel, headed to who-knows-where. While it's unlikely he even knows we're on to him, I can't take the chance he goes out and starts prowling for another victim.

Any further hesitancy on our part could result in loss of life and that's just not something I'm willing to chance.

"Okay," I tell Liam. "Judge signed off on it, based on what we learned. And surprisingly I've got back up from Quaker's officers on the way."

"She offered to help?"

"Didn't blink an eye." I'm confounded too, but I'm not going to question it now. My main concern is right out in front of us.

Liam looks over. "Do we wait on them?"

"I think we can take an eighteen-year-old," I reply. "Let's see what we can get out of him."

Liam pulls forward until he's in front of Zach's truck, then slows to the point where he's forced to stop or run over us. Zach makes a handful of gestures at us through his windshield which leave nothing to the imagination.

I take a breath to steady myself and pull my service weapon. "Here we go," I say. I get out of the car and level my weapon at him. "Zachary Dempsey. FBI. Step out of your vehicle!"

His hands go up. "Whoa, what the hell?"

I position myself behind my open door to give me cover, in the event he has the gun on him. "Roll down your window, place your hands outside where I can see them."

For a second, he stares at me like he's not going to do it, then he rolls the window down and I see both his palms extend out.

"Open the door from the outside," I say and step out, keeping both hands visible to me at all times."

He does as I ask, stepping out of the vehicle while leaving it running and the door open. It's almost like he's done this before.

"Lay down on the ground, face down. Place your hands on the back of your head. Slowly." I say, making sure my finger is close, but not on the trigger of my weapon. It doesn't look to me like he's armed, but it's always the ones who don't look it who are the most dangerous.

"Are you insane?" he finally says, sinking down to his knees.

"Lay down flat, place your hands on the back of your head," I say again.

"You can't do this," he protests, but he takes another look at the weapon pointed right at his face and decides not to chance it. He gets all the way down on his belly, placing his hands on the back of his head. I circle around the car until I have a clear shot on him while Liam gets out of the driver's side and places a cuff on one of his hands before wrenching it to his back.

"Watch it!" Dempsey yells. I have to admit, he's not as frightened as I'd hoped he'd be. Which only leads more credence to my theory that he's our killer. Someone who has just taken two lives won't be rattled by the FBI. But an innocent person would.

Liam finishes cuffing him before standing him back up while I holster my weapon. "Zachary Dempsey, you are under arrest for the murders of Brady and Summer Sanford," I say, then read him his Miranda rights. The whole time he's looking at me with a mix of amusement and revulsion, like this is some big joke to him.

"Lady, I don't know who you think you are, but you're messing with the wrong person," he says as we lead him to my car and put him in the back seat. I hear sirens in the distance. Good to know Quaker didn't stonewall us.

"Is that what you said to Summer Sanford before you choked her to death?" I ask before slamming the door. I turn to Liam. "Pretty clean."

He nods. "The best arrest is one where no shots are fired."

"Agreed," I say.

Moments later the Mardel police arrive. I coordinate with them to transport Zach to their headquarters while we wait for a tow truck to come and transport his vehicle. As we're waiting, Liam and I take the opportunity to inspect the back-seats, though we don't immediately see anything. "Hopefully the techs can find something," I say.

"Yeah, I don't get the sense Dempsey is willing to give up a DNA sample," Liam says.

"Doesn't matter. Given what we have, we can compel him. And I'm pretty sure he's going to be a match to one of those two semen samples."

"What about the other man?" he asks.

I place my hands on my hips. "That's where this gets tricky."

An hour later Zach Dempsey's truck is in the police impound lot and Zach himself is in an interrogation room in Quaker's station. We arrive to the station just as I'm finishing up my update call with Janice.

"Sounds like you have your hands full down there," my boss says.

"Somehow, I always seem to get the complex cases," I tell her. "Has there been any update on my case yet?"

"I'm waiting to hear back from Zara," she says. "She was supposed to report in after she tracked down a lead this afternoon, but I haven't heard back from her yet. As soon as I do, I'll let you know."

"I'd appreciate it," I say. "In the meantime, we'll work on finding our second unsub."

"Good hunting," Janice says and ends the call.

"Any update?" Liam asks.

I place my phone back in my pocket and get out of the car. "Nothing yet. But Zara is working on it. If I don't hear back from Janice once we're done with Dempsey, I'll give her a call."

We head into the station only to find Chief Quaker standing right at the front desk, speaking with the sergeant on duty.

"Chief." I nod. "Where's our suspect?"

"In interrogation two," she replies, a smile on her face. It's a genuine smile too, not the sour one she left us with when we began searching the Sanford's home. I don't understand her extreme mood swings. I figured we'd made another enemy for life when we shunned her for opening an investigation on Black.

"Has he said anything?" I ask.

"Just that he wants his phone call and his lawyer," she replies. "So I'm afraid you're out of luck. Still, it's a good collar."

I furrow my brow. "Thanks. We'll take a shot at him anyway, see if he'll open up at all. But he strikes me as someone who has been through this before, so I'm not surprised he knows not to speak to us."

"Oh, he's definitely been in the system before," she says, grinning.

"Wait," I say. "Do you know him?"

"Of course," she replies, her grin growing even larger. "That's Big John's kid. Didn't you know?"

I exchange glances with Liam. "How would we have known that?" I ask. "He's got a different last name."

"It's his mother's name, he lives with her most of the time, down in Fairview. Kid has been a thorn in my side for years. If he's the one who really did this, it will be better for everyone in this community." She chuckles as she walks off.

"Great." No wonder she was so anxious to help us. "This isn't going to make things any easier." With Zach being Sheriff Black's son, it's only going to deepen the rift between the two communities. Not to mention it's going to call into question Black's original investigation. Now I have to determine if Black knew his son was involved and conspired to cover up the facts of the crime.

"What do we do now?" Liam asks.

"We'll deal with Black later," I say. "Right now, we have a suspect to interrogate. I'm going in there to see if I can get anything out of him. Can you run a check and make sure he doesn't have any brothers who might have done this with him? The last thing we need is to find out both our perpetrators have been under our noses this entire time." I watch Chief Quaker make her way down the hall. "I'm willing to bet the chief has changed her mind on giving you a space to work."

He nods. "You sure you don't need backup in there?"

I head for interrogation two. "Trust me, I can handle him."

Chapter Twenty-Five

I TAKE A FEW MINUTES TO READ THE FILE QUAKER HAS ON Dempsey. He's got a sheet going back four years, back to his first offense with vandalism in his early teens. Ever since then it's been a string of misdemeanors, though with each successive one, it seems Quaker has come down harder and harder on the boy, doing her ever best to convict him and try to lock him up. I don't know if she's this way with all her juvenile delinquents, but it certainly explains the animosity between her and Sheriff Black. It seems like Quaker has been waiting for this moment a long time, and I've just delivered for her.

While his sheet is longer than I would expect for someone of his age, I'm not entirely sure someone goes from shoplifting and drunk driving to murder, but stranger things have happened. I decide to leave the file outside the interrogation room and instead head in with nothing but my wits.

Zach Dempsey sits behind the metal table, looking bored out of his mind. He's slouched to one side, glaring up at the ceiling when I come in. He still wears the cuffs, though they've been transferred to his front, but they haven't locked him to the table yet. From his body posture and what I observe, I'm assuming Dempsey isn't in any discomfort here.

"Lawyer," he says before I can even get a word out.

I nod, taking my time before sitting down across from him. I don't say anything, just train my gaze on his face, doing my ever best not to break eye contact. He shifts in his chair a few times, then gives me a sardonic smile before going back to staring at the ceiling.

I see he's no amateur, so I can't treat him like one. I just lean back in my chair and begin tapping on the table with my fingernail, watching him, seeing if I can get anything from him.

"Really?" he finally asks after about a minute of tapping. "Is this your strategy? Try and unnerve me? I've already said I want a lawyer. I'm not telling you shit."

I give him a subtle nod and just keep tapping away, watching him the entire time. The longer I stare the more uncomfortable he becomes, finally turning away from me so he doesn't have to see me. But I don't break eye contact. I just keep watching the side of his head, and I catch his eyes flit to the side to see if I'm still trained on him.

"Look, you're wasting your time. Isn't this harassment or something?" he asks, turning back to me.

I don't even give him an iota of response, instead I just keep watching him. I've made sure my FBI badge is visible on my blazer from where I'm sitting, so every time he looks at me, he sees those big blue letters. I catch his gaze glance down every so often and I can tell it's having the desired effect. Had I come in here all combative, I'm sure he would have been happy to stonewall me to eternity. But this is a more calculated move, something to make him jumpier.

He makes a dismissive sound and turns away again; it seems Zach Dempsey can't take as much heat as he thinks he can.

There's a knock on the door behind me, but instead of getting up, I don't move. Dempsey however, looks over at the door. "Aren't you going to get that?" he asks. I just keep staring, only this time I narrow my eyes.

The knock comes again, more urgent this time. And still I ignore it. Dempsey looks from the door to me, like he's hoping I'll finally get up and grant him some relief. But I don't. I stay rooted to the spot, glaring at him like he's my next meal.

Finally the door behind me opens and I sense the presence of more than one person coming into the room. "Agent, what are you doing to my client?"

I still don't take my gaze of Dempsey to look at the speaker, but I can already tell by his tone and intonation he's the kid's lawyer. The light hint of Liam's cologne tells me he's right behind him.

"Just keeping an eye on him," I say.

"This is harassment," the lawyer says, and I finally look over at him. He's an older gentleman, probably in his early sixties, dressed in a well-fitting gray suit. His face is small, and most of his hair is already gone, giving him a bit of a babyface framed by circular spectacles. He's carrying a small briefcase which I'm sure contains Dempsey's entire record.

"What is harassing about sitting down across from a suspect?" I ask. "Your client is here on a murder charge. And we in the FBI don't like to take our eyes off our most violent offenders." I catch Dempsey's eyes go wide for a moment, as if he only now realizes just how serious all this is.

"That'll be enough, agent," the lawyer says. "I need to speak with my client. In private."

I give Dempsey a smirk before standing back up then turn to see Liam with a peculiar look on his face. He motions for me to follow him back.

"What's wrong?" I ask as soon as we're back out in the hallway.

"*SLATE!*" I turn to see Sheriff Black barreling down the hall, his face beet-red. He's pumping his legs as fast as they'll go without breaking into an all-out sprint. He looks like a bull about to charge down the matador. Immediately I'm on the defensive and I plant my back leg, not about to shy away or move from him. He stops inches from my face, and I can smell the sweat on him, the musk of a man who has been working all day. His breath his heavy and acrid, like he's been chewing on something, and his eyes are boring down into mine. "What in the HELL do you think you're doing?"

"My job," I say, getting even closer to him. "We have an eyewitness who places your son's vehicle at the scene of the crime. Something your deputies conveniently missed."

"How dare you," he growls. "A vehicle on the scene means nothing. Someone else could have been driving."

"Listen to me very carefully, Sheriff," I say. "Back off right now, and I'll forget this. Otherwise, you're looking at an inquiry at best and a full-out investigation at worst. We have semen samples from the men who killed Summer Sanford. And you can rest assured I'm taking a sample from your son before the day is over."

"You can't do that," he replies.

"In an instance where we have evidence your son may have been at the scene, I absolutely can. I don't even have to ask. I will strap him down to a table and take it by force if I have to. Don't think I won't."

"This is bullshit," he says, not backing down. "You can't just come in here and accuse my son of murder like some common criminal."

"Looks to me like he's had a pretty long sheet for someone of his age," I reply. "And right now, I don't care what you think. I'm following the evidence of the case. It just happens to lead back to your son. If I were you, I'd be more worried about what Internal Affairs is going to say when we tell them not only did your men miss key evidence on the night of the crime, they conveniently didn't interview the only witness. How do you think that's going to look on your department and on you? If you're not careful, I'll have you in that interrogation room next."

Black works his jaw, his glare as penetrating as I've ever seen. I can feel the tension in his body, he's as tight as a snare drum. I also expect to be cold-cocked at any second, but right now I don't care. I'm done putting up with incompetent officers, or possibly criminal. There's a good chance Black orchestrated all of this to protect his own son. No matter what happens, it isn't going to look good on the Nanticoke Sheriff's Department or for Black's re-election campaign, assuming he isn't arrested first.

"You're not going to get away with this," he finally says. "I will fight you to my very last breath."

"You're welcome to it, but the truth will come out. It always does."

Finally, he turns and leaves us in the hallway, pushing past one of Quaker's officers. I realize I've been holding my breath and I finally let it out. For a second there I wasn't sure what was about to happen, but I'm not surprised by his reaction. Either he helped his son cover up his crimes, or he was too stupid to know it was happening. Regardless, he's going to be upset.

I turn back to Liam, who is managing to suppress a grin. "I don't think you would have needed it, but I would have held him back if he got physical."

"Thanks," I say. "I wasn't sure myself there for a minute. The man clearly has a temper problem. Which I'm sure is great for his position, you know, trying to protect the innocent and serve the public."

"Sometimes they stay in the job too long and they feel like they can get away with anything," Liam says, no doubt thinking about his own former boss.

I look back at the interrogation room door. With a father like that, no wonder Zach thinks he can get away with anything. I wish we'd had a chance to interrogate him a little more before his lawyer arrived, but it doesn't really matter. Once we get that sample and compare it to what Sharon found, I'm sure we'll have our man. We just need to press Zach so we can find the second person in the car.

"They'll probably be in there a while," Liam says. "Wanna head out for that drink? On a job well done."

I'm hesitant to celebrate with the other killer still out there. "Maybe once we have the other one in custody. I don't want to jinx it."

Liam laughs. "I never would have taken you for the super-stitious type."

I shrug. "Eh, why tempt fate?"

Chief Quaker comes around the corner just as we're about to head out. "I heard I missed quite the show," she says.

"Just Black throwing his weight around to get everyone else to do what he wants," I say.

"Boy, I would have loved to have seen that."

There's that odd enthusiasm again. Though by this point I'm willing to chalk it up to a quirk of hers rather than anything nefarious. "We need a bio sample from Zach Dempsey before his lawyer tries to get him out of here," I tell her. "To compare to the samples Sharon found."

Quaker tilts her head. "Samples?"

"Yeah, the semen samples," I reply. "Did she not tell you?"

"Do you mean to tell me she went ahead with Summer Sanford's autopsy?" Quaker asks, her demeanor changing entirely again.

"She said Metcaffe was out of town. We didn't have the luxury of time. Is there a problem?" Again, I'm confused as to why she seems deferent to Metcaffe. The man is never around anyway.

"I see," Quaker says. "No, no problem. I'll make sure we have a sample from Dempsey."

I don't like the vibe I'm getting here. I don't know what it is, but something has changed about her. "On the other hand,

I need to make my report to my boss. We'll just stick around until they're done in there."

"Don't be silly," Quaker says. "You deserve a night off after all this work you've put in. Take some time for yourselves. Federal agents need breaks too."

I exchange glances with Liam, he seems as unsure as I am. "Okay. Just keep me in the loop."

"Not a problem at all," Quaker says and practically ushers us back down the hallway. "Trust me, we've got this. We're not about to let a violent criminal back out on the streets. If anything happens, I will let you know."

As soon as Liam and I are back outside, I dial Sharon's number. "Hello?"

"Sharon, it's Emily Slate. I know this is an odd call, but where are you right now?"

"Agent Slate, hello," she says. "I'm at home, why?"

"How quickly can you get back to the med lab?"

I hear rustling in the background, like she's getting up. "Why, is there a problem?"

"I'm not sure. I just want to make sure those semen samples are safeguarded." I look over to Liam again, his brows are knitted in concern.

"Well, they're in the refrigerator, which is locked. Only a few people have the key. What is this all about?"

"Just a hunch," I say. "Can you meet us there? I'd feel a lot better if we got eyes on them right now."

"Agent Slate, what is going on?" Sharon asks, her voice growing more concerned.

"I don't know yet. But I have a bad feeling something is about to happen to those samples." I don't like how Quaker seemed to change personalities again when I mentioned them. Like she didn't like that Metcaffe hadn't been the one to do the autopsy. Anyone else wouldn't have cared, as long as it was done professionally. And as far as I can tell, Sharon is more professional than Metcaffe anyway. But Quaker seems to have some strange deference to him.

"All right, I'm on my way. I can meet you there."

"Thank you, Sharon," I say and hang up. I look over at Liam. "Tell me I'm not crazy."

"Something is going on, but I can't figure out what," Liam says. "But I think you're right. Those samples are the keys to the entire case. And seeing how Quaker responded back there, I don't like it any more than you do."

"Good," I say, pulling my keys out. "Get in, cause I'm driving."

Chapter Twenty-Six

"EM, YOU GOTTA SLOW DOWN," LIAM SAYS AS I MAKE A hairpin turn down one of Mardel's streets. I'm rushing because I have a bad feeling deep in the pit of my stomach, one that I can't quite explain. Part of me wants to just let it all go, to take the evening off like Quaker suggested. But the other, stronger part of me needs to make sure those samples are okay. It's almost as if I'm not looking directly at them, they might disappear.

Which I know, *I know*, is crazy. They are in an official lock up behind two layers of security. They are evidence to a murder. No one would mess with them. Hell, most people wouldn't even know they're there. Still…something deep in my gut is telling me we need to get there as fast as possible.

"We're not going to be able to do anything if we're dead," Liam says and I hear the warning in his voice. He's right, I'm pushing it too hard, too fast. I'm being too reckless, which is something I never do. I'm the one who is always measured, who is always looking for the cleanest solution, the non-confrontational way out. Despite that, I seem to always find myself deep in it.

I slow the car. "Sorry, it's just—"

"You're worried, I know," he says. "Let's just get there in one piece. Quaker can't do anything before then. She sure as hell isn't driving faster than you."

I chuckle. "Do you really think something is going on? Or am I just being paranoid?"

He shakes his head. "I don't know. That woman is…odd. Sometimes her mood changes just like that. And other times it's almost like there's a purpose behind them. You wouldn't think she would have made a clean pass on the psych exam."

I concede the point. "That's true. If there was something wrong with her, like really wrong, she wouldn't have made it to police chief. I'm sure this is just me being overly cautious. I just want to make sure." I'm not sure if I suspect Chief Quaker of anything or not, but I feel like if we don't check on these samples, we're going to regret it.

About five minutes later I pull up to Mardel's med lab, and park right in front. The building is dark, a signal that all the staff has already gone home for the evening. Mardel doesn't strike me as the kind of place that operates a twenty-four-seven lab as they probably don't have that much to analyze.

We get out of the car and I begin a visual inspection of the building, though I don't see anything out of place. When I check the front doors, they're locked up tight, but I give them a good rattle anyway. The longer I stand here, the more I begin to think I just ruined Sharon's Friday night for nothing.

Speaking of which, she pulls in only a few minutes later, her low beams cutting across the parking lot. The sun has just disappeared below the horizon, so there's still a little light left in the sky, but not enough to drive-by. She gets out of her car, dressed in sweats and gives me a look that tells me I better be right about this otherwise I'm gonna get an earful.

"Sharon, thank you for coming," I say. "I'm sorry to call you in. This is probably nothing."

"No, it's fine, Agent Slate," she says. "Wasn't doin' nothin' but watchin' TV anyway."

"Pretty woman like you? I don't believe it," Liam says in an attempt to lighten the mood.

Sharon gives him a "really" face causing him to shrink a little. "Don't even start with me. Flattery gets you nowhere."

Liam looks as though he's paled a bit and I hold back a laugh. At least all her ire isn't directed on me, for which I'm grateful.

Sharon unlocks the main doors then flips on the primary lights and leads us down the hallways to the back. "There's a loading dock in the back where we have the bodies delivered," she says as we walk. "Makes things a little easier."

She takes us past where we went over the information on both Summer and Brady Sanford, to a back laboratory. But as soon as she flips on the light to the lab, it's clear something is wrong.

"What the hell?" she says, unlocking the main door quickly. Shards of glass litter the ground where one of the back windows to the building has been smashed. Based on the glass, the window looks like it was broken from the outside. Just as she's about to step into the room, I take her by the shoulder and pull her back.

"Wait here," I tell her, pulling my service weapon. Liam does the same and I motion for him to cover the doorway for me.

"But—"

I place one finger to my lips, willing her to be quiet. Whoever broke in might still be in there. The room itself is made up of what looks like three antechambers, all off the main room here. Liam checks the corner, even though glass partitions allow us to see into the lab itself. He motions for me to go ahead, and I creep into the room, staying low, and then hustle to the doorway to the left, keeping my back up against the wall. The room beyond is still dark. It's times like these when I wish I had my own night-vision goggles. Even though some light filters through the windows in the room beyond, it's not enough to illuminate it all, and I don't know where the switch is.

I reach up and fumble around for a switch on the inside of the room but find nothing. I take a breath and creep inside, noting that I'm stepping on small shards of glass as I do. I try my best to avoid them, but they're everywhere in here. My weapon is extended out in front of me, and my eyes are adjusting to the dark, but I don't see anyone. All I see is a sliver of bright light at the far end of the room, coming from what looks like the middle of the wall. Fortunately, the room isn't that large, and there aren't that many places to hide. The glass trail ends and I'm silent again, creeping ever closer. My heart jumps when I see the sliver of light belongs to a refrigeration unit.

"Dammit, no," I whisper as I reach it and push it open with the barrel of my gun. Inside vials and containers are strewn everywhere, some of them broken and dripping down into the bottom of the unit.

The light in the room comes on and I spin to see Liam standing at the doorway, having flipped on the overhead fluorescents. "Check the other room," I tell him. We both head out past Sharon and I motion for her to stay put. She has her arms around her shoulders hugging herself and nods. Now that we know where the switch is, Liam flips it. Inside this room are nothing but plastic storage containers, some of them stacked three and four high. No people at all.

"Clear," I say, holstering my weapon. I head back to Sharon and pull two pairs of gloves from my pocket, tossing her a pair. "Put these on and try not to touch anything," I tell her. Liam stays behind to examine the broken window while she and I return to the first antechamber. Sharon walks quickly over to the refrigeration unit and now that the lights are on, I see the lock that was on the unit is bent and broken over by the cabinets. A dented fire extinguisher sits up against the close end of the unit.

Sharon opens the cool door all the way and curses when she sees the carnage inside. She turns to me. "They're gone, aren't they?" I ask.

"How did you know?"

"Hey, Em," Liam calls. I bite my lip from saying something stupid when I don't have any evidence yet, but I need to have a serious talk with Chief Quaker. I head back to Liam, who has his own gloves on now and is examining something on the ground near the far wall. "Here."

I bend down to find a large rock, probably at least fifteen or twenty pounds. There are dents and skid marks along the linoleum tile where it landed and came to rest. "Method of entry, I'm assuming."

He nods. "That would be my guess."

"Sharon?" She appears in the doorway. "What time do you normally close up here on Fridays?"

"If there's not a current case, people tend to leave around four or four-thirty if it's a Friday," she replies. "But on the weekdays, they'll stay until six or later. Like the other night, when I was here all night doing the autopsy."

I check my watch. It's four after eight. Which means whoever broke in here did it within the last three hours. But I have a feeling it was much more recent than that. I'm thinking it was within the last thirty minutes. Ever since we informed Chief Quaker about the existence of the samples.

"We're never going to be able to prove she did this," I tell Liam.

"How could she?" he asks. "We came straight here from the station. She wouldn't have had time."

"Unless someone was helping her," I reply. I turn back to Sharon. "Who else knew about the samples?"

"A few of the techs, I suppose. I hadn't told Metcaffe yet because he's still on vacation and the man doesn't like to be bothered when he is."

"Big surprise," I say. "I'd say that narrows our suspect

pool. Can you give me the names and numbers of anyone who works here who might have known about them?"

"Agent Slate, I don't think you understand," Sharon says. "It's not just the samples from Summer Sanford that are missing. It's *all* of them. We had two other cases stored in there. And now they're all gone."

Chapter Twenty-Seven

"THAT'S RIGHT," I SAY INTO MY PHONE. "I THINK WE'RE looking at some kind of conspiracy here."

"That's a serious charge, Agent Slate," Janice says. "What's your evidence?"

"How about the fact thirty minutes after we told Chief Quaker about the semen samples, they've been conveniently stolen?" I ask. "Or the fact that Sheriff Black's son is our primary suspect? I'm telling you, Janice, something is going on. I need a backup team. We can't trust either of these units to have our backs."

"I understand where you're coming from, Agent Slate, what sort of backlash from the local LEOs will we be looking at? Will bringing in more agents put what you have at risk?"

She brings up a good point. Neither side likes the fact we're here. Bringing in even more agents could exacerbate the situation. Someone might get nervous and take chances they don't need to. "Unclear. At least it will allow us to investigate every avenue of this case without second-guessing ourselves. I wouldn't be making the request if I thought it was superfluous. I hope you know that about me by now."

There's a pause on the other end of the line. "Very well.

I'll start putting a small team together and send them your way as soon as I can. But you'll be on your own until they arrive."

"Thank you, I appreciate that," I tell her.

"In the meantime, you're going to have to follow normal procedure. But do not let Chief Quaker know that you may suspect her."

"What do we do with the facility?" I ask. "We have a crime scene here."

"I'll call the Chesapeake field office and see if they can't spare anyone. They should only be about two and a half hours from your location. Until then, secure the scene and wait."

Janice has known me long enough to know I don't "wait" well. Especially not when we're looking at what is beginning to amount to a conspiracy. "Yes ma'am," I say begrudgingly.

"Good work on this Slate," she says. "Keep me apprised of any changes." She hangs up before I can get another word in.

"Great talking to you too," I mutter, then head back over to Liam and Sharon. "Doctor, head back home. There isn't anything else you can do for us this evening. We have additional agents on their way up to help with the investigation. I'll let you know if we find anything."

Sharon huffs. "Be sure that you do. Those other cases were both sexual assaults. We were waiting for the all clear from Quaker before sending them off for analysis. That's two more predators out there that just got away."

I clench my fists. "Believe me, I'm as mad about this as you are. But until we have evidence to link someone to this crime, we have to treat it like any other case."

She shakes her head. "I don't like it. How did you know?"

I avert my eyes. "I'm sorry, I can't talk about it. Not while the investigation is ongoing."

Sharon purses her lips and heads back to her car. "Something stinks here, agent," she calls back. "I just hope you find out where it's coming from before it's too late." She gets in and drives off.

"Me too," I say.

"Waiting again," Liam says. "I see what you mean."

I nod. "The other agents from Chesapeake shouldn't be too long. I don't want to leave the crime scene until someone decides to come back to try and cover their tracks."

"Great," he says, leaning back up against the hood of my car. "And here I was thinking we'd get to spend Friday night celebrating."

"Nothing is ever that simple," I tell him, leaning beside him on my hood. "I guess we'll have to have that drink another time."

"Good things come to those who wait," he says with a completely straight face. I make a slow turn and glare at him before busting out laughing.

"What the hell was that?" I ask.

"Sorry, I am shit at flirting," he replies, his face going red, though he joins me in the laugh.

"You're not as bad as you think," I reply, and I realize I am dangerously close to the line here. But part of me doesn't care, part of me wants to see where this goes. I've essentially been alone for the past seven months. Were it not for Zara, I probably would have either lost myself completely in work, or I would have just stayed home on the couch for weeks at a time. It's only recently that I've been able to reconnect with what little family I have. And now this opportunity is here, staring me right in the face. And I'm not sure what to do. I like Liam…a lot. But at the same time, I don't want to ruin what we have. I think the guilt of losing someone else might be the final straw. And yet, at the same time, I'm curious.

My phone buzzing in my pocket interrupts my thoughts and I give him a quick smile before answering. "Slate."

"Em, hey."

I push off the car. "Zara, what's wrong? You sound…I dunno, anxious."

"Yeah, I've been putting off this call all day. I just spoke to Janice; she gave me an update on what's going on there. Are you okay?"

I frown. "Of course. Why wouldn't I be?"

"No reason," she says, though I'm not sure I believe her. "Did Janice tell you what happened?"

"No," I say, even more concerned now. "Why? What's going on?"

Zara hesitates. "That's odd. I wonder why she wouldn't tell you?"

"You're killing me, here. What is it already?" I ask, shooting a look back at Liam. His features are knitted in concern.

"Okay, don't freak out. Are you sitting down?"

"I swear, if you don't tell me right now, I'm gonna find a way to reach through this phone—"

"Okay, okay, jeez!" she says. "I just want to make sure you're prepared. I found Garrett."

Brian Garrett. Matt's boss at Covington. "Where?"

"In an office building down in Quincy Heights if you can believe it. He looks exactly the same."

"You saw him?" I ask. "Why didn't you call me earlier?" I can't believe she would leave me hanging like this.

"I spoke to him, Em. And guess what, he's scared stiff. Nearly twisted my ankle trying to run him down. He's also in amazing shape."

"Are you okay?" I ask.

"Sure, nothing that some ice and rest won't fix," she replies. "I'm actually icing it now. But that's not what I needed to tell you. Garrett is working downtown under a pseudonym. He knows what happened to Matt was no accident."

"Son of a bitch, I knew it," I say, turning in a half-circle away from Liam so he can't see the frustration on my face. "He was lying right to our faces all through the funeral."

"Yep," she says, conviction in her voice. "And you don't get to feel bad about this one, because none of us saw it. He's a trained liar."

"What did he say?" I ask. "Verbatim."

"He said we didn't know what we were getting ourselves into. That the FBI couldn't protect Matt, and that we wouldn't be able to protect you. I'm not sure if that was meant as a threat or a warning, but he knows something."

I feel like someone has released a thousand bees in my stomach. All of a sudden it's all in knots and I pitch forward, but manage to keep myself from going all the way down.

"Em!" Liam yells and in an instant he's got me by the arm and shoulder, helping me stand. I take the opportunity to lean my weight into him.

"Are you still there?" Zara asks. "Em, are you okay?"

"I'm here," I tell her. I nod to Liam that I'm all right and he lets go. "He knew. He knew this whole time."

"Seems like it," she says. "I don't know if he's in contact with the woman who killed Matt or not, but he has some information on it, that's for sure."

"Where is he now?" I ask.

There's that hesitation again. "Em, I'm so sorry. I tried as best I could, but he got away from us."

I barely manage to keep from screaming out loud. But I'm gritting my teeth so hard I think they might crack.

"We set up a perimeter, he got on the train at Georgetown but when it got to the next stop, the team couldn't find him. It's like he jumped off halfway, which is impossible."

"What about where he was working? What was he doing there?" I ask.

"I have no idea. The business has no identification and the lease was some business that doesn't exist down in the Caribbean. It had to have been a front of some kind, because when we went back, the place was already empty. Apparently only a few people had been working there. But one of the teams is doing a deep dive into the location now, trying to find out exactly who worked there, and what they were doing. I'm really surprised Janice didn't tell you any of this. She's been heading things up since we lost Garrett."

"She didn't say a word," I reply. I don't know if it's because she wants me focused on the job at hand here, or if she's intentionally trying to obscure things from me, but I don't appreciate it. And we are going to have a long talk when I get back.

"Em, I'm really sorry to tell you, but from everything I've found, it looks like Matt really wasn't who he said he was. None of his credentials are holding up. I don't know what he was a part of, but I can't find anything about it." I can hear the contrition in her voice. It's not Zara's fault; I know she's working as hard as she can to get to the bottom of this.

"I know you did your best," I say. "Thank you. And I really am glad you're okay. I don't want you putting yourself in danger for me, understand?"

She trills on the other end of the phone. "Heh, sorry Em, but I'm not about to break my streak. There hasn't been a lead yet that I haven't tracked down. Can't stop won't stop."

That elicits a small grin from me. "Just be careful. Please."

"You too," she says. "It sounds like you're in a war down there."

"Not far from it." I can already feel the energy draining from my body. It's like I've been hit by a Mack truck and am still spinning. But the ground is growing ever closer.

"Get some rest. Like I said, I wasn't going to tell you until you got back, but I figured you deserved to know."

"Thank you," I say. "I'd rather know than not."

"Take care, Em. I'll see you when you get back." We say our goodbyes and I hang up, then sink to the ground, where I take a seat on the pavement. My entire body feels numb. It's true, he really was lying to me throughout our entire marriage. I never even knew who he really was. And not only that, but he did it convincingly for four years. Anger and outrage suddenly replaces the numbness. I can't believe he would do that to me. I thought we had a good relationship. Sure, it was strained at times. But I was trying as hard as I could. And to find out that none of it was real to him...was I just part of some cover? Was I nothing more than a tool to him?

I can't help it; the tears spill out of my eyes. I hate myself for getting emotional over him. Over someone who clearly didn't love me, despite telling me that he did every day we were together. How had he done it so convincingly?

I gradually become aware of someone else crouching close to me. I turn and see Liam nearby. He's crouched down low, watching me with a careful expression. I wipe my eyes with the back of my arm. "It's...it's not great news," I say.

He shakes his head. "You don't have to tell me. I'm just here if you need something."

"Thank you," I say. I really don't have the energy to go through all of it again. I need to sit with this a while before I'm really going to be able to accept it. I just can't believe that assassin was telling the truth.

The case. Focus on the case. I take a deep breath, then exhale and get up. Liam makes a motion to help me, but I wave him off. I can handle this; I just need time. But as I'm standing, I realize he's closer than I thought. I can still smell his after-shave, and it feels familiar...safe. Before I know it, my lips are pressed up against his, hard. It's all I want in the moment, and I'm not even thinking of the consequences. For once, it feels good not to worry about them. I need this more than I've needed anything else in a long time.

Fortunately, he doesn't pull away, at least not at first. When I finally take a breath he takes me by the shoulders, looking deep into my eyes. "Emily...are you—"

As if to answer I push myself up against him, hard enough

that both of our bodies hit the side of my car and my lips are on his again. I fumble with the door handle to the back. Liam attempts to duck down while kissing me and laying backward at the same time, and only succeeds in thumping the back of his head against the door frame. We both can't help but laugh, which only dissolves any remaining tension between us. Liam slides into the backseat and I'm on top of him a moment later, finding myself lost in his smell, in his embrace, in his everything.

They say there's something raw and primal about sex in the back of a car. I think I finally understand what they're talking about.

The world drifts away and it's just us.

Chapter Twenty-Eight

THE PART THEY *DON'T* TELL YOU ABOUT SEX IN THE BACK OF A car is how uncomfortable it is. There isn't a lot of room so once the main event is over, it isn't like we can both lie next to each other, staring out the fogged-up glass with wistful smiles on our lips, my hand on his chest and his arm around my shoulder, covers pulled just high enough.

No, instead it's more like awkward positioning and trying to get clothes back on while not bumping into each other, the roof of the car, or the front seats. Neither of us has said anything, and I'm sure he's worried he's screwed up. I thought I would feel more guilty, but instead I feel a sense of release. It's like a weight has been removed from my back, one that I've been carrying for months. My inner self tries to make me feel guilty for not feeling more guilty and I just shove it all back down. I'm not getting into that cycle again—I've been there too many times before.

We finish dressing in silence and finally I get the door back open and step out into the evening breeze. The night has cooled off a lot. While Liam finishes in the back of the car, I head back to the med lab, stopping in the lobby where a vending machine sits. A minute later I'm back outside as Liam is attempting to get the wrinkles out of his jacket. Finally he gives up and tosses it into the backseat.

I smile and hand him one of the two waters I retrieved from the vending machine. I feel like I've sweated off the better part of a pound.

"Thanks," he says, though he won't meet my eye. I can tell he's embarrassed, though he shouldn't be.

"That's one way to pass the time," I tell him. "I guess I'll need to include that in my report to Janice."

His gaze snaps to mine, his eyes as wide as saucers, causing me to bust out laughing. Finally he grins then shakes his head, opening his water. "Very funny, Slate."

"I thought so," I say, then take a gulp of my own.

"You don't regret it?" he asks.

I pause, making sure I have his attention. "What's to regret? I had fun. Didn't you?"

He grins. "Maybe a little too much."

I "clink" my water bottle with his. "That's the best kind." I haven't been with anyone since before Matt died. And even then, our schedules made intimacy hard. He'd usually be asleep when I got home and out the door by the time I got up. Thinking on it now, I wonder what he was really doing, since he wasn't going to what I assumed was his job.

I don't let myself fall down that pit again. I'm sick of thinking about it. About him. I've spent entirely too much time worrying about my dead husband when it turns out he never was who he said he was. I'm much more interested in figuring out what's going on with this case.

"So…what does this mean, for the future?" Liam asks.

I shake my head. "I don't know. I guess we'll just see what happens," I say. What I'm really saying is I need time to figure things out. I don't know if I want another serious relationship. Though since Liam is in the Bureau, at least we would understand each other a little better. Then again, the total homogeneity might make things too familiar all the time.

All I know is right now a relationship is not at the top of my priorities.

It's another hour and a half before the other agents arrive. Thankfully Liam and I manage to shoot the breeze without making things weird, which I take as a good sign. I wish we could get back out there and confront Quaker, but given it's the middle of the night and we have no evidence that this was specifically her, it isn't like I could go off and accuse her anyway.

We give the other agents the rundown of the scene, showing them everything and giving them a heads up about Zach Dempsey and everything we've learned. The Agent-in-Charge, Jennifer Becker, seems like she has a good head on her shoulders. She's a senior agent, having been with the Bureau twice as long as I have. Thankfully, she doesn't try to take over the investigation, and leaves us to continue heading it up while her team works as our backup.

Once I'm convinced they have things at the medlab under control, Liam and I head back to the hotel for some rest. We've been going nonstop all day and we both need sleep. Though I find once I'm in bed that I'm wide awake, thinking about all the events of the day. The particulars of the case whirl around my brain, all these disparate elements that won't come together. I know everything fits together; I just can't see it all yet. Why would Zach Dempsey help commit a double homicide? Because he's the sheriff's son and thinks he can get away with it? Seems like a stretch unless he really is a sociopath. But since I can't interrogate him, it's difficult for me to make that determination. I know he's got a healthy hatred of authority, probably from growing up with his dad in a house that was defined by the law. No wonder he started rebelling early. But it's a big jump to murder and I'm not sure Dempsey has it in him.

Regardless, we're going to have to confront Quaker tomorrow and I don't know whether to play stupid and try to take her back into our confidence or if it would be better to lay out what we know and see if the pressure makes her snap. Whatever we end up doing, we still have one more killer out there somewhere. And now that we no longer have the semen samples, I fear we'll have to let Dempsey go.

I end up tossing and turning half the night. It might be my imagination, but I think I hear Liam in the next room over doing the same thing. It's funny, the two of us, separated by nothing but a wall, both probably restless all night. Though I'm willing to bet he's restless for a different reason. I don't know what he's thinking, or what his plans for the future are, all I know is that ever since I've met him, I've felt this magnetic pull toward him. And after everything that happened tonight, I still feel it. Which makes me think I made the right decision. I hope so at least.

"Morning," Liam says as I reach the hotel's small lobby. He looks freshly pressed and is wearing a different suit jacket than yesterday. Remembering what happened to the other one makes me smile a little.

"Morning, unfortunately I think we'll have to skip the biscuits and gravy. I want to get back over to the station."

He nods. "Understood. What do we do about Quaker?" I'm glad to see he's not letting last night affect his work. We're both back to being professional this morning, another good sign.

"We wait until we get something back from Becker," I say. "I don't want to go back in there accusing her of something she may not have been a part of. Could it have been a huge coincidence that right after we tell her the semen samples exist, someone breaks into the medlab and steals their entire stock? Yes. Do I believe for a second she wasn't involved? Not at all. But if we accuse her without something to back it up, we're screwed."

"So, we just say nothing?" Liam asks. "She could be responsible for allowing two killers and possibly two other rapists to go free."

"I know, I don't like it either," I say. "Hopefully Becker's people can find something. But we'll have to make a decision on Dempsey. Either we charge him or let him go. And without the DNA to match, I'm not sure we can hold him."

What I can't figure out is if Quaker is involved, why would she want to protect Dempsey? He's the son of her sworn enemy. With those samples we could have nailed him to the wall for good. I'm still going to insist he give us a sample because as soon as his lawyer finds out we've lost some of the evidence we had for the case, he'll go straight to the D.A.

"This whole thing is a mess," Liam says.

"Damn right." We head out to the car and make it back to the precinct before there are too many other cars in the lot. However, one large black car stands out among all the others. I curse under my breath as we both get out and head into the building.

"I don't care what evidence you have; he's not staying here a second longer!" a booming voice announces as we walk through the front door. Sure enough, Sheriff Black and Chief Quaker are mere inches from each other's faces, both of them looking like they've been screaming at the other for the better part of an hour.

"I've got an eyewitness John," Quaker spits back. "So get used to it. He's not going anywhere." She turns when she sees us out of her peripheral vision. "Right, agents?"

Black turns as well, and it looks like a couple of capillaries have burst in his eyes. His entire forehead is covered in a slick sheen, and he's doesn't look like he's changed since yesterday when we last saw him. "I want to talk to this witness," he says. "This is all bullshit and I'm not gonna let you get away with it.

He has an alibi that night, somethin' his lawyer has repeatedly tried to tell you."

My stomach drops. I hadn't heard anything about an alibi. "Is that true, Chief? Does he have an alibi for Sunday?"

Quaker just rolls her eyes. "After you two left last night, his lawyer said he was home all night."

"Ask me how I know that," Black says. I wait for him to continue. "It's 'cause it was his weekend to stay with me. So I know where he was."

"You saw him all night?" I ask.

Black stops for a second, then regains him posture. "He was in his room."

"And is his room on the first or second floor of your house?" I ask.

"First."

"Has he ever snuck out at night before?"

I didn't think Black's face could get any redder. "That's not the point," he yells. "I know he was in there all night."

"Did you check on him?" I ask. "Did you make sure he was in there like he says he was?"

"He's not five, I don't need to check on him. He's an adult for chrissakes."

"So he could have snuck out and returned without you knowing," I say. Black looks like he's about to blow a fuse. I turn to Quaker. "Do we have a DNA sample from him yet?"

"They're prepping him now. We kept him in the overnight lockup. His lawyer said he'd be back this morning as well."

Great, just what we need. What's strange is Quaker seems adamant about keeping Dempsey here, just as I figured. Nothing about this case makes any sense and it's beginning to aggravate me.

"I'm done arguin', I'm takin' my son," Black says. "I'll hold him at my station if I have to. I don't care what any of you say." He begins to head through the back.

"That's right John, you go ahead and try to remove a

suspect from my custody. See what happens," Quaker calls after him. It doesn't slow him down. This situation is quickly spiraling out of control. If I don't do something, these two are going to end up killing each other.

"Sheriff, don't force my hand," I call after him. "This is not your precinct and not your jurisdiction here. You try and remove your son it's aiding and abetting a suspect, which means we'll have to arrest you." That stops him. He turns and looks over his shoulder. "Don't make this any worse for your-self than it already is," I tell him.

"Is there a problem here?" I turn to see Dempsey's stick-like lawyer, standing at the entrance to the door. He wipes his glasses with a small rag, then returns them to his face.

"Your client's father is about to commit a felony," I say.

The lawyer breezes past me, ignoring the rest of us. He walks up to Sheriff Black and begins whispering in his ear. A moment later Black's shoulders begin to drop as the fight goes out of him. The lawyer turns back to Quaker. "I under-stand my client is due to provide a DNA sample this morning."

She nods. "We're getting him ready right now."

"I will need to be present," the man says. Quaker nods and leads him to the door to the back, ignoring Sheriff Black. Black remains rooted where he is. I'm not sure what his plans are, but his son's weak alibi will never hold up. We might still have a case even without the DNA. I motion for Liam to follow me and we both head in the back, leaving Black alone with the desk sergeant up front.

"This is really getting to him," Liam says.

"You're right," I say. "He seems determined to get his son out of here." As we head to the back, I stop one of the clerks and ask them for Dempsey's file again. I only gave it a brief once-over yesterday, but I want to take a closer look.

She returns a minute later with the file and Liam and I take a couple of empty desks. "Pull Dempsey's file here," I tell him. "I want to look at known associates. Let's see if we can figure out who is most likely to be our second suspect."

"What do you make of Quaker?" he whispers as he's typing.

I admit I'm having a hard time figuring out her motivations. It's like part of her wants to put Dempsey away forever, but another wants the evidence against him to disappear? I don't get it.

After looking over Dempsey's rap sheet again, nothing new stands out to me, other than the fact his father was the one who always bailed him out. From what I can tell the first few times were somewhat amicable, but as time went on and the offenses increased, so did the tension, and the fines. Finally, last year for petty theft, Black had to pay the three-hundred his son stole, plus another fifteen hundred for the precinct's trouble.

"I have a list," Liam says. "But they're all schoolmates. No one out of the ordinary."

"That's not surprising," I say. "It's too bad school is already out for the summer or we could go and interview some of them. Give me your top five and we'll track them down, see if they know anything." Dempsey has to have a few good friends that haven't left for college yet. At least I hope he does. And I hope he's got a loud enough mouth at least one of them will know something.

"Okay," Liam says after about fifteen minutes. "Top five, with an additional five just for fun. The first ones were either accomplices or had first-hand knowledge of all Dempsey's priors."

"Perfect," I say, closing his file and standing. "Let's get moving."

Chapter Twenty-Nine

LIAM AND I SPEND THE BETTER PART OF THE MORNING AND early afternoon chasing down Zach Dempsey's friends and former girlfriends. Not surprisingly, the former girlfriends have little good to say about the kid, and his closest friends aren't willing to go behind his back, even when I insinuate it could be very bad for their futures. But they're smart kids; they're not about to incriminate themselves or him. Still, I don't get the sense that any of them are killers. Or that they had any knowledge of Zach being out that night. Unfortunately, no one can place him anywhere other than at his father's house. It doesn't mean he didn't do it, it just means no one saw him leave and come back. Right now, our only witness is still Orlando.

As we're headed to the last name on our list, my phone vibrates. "Slate," I say.

"Agent Slate, this is Becker." The older agent reminds me some of Janice, though she's not quite as serious. "We have some good news for you. Managed to pick up an errant fingerprint on that rock that came through the window." I put the phone on speaker so Liam can hear as well.

"You got a fingerprint off a rock?" I ask. "How?"

"The backside had enough of a smooth surface that we pulled a solid partial," she says. "Even better, we got a match. Ryan McKenzie. He works over at the local lumberyard. Twenty-two, solid build. He's got a record."

"Anything serious?" I ask.

"Not as far as I can find," she replies. "There are a couple redacted from when he was a minor, but nothing much since then. A couple of drug possessions, and possession of an unregistered firearm. A rifle."

I look up at Liam. "What caliber?"

"A .22. But it was seized a year ago after he was caught with it during a traffic stop." I'm not sure if I'm willing to believe that's a coincidence. If McKenzie was the other person in Zach's truck that night, it would make sense why he would want to keep anyone from examining the DNA. But how could he have known about it other than a warning from Quaker?

"That's...amazing work, Agent Becker, thank you. Do you know where McKenzie is now?"

"Just doing our part to help, Agent Slate," she says. "I had one of my guys ping his phone. He's still in town, and it looks like he's at work at the lumberyard. It's four-nineteen Pine Avenue. Looks pretty big from the satellite."

"We can be there in fifteen minutes," I say. "Backup?"

"Absolutely," she says. "Just tell us where you want us."

"Thanks, Becker, I owe you a beer after this," I tell her.

"Make it a whiskey and you've got a deal."

I hang up and turn to Liam, but he's already headed back to the car. "You read my mind," I say.

He chuckles. "It wasn't hard. Let's see, do we keep chasing dead ends or go and pick up the guy we know broke into the medlab last night?" He heads for the driver's seat.

"Uh-uh," I tell him, holding my hand up for the keys. He hesitates before tossing them to me. "I promise I won't exceed the speed limit by more than fifteen," I tell him. Liam narrows his eyes. "Fine. Ten. But that's it."

"Fine," he grumbles, drawing out the word before tossing the keys to me. I smile and slip into the driver's seat.

"On the way, look and see if you can find any connection between McKenzie and Quaker."

"You think they might be related?" he asks.

I shrug. "Look at Sheriff Black and his son. There have been too many strange coincidences in this case. I want to make sure we're not dealing with another one." I turn the car over and back up, a renewed sense of vigor flowing through my veins. This is just the break we needed after spinning our wheels. First Dempsey, now McKenzie. I have little hope that the DNA samples survived; he probably destroyed them not long after stealing them. But I'm really more interested to speak to him and find out *why* all of a sudden he decides to break into a medical facility.

By the time we reach the lumber yard, Becker and her team are already there. We pull close and coordinate a system where at least two agents will cover every exit. Liam and I will go in the front and hopefully apprehend McKenzie without any fuss. But if anything goes wrong, he won't be able to get away.

"I read the case file on this one as we were driving up last night," Becker says as we move into position. "They're never simple anymore, are they?"

I shake my head. "Doesn't seem like it. I'm just glad we got lucky with that rock," I say.

"More like he got sloppy," Becker says. "Any experienced burglar would have worn gloves, or at least avoided anything that could have picked up a print. It looked like he might have put on gloves after he got inside, but not before."

Interesting. I'm now more convinced than ever that one of those DNA samples belonged to McKenzie, as leaving it behind was sloppy as well. It doesn't speak to someone who is experienced in this kind of thing, which makes me think this was McKenzie's first murder.

Liam and I split off from Becker and her team and head to the front of the yard. It's a large place, with a tall chain-link fence all the way around. But the main gate is open as large trucks are leaving the yard at irregular intervals, some full of wood, others that are just the cabs, probably headed out until their trailers are full.

Liam and I make our way to the main office in the front and inquire about McKenzie. The yard manager points us to a tall, skinny-looking guy holding a couple of orange flags as he walks behind a front-loader carrying a pile of unprocessed lumber. While we could go out there after him, it's probably safer to bring him here to us. I ask the yard manager to call him in, which he does, over the yard's loudspeaker.

A few minutes later, McKenzie comes into the main office, sans flag, but still with the orange vest on. He's got a greasy look about him, like he hasn't bathed in a few days, and his black hair hangs down into his eyes, which are slack. I wouldn't be surprised if he was high right now.

"Ryan, these people need a word with you," the yard manager says, indicating us.

McKenzie only now seems to have realized there are more than two people in the room. He looks over at us and I see the recognition in his eyes. He turns to run back through the factory but before he can take two steps, the yard manager has tripped him up. I already had my weapon out and was ready to sprint.

"Nice job," I tell the manager as Liam struggles to get McKenzie's hands into cuffs. I replace my weapon and hold McKenzie down long enough for Liam to clasp both hands.

"Thanks," the manager says. "If the FBI are here, then it's serious. And I don't need any additional drama." He leans down to look at McKenzie in the face. "Ryan, you're fired."

The kid responds with a huff, but when we pull him back

up on his feet, he's got a smile on his face like this is the funniest thing he's ever seen. He's definitely high. "You might want to start drug testing your employees," I tell the manager as we're making our way to the door.

"We tried," he calls back. "Couldn't keep any help. Necessary evil, I'm afraid."

I give him an appreciative nod as we take McKenzie back out. I pull out my phone and call Becker. "All clear. We got him."

"Nice and clean. I like your style Slate," she replies.

"I wish I could take the credit. Do me a favor and accompany us back to the station. It's time to put some pressure on Quaker." I give Liam a knowing nod. He never found anything connecting the two, but I have some suspicions that I need explained.

"We're right behind you," Becker says.

As we walk into Chief Quaker's station with Ryan McKenzie in tow, I keep a close eye on everyone to see if I can pick up any signs of recognition. I have to consider that someone *under* Quaker may have ordered for Ryan to break in as I don't know who else she told about the semen samples. Regardless, we can't trust anyone in this station. Fortunately, I have Becker's team at my back, and we come through the doors like the Men in Black. The desk sergeant stands as soon as he sees all of us, his face etched with concern.

"Agent Slate." He looks around me to the other six agents behind us. "What's going on?"

"Bringing in a suspect," I tell him. "We're going to need access to your facilities so we can process and interview him."

"I'll...I'll have to check with Chief Quaker," he replies, reaching for the phone.

"Trust me," I tell him, "No you don't. If I need to, I will

get the USAG to call down here to confirm our authority. Now open the door."

He looks at me a moment, then decides this isn't a battle he wants to wage. He hits the button and the glass door to the back opens. We file through and Becker's people begin processing McKenzie, while Liam and I make sure one of the interrogation rooms is ready for him.

"What's going on?" Quaker asks, coming out of her office. She has a cup of coffee in one hand and concern is etched on her face. But I can't tell if she's concerned because we've just come in and taken over her operation, or because she knows she might now be in the crosshairs.

"Because this case was becoming more complex, I requested additional resources," I tell her. "This is Special Agent Jessica Becker, from the Chesapeake office, and her team," I say, indicating the other agents.

"Agent Slate, this is highly irregular," Quaker says after giving Becker a curt nod. "You can't just come in here and—"

"Are you saying you're refusing to cooperate with a federal investigation?" I ask. Before, when it was just the two of us, she might have thought she had the upper hand. But the truth is she never did, and now that she sees the reinforcements in person, Quaker isn't nearly as cocky.

"Well, no, we want to bring this case to a conclusion as soon as possible," she says, glaring at McKenzie. "Who is that?"

"Ryan McKenzie," I tell her. "Apparently he broke into your medlab last night and stole the semen samples from Summer Sanford," I say. "Along with samples from two other cases. We're about to interview him."

"I see," Quaker says. She seems very solemn for a moment. But when she turns to me, her face is stretched in a grin again. There's that damn switch she seems to be able to turn on and off at will. "Glad you managed to catch him. I'll need to let Metcaffe know; I wish you'd told me earlier."

"We already informed Sharon," I tell her. "No doubt she'll let her boss know."

I see something flash in Quaker's eyes. But it's gone before I can identify it. "Of course." She gives me a small salute with her mug. "Let me know if there's anything I can do to help." With that, she retreats back to her office and closes the door.

"Thoughts?" I ask Liam as I cross my arms.

"I don't know. Maybe this is just because I'm so new at this, but she seems hard to read."

"No, you're not wrong," I tell him. "She's giving off a lot of mixed signals. That's a good way to avoid being profiled. But it also makes her a loose cannon. We don't know what she'll do."

He nods at McKenzie, who is having another set of fingerprints taken. "Do you think he'll rat out whoever ordered him to break in? Because he doesn't seem like the kind of person who is a self-starter."

"I don't know," I tell him honestly. "I really don't."

Chapter Thirty

It didn't take very long to process McKenzie. We got a urine sample from him which we sent off to the medlab. I'm sure when Sharon comes back with the results it will show he's got at least one substance in his system, maybe more.

But right now, I don't care. If he's coherent enough to work, he's coherent enough to answer some questions. But just as I'm on the way to the interrogation room with Liam at my side, I catch sight of Zach's lawyer striding confidently toward us.

"Ah, shit," I mutter.

"Agent Slate," the lawyer says, stopping a few feet in front of us. "I understand you have lost some evidence pertaining to my client."

"We're working on recovering that evidence right now," I tell him.

"But you no longer have it. And unless I'm mistaken, it was this evidence which brought the murder charges against my client in the first place. I would like to assume that since the evidence no longer exists, the charges will be dropped."

"That's to be determined," I tell him.

"Let's see what the attorney general has to say about it,

shall we?" He takes a moment to remove his glasses, attempting to penetrate us with those dark brown eyes of his before wiping the glasses with his handkerchief, then replacing them. "I'll be in touch shortly." He strides past us, his head held high.

"God, I hate lawyers," I tell Liam.

"Who doesn't? But he's got a point. Without the semen——"

"We still have Orlando's testimony," I say.

"Orlando saw the truck, not the driver," Liam reminds me. "We won't be able to hold him on that."

I bite my lower lip. He's right, I just don't want to admit it. "You're too much of a boy scout, you know that?"

"Are you saying you want to make something up to keep him in custody?"

"No," I say, blowing out a long breath. "But maybe Ryan is stupid enough to flip on him. If we can get something before Zach's lawyer speaks to the AG, we don't have to let him go. If he leaves this station a free man, Black will use every resource at his disposal to get his son out of the state, even out of the country if he needs to."

"I think you're right about that," Liam says.

When we walk into the interrogation room, Ryan barely looks up. He's closed in on himself, like he's cold, but it's a normal sixty-eight degrees in here. I take a seat right across from him as Liam leans up against the nearest wall, both of us staring at the man.

He seems completely out of it, and suddenly I'm not sure we'll be able to get anything out of him. If he comes across as too dazed, his lawyer could argue that anything he told us was a fabrication as he wasn't in his right mind.

"Ryan," I say, leaning forward fast.

He jumps back, his eyes snapping all the way open. "Hmm."

"Are you with us?" I ask.

"Yep, I'm here," he replies. I don't see any further sign of his "sleepiness", so I decide to continue.

"Here's where we are. We have your fingerprints on the rock that was used to break into the medlab. We know that you broke in, stole some samples, then left late yesterday evening. Isn't that right?"

He shakes his head. "Nope, wasn't me."

"Ryan," I say again. "We have your *fingerprints*. We know it was you."

"Okay," he says, shifting in his seat. "But I was just doing it for a goof. For fun."

"For fun?" I ask, my neck suddenly becoming hot. "Do you realize what those samples were? Two were for rape cases, which means without those samples, whoever raped those women is free to do it again."

"Oh, man, that sucks," he says, then brushes some of his hair out of his eyes. It falls right back into place. We're not going to get anything on the empathy route with this guy.

"So Ryan, what do semen samples go for on the secondary market these days?" Liam asks. "Can't be a lot."

"What?" he asks, looking up.

"Obviously you stole them to sell them. But I'm kind of wondering why. You know you can sell your own semen, right? You don't need to steal it." He pauses for dramatic effect. "Or do you?"

It's brilliant. I wish I'd come up with it.

"Hey man, what are you saying? I don't have any problems down there," Ryan says, his voice more animated than at any other time so far.

"Then why steal them?" Liam asks. "If not to sell them."

"I uhh...I didn't know what they were," he finally says.

"You didn't know what four vials marked 'semen sample' were," I say incredulously. "Look Ryan, I know you're not a bright kid, but you're not *that* dumb."

"I'm not dumb," he protests.

Liam steps forward. "Yeah? Then why'd you leave your fingerprint for us to find?" I ask. "Or why not take the rock with you? It was a real rookie move. Professionals know better than that. Whoever hired you made the wrong call."

"Naw, man, I got the job done," he says, his voice confident and full of arrogance.

"Then why are you in here?" I ask. "If you're so good at your job?" He just gives me a noncommittal shrug. "Tell me, was it your idea to steal the samples or someone else's?"

He doesn't look directly at me.

"Ryan, time is ticking," I say, motioning to an imaginary watch on my wrist. "The longer you draw this out, the worse it's going to be for you. The sand is running out of the hourglass, my friend."

"I...uh," he says, then stares off into space again. I need to pull him back.

"Okay then, we're going to have to assume you stole them because they could have incriminated you. Which means you are now our number one murder suspect."

His eyes focus again. "I was just doing what I was paid to do," he finally admits.

Finally, we're getting somewhere. "And how much did you get paid for this amazing job you pulled?"

He doesn't say anything.

"You know, all it takes is a quick search of your bank history," I tell him. "We're going to find out one way or another. The more you cooperate now, the better this goes for you. The more you piss me off..." I don't need to finish the rest for him.

"Ten grand," he finally admits.

I let out a low whistle. "Wow, semen really *is* going for a lot on the black market these days. Where are the samples now?"

"Tossed 'em in the river," he says. I'm not surprised, but still, my heart sinks. I had really hoped there was a chance they'd survived. But unless someone had kept them refrigerated, it wouldn't have mattered anyway.

"Ryan, who hired you?" I ask, point blank. He doesn't answer. Only looks at the table.

"Ryan, this is serious. Who hired you to steal those samples?" Liam adds. He's probably hoping the added pressure might just make the kid crack. But I'm not so sure.

"I...uh..." He's so close. We just need to give him a little more incentive. He looks over at the glass partition, where a tech is recording everything we're saying. "Nobody hired me."

I sigh. "You just said you were paid ten grand to steal those samples," I remind him. "Did you pay yourself?"

"No, I made that part up," he says.

If this table wasn't bolted to the ground, I would have flipped it by now. But what did I expect from a burnout? A full, credible confession? Maybe if this was an episode of *Law and Order*. Unfortunately, it doesn't work that way in the real world. Criminals will do everything they can to keep from going to jail. Including claiming they made part of their confession up. This is really going to set us back.

I rub my temples for a moment. "So you've perjured yourself. Congratulations. That means you're definitely going to prison. I should—"

Liam steps forward his hand on my shoulder. "Let's take five minutes," he says.

I push a breath out through my nose. "When we come back, I'm going to ask you again. And I want you to think long and hard about what your answer will be, got me?"

McKenzie keeps his head down, not looking at me. He seems to have shrunk in on himself even more. I don't know if we're ever going to get the truth out of him. But at least he hasn't lawyered up yet.

I stand with some force, startling him, and Liam and I head back out into the hallway. I'm so mad I want to slam my fist into the wall, but that would only break my hand, which wouldn't do me any good right now.

"He'll talk," Liam says as we make our way down the hall. "He just needs to think about it for a minute."

"I dunno," I say. "I think there's something else going on. Why not just give up the person who hired you? He'd be looking at what, three years, max? But by stonewalling us, he's risking ten to twenty. Why?"

"I don't know," Liam replies.

"Agents." We turn to see Becker trotting up to us. "I was just coming to get you. I don't know if this is relevant or not but given what you've told me about this case so far, I believe it is. Chief Quaker just left, and she looked like she was in a hurry."

"Dammit, I knew it," I say and all three of us start running for the exit. "How long ago?"

"Just a few minutes."

"In a squad car?" I ask. Becker nods. I stop and return to the bullpen, heading for the precinct's tech services division. "I need to know where Chief Quaker's car is, right now," I tell them.

"That's for internal use only," one of the techs says, a redhead with a smattering of freckles all over his face.

I show him my badge. "I'm overriding that authority. Track the vehicle, now."

"Yes, ma'am," he replies, and begins typing. "It's here, headed south."

"She's going over into Maryland," I say. "Why? What's down there? She wouldn't be responding to any calls because that's Sheriff Black's territory."

"Unless she's going to meet Black," Liam says.

"But why? He was just here, giving her the raw end of the business stick for us arresting his son."

"I don't know," Liam says. "But ever since we've gotten here, it's always been about those two, in one way or another. What if they're in on this together? Zach could be nothing more than a setup."

I'm not convinced, but at the moment, we don't have a lot of time to argue. "I need you to tie that into my phone," I tell the tech. "I want to be able to track where she goes."

He hesitates a second, then relents. "I can set up remote access. What's your number, I'll send you the link."

I rattle off the number for him and a moment later, I have the live link that shows her vehicle's location. "She's just crossed the state border," I say. "We need to get after her."

"Want backup?" Becker asks.

"We can handle Quaker," I tell her. "You and your team stay here and make sure nothing funny happens while we're gone. We have no idea if anyone else is in her pocket or what she even told them. The last thing we need is some unsuspecting officer doing her dirty work for her."

"Go get her," Becker says before Liam and I head for the doors again. I take one look at him as we reach the car, and he rolls his eyes before tossing me the keys again.

"Just keep it under a hundred if you can, okay?"

"No promises," I say with a smirk.

Chapter Thirty-One

THE WHOLE TIME WE'RE DRIVING, I'M TRYING TO PUT MYSELF inside Chief Quaker's head. What is her plan? Who is she loyal to? And each time I try, I draw a blank. The woman is a chameleon, able to change her mood at the drop of a hat. That doesn't bode well for someone like me who has built their career on being able to determine what a person is going to do based on what they've already done.

But her leaving right as we're in the middle of interrogating our new suspect isn't a good look. She has to know that. So whatever this is, wherever she's going, it must be urgent. Enough that she's willing to risk everything.

"We still don't have anything on her," Liam says as I floor the accelerator.

"I know, but she's involved somehow." I check my phone, following the small cursor as it travels down the streets of Fairview. She's closing in on the middle of town.

"You're sure we shouldn't call Becker for backup?" Liam asks.

I shake my head. "We can handle this. I'm not letting this woman best me. She's been screwing with us ever since we got here; it's time to put an end to this." Somehow this is all connected, I just need the final piece. I had hoped Ryan would give us everything we needed, but he didn't even mention Zach, which worries me. He doesn't seem like the kind of guy who can hold out during a sustained interrogation. I'm hoping when we get back, we'll finally be able to get the truth out of him. But by then I'm sure Zach's lawyer will have him out. Without the semen, the D.A. won't be willing to charge him anymore.

"C'mon, c'mon," I mutter as I push the car faster and faster.

"Em, you promised," Liam says.

I nod, pulling back on the accelerator a little. I just want to get there.

Finally, Quaker's car stops in what looks like a residential neighborhood close to the town's center, but not quite. "Abermarle Road," I say. "What could be there?"

Liam shakes his head. "No clue."

Could he be right about Quaker and Black being in on this together somehow? But why? How would that help either of them? Maybe I've been looking at this the wrong way. What if Zach committed the murders, but instead of trying to expose him, Quaker is trying to cover it up? All behind the guise of this feud with Black? Maybe it's a way to throw any suspicion off either of them, that they're always at each other's throats. Could they be that good of actors? Quaker certainly has the capability to change her mood at the drop of a hat…Black I don't know about.

But how does Ryan fit in? Did Quaker just hire him to get rid of the samples? And if so, why is he risking extra jail time for her? What did she promise him in return? It would have to be substantial. If there's one thing I hate, it's dirty cops. No matter what we find, these two can bet the FBI will be launching a full investigation into both of them.

I turn down the sleepy residential streets, following the map until we reach Quaker's marker. The houses around here are all old, but historic. They look like they were built around the turn of the twentieth century, as they all have ornate gables, large porches, and lots of high peaks to their roofs. Many look to have been restored, which means the people here have plenty of money to spend.

Chief Quaker's car is parked along one side of the street, though there is no sign of her. I have to assume she's either in the house she parked in front of, or the one directly across the street. "You take that one over there." I nod as we pull up behind her car. "I'll check over here. If either of us doesn't find anything, head to the other side of the street."

"Got it," Liam says. "What are we looking for, exactly?"

"I don't know. But I'll know it when I see it," I reply. I can practically *hear* Liam rolling his eyes. I'm right about this, I know I am. We just have to catch Quaker and Black in the act.

After closing our doors softly, Liam heads across the street while I head to the house on this side. The small gate which is part of the white fence in front of the house offers no resistance when I open it, making sure I stay quiet. The yard itself is in immaculate condition, and a variety of flowers are in full bloom. The brick walkway up to the house is clean and free of any weeds growing through, which tells me whoever lives here takes really good care of their property.

The home itself is painted white and is free of any dirt or algae. Some of the windows on the uppermost floors are stained glass. Even though it isn't that large, it must cost a small fortune to live here.

I make my way up the small porch and begin checking the windows to the inside of the house. I can't knock, because if Quaker *is* inside, she might have time to get away. No, I need to catch her in the act. Unfortunately, the front foyer is dark, and I don't see anyone in any of the rooms from the front porch. I follow it around, checking the rest of the windows until I finally see shapes moving near the back of the house. I duck down below the windows and crawl forward until I'm close to the windows on the back of the house. I can hear people talking inside, but I can't make out individual voices yet. But it sounds like two people arguing.

I reach the next corner which takes me around the back of the home, to the back door, which is open, and a screen door is the only thing keeping the bugs out. But the voices are becoming clearer, and I can finally make out the two distinctive ones: Quaker is one, and the other I've heard before, but I can't immediately place. It's not Black. I hope Liam has finished with his house and is on his way over. I pull out my phone and send him a text anyway, just in case.

"—I won't do it. There's nothing you can say to convince me!" the male voice says.

"You're out of options," Quaker replies, her voice more serious than I've ever heard it.

"No, I can still leave," he replies. "Start again."

"Afraid not," she replies. "This is what's best for everyone."

"How could you do this to me?" he asks. "I thought we were in on this together."

"You need to shut your trap right now unless you want me to blow it off. I've got no problem with you resisting arrest. It makes things easier for everyone," she says.

"So that's it then. You're throwing everything away because you got sloppy." His voice is becoming heated. And I can tell Quaker is growing frustrated. But whoever this is, he knows something about her. He knows she's involved. He's just become my star witness. I pull my gun from my holster. Where the hell is Liam? I check my phone but there is no response.

"Me? What about you?" Quaker says, her voice rising as well. "None of this would have happened if you'd just used a condom."

A shiver runs down my spine. Is she talking to the person who killed Summer Sanford? It sure seems like it. I can't wait any longer. Quaker might decide to cut her losses and kill this guy so he can't say anything. And right now, I need them both alive.

I spin into the doorframe and pull the screen door open in one swift move, training my weapon on the scene in front of me. "FBI, no one move," I say.

Quaker turns to me, her eyes burning with rage. I have my weapon pointed directly at her. "It's over, Chief. Remove your weapon, slowly, and kick it over to me." My eyes flit over to the other figure in the room and I have to do a double-take. "Metcaffe?" I knew I recognized the voice, but because he spoke so little in the medlab it never really solidified. I certainly didn't think Mardel's chief medical examiner would have been involved with this.

"You're just in time, Agent Slate," Quaker says, putting on her sweet demeanor. "I was just about to apprehend Dr. Metcaffe. He's guilty of murdering Brady Sanford and raping and murdering Summer Sanford."

"You treacherous bitch," Metcaffe says. I manage a quick glance at Metcaffe's exposed arms and see the remnants of scratches on both. Arms that had been covered up when he showed us Brady Sanford's body.

I don't take my weapon off Quaker. "Nice try, but I heard you conspiring with each other," I say. "You're involved in this too, chief."

She shakes her head, but I can see a flash of panic in her eyes. "No, not at all. I'm just here doing my duty."

"How did you know to come here then?" I ask.

"I recognized the boy you brought in," she replies. "He takes care of Robert's lawn and gardens," she explains. "It took me a minute to remember who he was, but when I realized he was in for the B&E, I knew Robert had to be involved. How else would he have known?"

"Because you told him," I say. "You were the one who got him to break in and steal the samples. I'm not an idiot, chief. It happened less than half an hour after I told you Sharon did the autopsy."

Metcaffe begins cackling. "She's got you there. Not so clever now, are you?"

Quaker turns to him. "Shut up, you're under arrest." She redirects her attention to me. "Agent, I'm sure once we get Robert here in and booked, we can straighten all this out."

"If you think I'm not singing like a songbird, you're crazy," Metcaffe says. I want to tell him to shut up because I don't know what Quaker is capable of. She can change her emotional mood at the drop of a hat.

Quaker smiles at me, ignoring Metcaffe. "What do you say, Agent? We can bring him in together."

Whatever Quaker is thinking, she must have a pretty low opinion of me to think I'm stupid enough to fall for this. I don't lower my weapon. "I won't tell you again, chief. Your weapon."

Her face contorts into a rage. Metcaffe yells out and that's when I see the second, smaller pistol in her hand that had been at her side. She must have had it concealed and I hadn't seen her go for it. I barely have time to swivel back around as bullets slam into the old wood on the other side of the door frame.

"Fuck," I say, knowing I just barely escaped death. The shots are all head height. She's a good shot.

Metcaffe cries out after another two shots. I chance a look into the doorframe again to see him lying on the ground, a pool of blood forming around his torso. I do a quick check and don't see Quaker anywhere, so I head in and see if I can staunch the bleeding. But his eyes are already closed. The wounds are both in the center of his chest and I instinctively know there's no saving him. She just murdered my only witness against her.

Another shot rings out, but this one is further away. I stand and place my back to the nearest wall, waiting for another barrage of bullets, but they don't come. I turn the corner, keeping low and follow the sound. It didn't come from above...and that's when I see the front door is open. My heart racing, I don't even check my surroundings before barreling through the door into the sunlight.

And there, on the front walk, lays Liam, holding his side while crimson blood flows freely around his fingers. I catch sight of Quaker at her vehicle. I think for a second she's going to drive away, but instead she re-emerges with the vehicle's shotgun in hand.

I squeeze off three rounds, which all hit the car around her, causing her to duck. In that short time, I jump off the porch and run over to Liam. He's still breathing, but it's rapid and shallow as he holds his wound. "Look out," he says.

I have just enough time to raise my weapon and fire one more time as Quaker encroaches on our position, the shotgun extended in front of her. The bullet ricochets off the barrel of the gun itself, giving me an opening. I jump up and slam into Quaker, taking us both to the ground. She might be a good shot, but she's no fighter. I quickly incapacitate her with a well-timed blow right up under her ribs, which knocks the air out of her. As she's gasping for air, I flip her to the side, pull the cuffs out of her own belt and use them to restrain her arms behind her back.

By the time she's regained her breath, I'm already back over to Liam and am on the phone with emergency services. "It's okay," I tell him. "They're coming. They're on their way right now."

He doesn't say anything, which is good. Best not to aggravate anything further. But he looks into my eyes the whole time, not breaking the gaze until his lids begin to droop. "No! Stay awake," I tell him. "This is just like when I got stabbed, remember? Just in reverse. You're going to be okay."

He nods and gives me a faint smile. As I hear the sirens in the distance his eyes flutter once more. By the time the ambulance arrives, he's lost consciousness, and I can't wake him.

My stomach drops.

Chapter Thirty-Two

I FIND MYSELF IN A VERY STRANGE POSITION. NOT ONE I EVER thought I'd find myself in again.

I'm sitting in what has to be the most uncomfortable hospital chair I've ever sat in. It has no cushioning whatsoever, like it was built by the same person who designed church pews. Across from me lays Liam, unconscious for five days now. They had to induce a coma due to the blood loss, and he was in surgery for a good eight hours. The bullet Quaker fired at him tore through his spleen, his kidney and narrowly missed his appendix. Had the ambulance been any later, he would have bled out on the brick walkway in front of Metcaffe's house.

Despite the whirlwind the past five days have been, I've tried to be here as much as possible, even though they said he wouldn't wake up until they were sure he was stable. They called three hours ago, saying they were bringing him out of it, but it could take him some time to finally wake up, and it would help if someone was here with him. Thankfully, Becker took over for me at the Mardel station, allowing me to sit here by his side.

I can't help but see the parallels between Liam and my

husband. I never got to sit by Matt's side—I wasn't even there
when he died. But at the same time, I'm once again faced with
someone I care deeply about possibly being taken away from
me. I'm not sure if I can stand it.

Liam begins to stir, and his hand reaches out before
anything else. I take it in mine and his eyes slowly open before
he looks over at me and smiles. There's something about those
hazel eyes that I just can't resist, and I smile back. He moves to
speak but can't really seem to get the words. He points to his
throat, and it occurs to me he hasn't said anything in almost a
week. After all the drugs they've had him on and being out of
it, his throat must be dry. I hand him a Styrofoam cup full of
half-melted ice chips which he drinks all he can before
crunching on some of the chips.

"I'll be right back," I say, patting his hand. "I need to get
the nurse." He smiles and nods again. Good, at least he can
still understand me. They weren't sure if he would have any
brain damage or not.

After the nurses spend about ten minutes with him,
making sure he can sit up under his own power, and after
helping him to the bathroom and back, he already looks a lot
better. His face is flush with color again and he seems more
alert.

"I guess now you know how I felt that day," he finally says,
once he's comfortable in the bed again.

"What day?"

"The one when you got stabbed," he says. "I remember
watching you after they brought you out of surgery. I was
scared I'd never get to see you again."

Heat rises in my cheeks. I hadn't realized the depth of his
feelings, even back then. "Yeah, well this sucks. Let me tell
you."

"Are *you* okay?" he asks.

I nod. "I will be. Once we finish nailing Quaker to the
wall. The woman has an answer for everything. She's proving

much wilier than I expected." He moves to protest but I settle him. "Don't worry, we've got her cold on your attempted murder and Metcaffe's murder."

"Metcaffe?" he says.

That's right. He never got inside the house. The best he did was make his way up the main walk just as Quaker was coming out, her gun blazing. "That was Metcaffe's house," I tell him. "I found them in there arguing. From what we've been able to piece together from Ryan's confession, as well as some ancillary evidence, they were in on it together."

"The police chief and the chief medical examiner?" he asks. "Why?"

"Well, apparently, according to some files Sharon found, Metcaffe was quite the sexual deviant. Summer Sanford was just the last of a group of women he assaulted, then covered up by tampering with, or disposing of evidence. But after searching his house, Becker and I found trinkets from each of his victims, along with a photo diary he kept."

"So he was the one who raped and killed Summer? And her husband?" he asks.

"We're still working on that. Apparently, the other person in the truck that night *was* Ryan. Quaker had decided to use the opportunity to finally try and frame Sheriff Black's son after years of aggravation. Ryan admitted that she'd hired him to get Zach's truck, and since he already worked for Metcaffe, it was a good fit." My stomach turns when I think about it, especially about what both of them did to Summer Sanford. I'm not even sure Ryan was aware enough of what was going on to process what he was doing, or maybe Metcaffe forced him in some way. Regardless, the pictures on Metcaffe's computer proved both of their culpability.

"Dempsey was never involved?" Liam asks.

I shake my head. "Not that we can find. All the evidence we ever had against his was circumstantial. And because the original semen samples were destroyed, we couldn't test them.

But given there are no pictures of Zach that night on Metcaffe's computer, I'm satisfied he didn't have anything to do with it."

"Quaker just wanted to get to Black that bad, huh?" Liam asks.

"They've had a long feud," I say. "Going back at least fifteen years, to when she used to live in Fairview. Becker and I managed to find that Quaker and Black had gone for sheriff at the same time, and the results were close enough for a recount. Quaker was convinced that Black paid someone off in the end as she seemed to have more grassroots support. And ever since then she's never been able to let it go. It's just built up, year after year after year."

"But why was she so adamant about helping Metcaffe?" Liam asks. "Why not just turn the sicko in?"

"Because they were in love," I say. "At least, that's her explanation as to why she didn't turn him in earlier. She's still denying culpability in setting Zach Dempsey up. But she says they've been having a secret relationship for years."

Liam sits up a little more. "No wonder she was so reverent around him. I knew there was something weird going on there."

"We still don't know the full extent of their relationship," I say. "But it appears that she knew full well what Metcaffe was doing and did nothing about it. In fact, she worked to cover it up."

"Then she was the one who got Ryan to break in and steal the samples," Liam says.

I nod. "She knew one of them was Metcaffe's. But because he hadn't done the autopsy, he hadn't been able to destroy the evidence that would have implicated him. Which is his own fault, really. Had he not been so adamant about staying on his schedule, it never would have happened. But given what we've learned about Metcaffe, we've found he was a creature of habit. If it wasn't on his timetable, it didn't happen."

Liam turns his lips down in disgust. "God, they weren't kidding. We really do deal with the worst of the worst here, don't we?"

I nod. "Odds are those other two rapes were him as well, but he processed those samples, which means he could have changed them out or tampered with them to keep himself in the clear. We don't have any hard proof of that yet, but Becker is still working on it."

"What happens now?" he asks.

"Quaker is currently sitting in her own jail cell, until the D.A. can remand her to the state prison, where she'll await trial. In the meantime, Becker and her people are performing a full investigation of the Mardel police department. A second team from Baltimore arrived two days ago to help, and they're also doing a deep dive on the Nanticoke Sheriff's Department. No one is getting away from this one, trust me."

He grins and lays back on the elevated bed, relief spread all over his face. "You never cease to amaze me."

"Liam—"

"No, really," he says. "Look at what you uncovered here. What started out as a random drive-by shooting turned out to be a conspiracy involving the entire city's police department. C'mon, you have to admit that's pretty awesome."

There's that heat in my cheeks again. I'm not fishing for compliments, and they make what I'm going to say next even harder, but I appreciate them all the same. "Thanks."

"You should be really proud of yourself," he says. "I'm glad I got to see you in action again." That silence stretches between us again, and I'm trying to work up the nerve to say what needs to be said.

"Liam, I'm not sure this can go anywhere," I finally screw up the courage to say. The look on his face breaks my heart, but I don't have a choice. "I've been sitting here, during every free waking hour I've had. And I've spent that entire time thinking. And the fact is, I can't go through with you what I went through with Matt. Even though he ended up not being the person I thought he was, his death nearly *unmoored* me. I almost lost myself. I don't think I could do that again. If we were together and you were killed in the line of duty…I just…" I feel a flood of emotions threatening to take over, like a giant wave, cresting and ready to crash down on me.

"Em," he says, reaching out his hand again. I hesitate but take it anyway. "I get it."

"Do you? Because I care about you, I really do. But I can't do this again. I can't be sitting at another funeral, watching them lay to rest someone I love."

"No, I really do," he says. "I care about you, deeply. But you have to do what's best for you. I wish it were different, but I won't try and guilt you into a relationship. Neither of us knew where this was going to go, so it's not like we're losing anything. But it was amazing while it lasted."

"It sure was," I say. "Thank you for understanding."

"I'll always be here for you, Em. In whatever way you need me to be." My heart lurches a little and I briefly consider going back on my words. But I can't do that. I am too mentally frail right now. Maybe sometime in the future when things have calmed down and I'm more centered. But I can already tell if we were to continue with this relationship, my obsessive nature would have me worried at all times of the day, which would affect my performance in the field. And I definitely can't have that again.

He lets out a long breath and gives my hand one last squeeze before letting it go. "So when are they going to let me out of this place? I think I've had my fill of Mardel."

"I'll talk to the nurses again. They'll probably want to keep you a few hours for observation. That and you do have a large hole in your abdomen."

He looks down under his gown for the first time, as if he's forgotten about that. "Oh, yeah. I guess there is that."

I chuckle and get up, headed for the nurse's station. As I reach the door I stop and look back at him, and there's a soft smile on his face. He mouths *thanks* and watches me until I turn the corner.

As I head to the nurse's station, I feel like part of my heart has been ripped out anyway. But it's still small and manageable at this point. If it had gotten any bigger, things would have been much worse. I straighten my shoulders and raise my head; confident I've made the right decision.

After all, there's more work to be done.

Chapter Thirty-Three

AT QUARTER PAST ELEVEN, I PULL MY VEHICLE INTO THE underground parking lot of the J. Edgar Hoover building. It feels like I've been gone a month, when it's really only been less than two weeks. But given how long it took to wrap everything up in Mardel, not to mention I had to assist Becker's team with making sure the police department didn't need a full restaffing, it seems like I've been gone much longer. I haven't even been home yet. Liam and I left Mardel this morning and after I dropped him off at his place, I headed straight here. I'd rather finish all my reports before heading home to relax.

As soon as I get out of my car, I spot a familiar face standing near the elevators. Her platinum blonde hair has been cut even shorter than I last remember it, and she's styled it so it stands up, but still looks reasonably professional.

"What's this, a new look?" I ask, smiling. Zara offers me only a half-smile in return. "What's wrong?"

"Janice wants to see you—us, right away," she says. She finally meets my eyes. "I'm really sorry, Em. I thought I had him, but I let him get away."

I pull her into a hug. "I don't care about that," I say. "I'm just glad you're okay."

"But I had him, he was right here," she says, making a fist with her hand. "We should have gone after him together."

"Honestly, after what you told me, none of it matters anymore," I say. "I'm done worrying about Matt and whatever he was doing. It's obvious he didn't care about me, otherwise he wouldn't have spent our entire relationship lying to my face. As far as I'm concerned, the matter is closed. It's your case now, you run it as you see fit."

Zara grins. "Wow. I guess good things really can happen in Delaware. Maybe I should take a trip over there, try and find some newfound clarity on life." She holds on to my shoulders a second, looking into my eyes. Her intensity begins to unnerve me. "Oh my God."

"What?" I ask.

"You did it, you had sex with Liam."

I pull away from her, knowing my entire face has gone beet-red. "What?"

"Emily Rachel Slate," Zara says with the biggest grin I've ever seen. "You got the big D in Delaware!"

"Okay," I say, pushing past her.

"No, wait, you gotta tell me what happened. Seriously, what *happened*? Are you guys an item now?"

I shake my head. "No, after he got shot, I realized I couldn't watch someone else I cared about die," I tell her.

"Yeah, that makes sense," she replies. "Oh, man. So, was it like all the time? Were you two just going at it like weasels?"

I stop and turn to her. "Like *weasels*?"

"Weasels are known to have large broods," she says. "C'mon woman, I need the deets!"

I resume heading back upstairs. "Then I'll have to disappoint you. The deets aren't that salacious and I'd rather not talk about it." Though, every time I look at the backseat of my car, I smile.

"Fine. But there will come a day when you *do* want to talk about it. And when that day comes, I'll be ready with a cup of tea and an open ear." She grins again.

I just roll my eyes and press on.

Fifteen minutes later we're both sitting in Janice's office while she finishes up a phone call. Zara won't stop grinning at me no matter how many times I tell her to quit it. I don't even want to know what's going to happen when Liam comes back into the office.

"That was SSA Davenport, down in Chesapeake. He said Agent Becker had a lot of good things to say about you and Agent Coll," Janice says after hanging up.

"Becker runs a tight team," I say. "We couldn't have done it without them."

"You both did good work down there," she says. "As I knew you would." I nod a thank you. Any praise is high praise coming from Janice. She turns to Zara. "Have you given her the update yet?"

Zara loses the smile. "I wasn't sure how much you wanted me to say."

"What's going on?" I ask.

Janice folds her hands in front of her. "Given what Agent Foley discovered about Brian Garrett, or as he's also known, James Renquist, we've been ramping up our investigation. However, we are running into a lot of dead ends."

"What do you mean?"

"The 'company' where he worked has no legal entity status, here or anywhere else in the world," she says. "We can't even find its name. We managed to track down the secretary Zara spoke with the day she went over there; however she has proved to be...less than useful. Her knowledge of the operation was that it was a consulting business of sorts and even though she saw people come and go all day, she can't give us any names that lead anywhere. It seems everyone was using an alias."

I furrow my brow. "What does that mean? Are they part of another governmental agency? CIA?"

"Not as far as we can find. We suspect it might have been a front for some foreign government, so we're partnering with the CIA to try and find more. Whatever your husband was involved with, it isn't good," she says.

"What about Garrett?" I ask.

Janice exchanges another look with Zara and I know whatever is coming next isn't good. "He was found yesterday morning, a bullet hole in his head. It's not clear whether it was self-inflicted or not."

"Where?" I ask.

"Rock Creek," she says. "Right on the trail. No one we've interviewed heard the shot."

I sit back in my chair, stumped.

"I also received a report from Agent Coll stating he never witnessed any threat to you and this woman was never spotted. My hope is that she's decided to move on, but we're still on the lookout for her."

"Well, that's fine by me," I say. "As I told Zara, I'm done looking into Matt's death. As far as I'm concerned, that's a Bureau matter now. Or agency. Whichever ends up with it. And as long as I'm not looking into it, I don't think she'll come after me."

"Glad to hear it, Slate. You'd be much too close to this case anyway. I'll be keeping Agent Foley on it for the time being, that is until we've determined the nature of the threat and where it originates."

"Fair enough," I say. "I'm ready to get back out there and start fresh."

Janice waits a beat, then pins me with her gaze. "Unfortunately, the Deputy Director became aware of your...excursion. Needless to say he isn't happy. And until we discover who or what is running this organization, he wants you sidelined, no more excuses. I'm sorry, I did everything I could for you."

I pinch my features together. I had really hoped since I was willing to let it all go, I could just go on with my life like normal. But I guess that was too naïve. Still, I can't even conceive of not being able to come back to work tomorrow. "How long?"

"I'm hoping no more than a few weeks."

"You know, working yourself to death isn't heroic," Zara says. "Some time off will do you good. Go take a bath or something."

I'll admit, sitting in my tub, soaking for a few hours does sound nice. Plus, if it really looks like the assassin has moved on and isn't a threat, I can bring Timber back home. But I'll need to get the apartment ready for him again. Maybe I could spend the day doing that.

"I guess I don't have much of a choice," I finally admit. Maybe part of me does want some rest. My last two cases have been tough. Add into the mix everything with Liam and what I've learned about Matt and a break doesn't sound half bad.

"I will keep you up to date as soon as that changes," Janice says, resignation on her face.

I give her and Zara a quick nod, then head back out, not willing to prolong the goodbyes. I'll take a few hours to get my place ready, then give Dani a call and let her know I can probably pick Timber up this evening. That still gives me a few hours to relax in the meantime. If I have to be home for two weeks, I'm not about to be there alone.

As I drive back home, I must admit, I feel lighter than I have in months. Maybe even years. Maybe some part of me, deep inside, knew something was wrong about Matt, and it just stayed there in my subconscious. But now that I've let all that go, I'm beginning to feel more like myself. At least, more like the person I used to know all those years ago. Not starting something with Liam right away was the right move. I need time to myself, to rediscover who I really am before I go off and try to make a life with someone else again. Plus, I've got plenty of time ahead of me, there's no rush.

I pull into my parking space and pull my small suitcase from the trunk of the car. I ended up wearing every outfit inside at least five times. But I've never been the kind of person who cares much about what she wears. Maybe the new Emily is, though. Maybe I should take some time to figure out what I really like and try some new things.

Then again, that sounds like a lot of discomfort. I wear what I wear because it's comfortable, flexible, and professional. Why mess with a winning combination?

As I put my key in the deadbolt, I start to imagine just what that bath might be like. I might even pour myself a little wine and enjoy some day drinking while I soak. After all, it's like Janice said, I deserve a break.

But when I open the door, I realize something is wrong. There's an unfamiliar smell in the place, and all my senses go on high alert. I let go of my suitcase and go for my weapon before a familiar voice stops me.

"I wouldn't do that if I were you," she says. I turn and see the woman I've been searching for ever since I first saw her in Stillwater. Her blonde hair falling in cascades over her shoulders. She's exactly as I remember her when we passed each other on the elevator. She's even smiling the same smile, with her ruby red lipstick. And she's standing right inside my doorway, with a Glock 9mm trained on my midsection.

"Welcome home, Emily."

The End?

To be continued…

Want to read more about Emily?

"Don't Make me Ask Twice."

After coming to terms with her husband's death, Special FBI agent Emily Slate thought she'd finally be able to move on with her life. But when the assassin who has been hunting her shows up on her front door with a gun in her hand, Emily knows it's far from over.

It seems the assassin has been betrayed by the same Organization who hired her, and must now rely on Emily to help her enact her revenge.

But when Emily refuses, the assassin raises the stakes, putting Emily's personal life in danger and giving her no choice but to comply.

In order to take down the Organization that's been plaguing her for the past eight months, Emily will need to track down the whereabouts of a US Representative's missing daughter.

If Emily can find her, then her captors will lead them back to the Organization and Emily will be done with this once and for all.
But Emily knows she can't trust the woman who murdered her husband. And as the consequences of her actions begin to unfold, Emily will discover the Organization is a lot closer than she suspects.

This time, she'll be faced with an impossible choice.

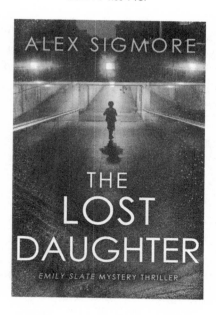

To get your copy of THE LOST DAUGHTER, just scan the QR code below!

FREE book offer!
Where did it all go wrong for Emily?

I hope you enjoyed *Her Final Words*. If you'd like to learn more about Emily's backstory and what happened in the days following her husband's unfortunate death, including what almost got her kicked out of the FBI, then you're in luck! *Her Last Shot* introduces Emily and tells the story of the case that almost ended her career. Interested? Scan the code below to get your free copy now!

Not Available Anywhere Else!

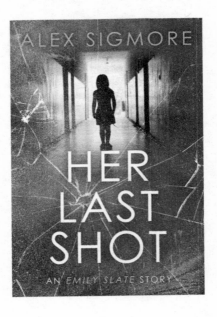

You'll also be the first to know when each book in the Emily Slate series is available!

Scan this code to download for **FREE!**

A Note from Alex

I can't tell you how much it means to me that you've taken the time to read my work. I really hope you enjoyed *Can't Miss Her*, and all the books in the Emily Slate FBI Mystery Series. My wish is to give you an immersive story that is also satisfying when you reach the end.

But being a new writer in this business can be hard. Your support makes all the difference. After all, you are the reason I write!

Because I don't have a large budget or a huge following, I ask that you please take the time to leave a review or recommend it to fellow book lover. This will ensure I'll be able to write many more books in the *Emily Slate Series* in the future.

Thank you for being a loyal reader,

Alex

Made in United States
North Haven, CT
07 November 2022

26394462R00157